A Place
Called
Home

Also by Preeti Shenoy

A Place Called Home

PREETI
SHENOY

HarperCollins *Publishers* India

First published in India by HarperCollins *Publishers* 2022
4th Floor, Tower A, Building No. 10, Phase II, DLF Cyber City,
Gurugram, Haryana – 122002
www.harpercollins.co.in

2 4 6 8 10 9 7 5 3 1

P-ISBN: 978-93-9440-740-4
E-ISBN: 978-93-9440-704-6

The views and opinions expressed in this book are the author's
own and the facts are as reported by her, and the publishers are not
in any way liable for the same.

Preeti Shenoy asserts the moral right
to be identified as the author of this work.

Typeset in 11/14 Minion Pro at
Manipal Technologies Limited, Manipal

Printed and bound at
Thomson Press (India) Ltd

To all the coffee growers and coffee lovers around the world!

Part One

Leaving Home

'In the sea there are countless treasures,
But if you desire safety, it is on the shore.'
—Saadi

1

2003

A Secret

THERE ARE TWO KINDS OF SECRETS. SOME WE WEAR LIKE an invisible cloak, which we don when we need to be shielded from the judging eyes of society, and discard over a few drinks in the company of friends. These are harmless secrets. Others are the kind that weigh you down like a stone. You bury them deep, deep within you. You carry them around for so long that they become an intrinsic part of you, till you no longer see them as burdens. These kinds of secrets you take with you to the grave. Or at least you intend to.

But the problem with a secret is that when it is between two people, you can never have complete control of it. You can only trust the other person to keep it, and carry on with your life.

As Alka walked briskly up the winding, curved mountain trail of the coffee estate in Sakleshpur that neatly sliced the dense forest in two, she was not thinking about her secret at all. It was the last thing on her mind as she passed the pepper vines that climbed the tall silver oak trees. They had been planted specifically to provide shade for the newer coffee bushes. She inhaled the cool nippy air, stuck her hands in the pockets of her hoodie and trudged on, listening to the birdsongs, the cicadas and the ceaselessly chirping crickets, trying to make sense of the thoughts that were hurtling inside her head like avalanches. She thought about how young she was when she had first set foot in this coffee estate. It had only been ten years and yet she felt so much older now. Before she had her girls, she could have climbed this path easily, without stopping even once. Now she wasn't even half way through and she was already panting. Childbirth. It did that to you. Motherhood was great, but it demanded its price, taking a toll on your body.

She took a deep breath when she reached Shepherd's Point, the plateau (*her very own* plateau) named by the British planters from whom Subbu's great-great-grandfather had bought the planation in the 1800s. When Subbu's father inherited the plantation, he had renamed it Anandi Estate after his wife, but had let all the British names within the property—Silver Brooks, Gurgling Waters, Laughing Meadows, Misty Blue Cottage and Poet's Paradise—stay intact. First-time visitors to the 400-acre coffee estate were fascinated by the quaint British names. Alka, however, had got used to them.

What was still fresh for her, was this glorious sight that stretched out before her. This magnificent, spectacular scene that she never got tired of—the deep green mountain peaks tiptoeing to kiss the cobalt-blue clouds. Every single day the sky changed. It was sometimes a deep purple, sometimes orange; at times a wispy white and, on a day like today, it was the brightest and loveliest blue. Looking at this sight, the troubled thoughts in her head faded away and for a few moments, she felt at peace as she gazed at the magnificent white clouds.

Alka sighed as she sat down on *her* rock. It was hidden from view, because it was surrounded by thick Nilgiri champa bushes that were in full bloom today. The white flowers danced in the breeze and the branches seemed to take Alka into their fold as she took a deep breath, inhaling their sweet scent. She reached into her backpack for her water bottle, greedily gulping the cool water. Sweat trickled down her forehead and she wiped it away with a small towel she retrieved from her bag. Closing her eyes, she lifted her chin to feel the cool mountain breeze on her face.

Alka was relieved that it wasn't raining and she could be here. Today, she needed to get away from all of them. She wanted time to think. She had to squash the thoughts trampling on each other inside her head. She forced herself to think of the choices she had made, and why she had made them. Mostly, she reminded herself that she was a married woman and a mother now. She tried not to think about a different life, one where she was not bound, tied down by duties and obligations. For all these years, she had convinced herself that she was perfectly happy, and she'd felt absurdly grateful for all she had. But now? She wasn't so sure anymore.

She'd never thought that being around Krish would be *this* hard. She had, several times over the course of the past many years, given careful thought to what she would say to him when they met again. She had known for certain that they would meet. What she had not anticipated was that he would forgive her—not after what she had done to him. But today, he had proven her completely wrong.

'The passage of time changes many things—but mostly it changes our perspective. We think about the unforgivable things that people we loved did to us, and with time, we forgive them. We think that we will never talk to those who wronged us—and there was a time when I thought I'd never again speak to you—but then, we discover the love we felt for them is still there. We think we never want to cross paths with someone again, but when we do, we are glad it happened. That's how I feel towards you, Alka,' Krish had said.

Alka was shocked at how his words had cracked everything open. It was as if he had thrown a grenade into the heart of the life she'd made for herself. Eight years of a solid marriage, two adorable daughters, a 200-year-old heritage bungalow she called home, a stable, comfortable life that she'd worked hard to create—now all of it seemed to have been built on a hollow foundation. How little it took! A few sentences uttered by a man she had sworn to put behind her, a man who was also her husband's brother. Her heart pounded and she took deep breaths to calm the turmoil rising up inside her.

Her eyebrows knitted in a frown, she sat lost in her thoughts, oblivious to her surroundings, till she heard a distinct low bellowing sound. From her vantage point, she could see a group of Chitals grazing. The locals believed that when you spotted a deer, it was a symbol of harmony, peace and longevity.

But what Alka was feeling was far from harmonious. Krish's words had destroyed her peace of mind.

What had made Krish say all these things to her? He had a wife and a child too. What did he even think would happen anyway? Did he think she would throw away all of this to go off into the sunset with him?

To be fair, he had gone on to clarify that he didn't expect her to do anything; that he didn't want anything from her. Alka couldn't understand why then had he expressed his feelings. Why hadn't he let the unfinished business between them stay that way? Why in the world did he tell her that he still loved her? How dare he throw her heart into turmoil like this?

One part of her was angry. He had no right to walk in here and say all those things to her, and stir feelings she didn't know what to do with. But another part of her also knew how ridiculous she was being. It was his home too! How could he not come back to his ancestral home? Subbu too was overjoyed at seeing his brother after so long.

When she finally stood up, there was an expression of calmness and certainty on her face. She'd made up her mind, and as she walked back towards her home, she knew the way forward. Whatever Krish felt towards her was his problem, she decided. With every step, the thoughts going around in Alka's head gradually untangled themselves. Walking helped her think clearly and as she approached the house, she became more and more sure of her decision.

She would do nothing. He would leave in a few days. Hopefully, when there was once again some distance between them, things could go back to normal. She had managed to suppress her feelings for so long. She had shut them up and put them away. She could do it again. And this time, she wouldn't allow them to resurface. She would put them in a box and keep the lid tightly on. She couldn't do this to Subbu. Subbu might not be a great husband, but she had made a choice and she would honour it.

Alka's gait grew slower and her heart became heavier with each step she took. Though her mind was made up, she also knew that deep down, nothing had changed. She felt the same way towards Krish, like she had all those years ago. Theirs was a relationship that had sprouted in secret, been nurtured in secret and now she would kill it too, in secret.

As she reached the bungalow, she was glad Krish was nowhere to be seen. She would do her best to avoid being alone with him from now on, till he left. But she was surprised to spot Subbu standing at the top of the steps. He was usually never home at this time. She smiled and waved at him, but he did not smile back.

She saw Krish then, emerging from the house, freshly showered, wiping his head with a towel. He came up to the door and stood next to his brother.

'Good walk?' he asked Alka, his eyes never leaving her face.

Alka nodded.

She looked properly at Subbu then. His face was dark with rage. His lips were a thin line.

Alka felt her pulse racing. She felt a surge of guilt submerging her. Panic followed. Did Subbu know about her and Krish? No, it wasn't possible. She knew Krish would never tell him. Krish would never do anything to harm her. Or his brother.

Subbu's eyes were blazing and he was staring at her with a look she had never seen before. It was a look of disgust, hatred and anger.

It was a look that could only mean one thing. Subbu knew her *other* secret. The one she had hidden from everyone, including Krish. She didn't know how he knew, but suddenly, she was certain he did. Her worst nightmare was unfolding in a way she had never expected it to. She looked down, unable to meet his eyes.

'Krish—please excuse us. Alka, we need to talk,' Subbu said, still staring at her. 'Come upstairs,' said Subbu as he marched up the stairs and into their bedroom.

Alka quietly followed.

~

2

1981

Mrs Shetty's Home, Delhi

Delhi

'ALKA, TANVI'S BED IS NOT MADE AND YOU HAVEN'T picked up her uniform from the floor either! How many times do I have to remind you? You need to get to these things as soon as you come back from school, understand? Not later.' Ranita Shetty's voice boomed through the house, making Alka hurriedly swallow the lukewarm tea her mother had kept for her. She rushed out, wiping her mouth on the sleeve of her T-shirt, her favourite one with the picture of a cartoon cat on it. It was the best among the hand-me-downs she got from Mrs Shetty, who gave her many of Tanvi's old clothes.

'Sorry, madam, I am doing it right away,' Alka said as she entered Tanvi's room. She picked up Tanvi's school bag and, after taking out the books and arranging them on the bookshelf, put it away. She took Tanvi's shoes and laid them neatly inside the shoe rack in the hall. She collected the discarded socks, the school uniform and the underclothes that Tanvi had left in a trail on the floor. She patiently cleared away every single item. Next, she went to the kitchen, got out the dusting cloth and cleaning liquid and began wiping Tanvi's desk. Tanvi lay on the bed, her eyes closed, and her head phones plugged into a Walkman that was beside her. She was smiling, swaying her head to the beats of the song. A few days ago, she had proudly shown Alka the headphones as well as the Walkman. Her father had gifted it to her when she visited him for the holidays. Tanvi told Alka that he'd got it from the US, and it wasn't available in India. She said that her father would most likely be moving to the US and she'd be visiting him there over the summer holidays. She described the tall buildings in New York City, the cafes, the parks, the trams, all of which her father had told her about. To Alka, it sounded like a fairy tale. She wasn't sure if Tanvi was making up these things, but she had nodded dutifully to every word Tanvi had said. She knew if she listened carefully, Tanvi would be pleased.

'You are so lucky,' Alka had said, her eyes never leaving the Walkman, and Tanvi smiled and replied that she was.

Then Alka had asked if she could listen too, and Tanvi allowed her to use the device for a few moments. Alka had never heard anything like it, and her eyes widened in surprise as the crystal clear notes formed a melody in her ears. She listened till Tanvi snatched it back. After that day, she had never allowed Alka to use her Walkman.

'Are you done with cleaning, Alka?' Mrs Shetty's voice rang out.

Tanvi removed the headphones and paid attention to what Alka was doing only then.

'I have told you not to touch my desk. Look how you've messed it up!' Tanvi cried angrily.

'I only tidied it. I haven't—'

'Maaaaa! I told you not to get her to clean my stuff. How many times do I have to keep repeating it?' Tanvi ignored Alka and yelled out to her mother.

'Alka, don't touch her desk,' Mrs Shetty called out from the hall.

'Yes ma'am,' Alka said automatically, suppressing her annoyance. It was Mrs Shetty who had instructed her to clean Tanvi's desk, and now she was singing a different tune. Alka knew from experience that a few days later she would be reprimanded for letting dust gather on the same desk. Mrs Shetty could never say anything to Tanvi.

'Are you done there, Alka? If you've finished, come to the hall and press my feet,' she said.

Of all the duties she was assigned, this was the one Alka hated the most. Mrs Shetty's legs were lumps of lard which Alka had to knead.

'A little harder, a little more pressure,' Mrs Shetty commanded as she rested her feet on the stool and sank back into the cushioned chair. Alka sat on the floor and knew that she would have to keep pressing till Mrs Shetty asked her to stop. Alka detested touching her feet.

'Seema, bring me some chai please. And use a lot of ginger. I have indigestion,' Mrs Shetty called out to Alka's mother, her eyes closed.

'Yes, madam,' said Seema. She always took care to make the tea exactly the way Mrs Shetty liked it.

'Aaah, this is bliss,' Mrs Shetty said as she took a sip of the tea Seema brought to her a little later. Alka was hoping she would tell her to stop. She had a lot of homework to do. But it seemed like today, she was in no mood to let her go easily. When at last Mrs Shetty finally told Alka to stop, it was already past 6.30 p.m., which meant that there was no time to play in the park today.

~

Alka's teeth chattered as she washed up hurriedly, scrubbing her hands furiously under the tap in the bathroom she shared with her mother. The ice-cold water turned her hands an angry red. She wasn't allowed to use the other bathrooms in the house, and the one attached to their tiny room did not have running hot water. Every morning, before Alka left for school, Seema would heat water for her on the stove. Alka mixed it with cold water in the bucket and took a bath. But she couldn't ask Aayi to heat water just so that she could wash her hands.

That night seemed like one of the coldest nights. Alka hugged her mother tight as they lay huddled together on the floor on a thin mattress, covered in the fleece blanket they shared. Alka asked her mother whether they could ask Mrs Shetty to buy a room heater for them.

'It is so cold, Aayi. My teacher said that this is one of the worst winters Delhi has faced, and a few people have died as well because of the extreme cold,' she added.

'Shhh—no Alka. I've told you many times not to ask for things. We should be content with what we have.'

'Why Aayi? Why should we be content?'

'Ranita madam is already doing so much for us.'

'You are doing so much for her too.'

'You won't understand. We have to be grateful to her.'

'Why won't I understand Aayi? I am nearly ten now.'

'Did you finish your homework?'

'Yes, Aayi. But I know you are changing the topic. They have a room heater in the guest bedroom which no one uses. I am sure Mrs Shetty won't mind us using it.'

'Alka—I said no. Go to sleep now. As long as we have each other, we will be fine,' Alka's mother pulled her closer and held her till she fell asleep.

Next evening, after Alka had returned from school and finished cleaning Tanvi's room, she approached Mrs Shetty, who was speaking on the phone to her friend. She waited patiently till the older woman disconnected the call. Then she said, 'Please madam, it is very cold at night. Can we have a room heater that no one is using?'

Before Mrs Shetty could reply, Alka's mother came running out from the kitchen and gave Alka a smack on her head.

'Sorry madam … She doesn't know what she is asking. Apologize immediately, Alka.'

'But why should I apologize?' Alka asked. Her teacher had told her that we should apologize when we have wronged someone. She didn't think she had wronged anyone.

'Alka—you are being arrogant. This is not right. Is this what I've taught you?' Seema's voice rose as she scolded her daughter.

Mrs Shetty looked at Seema and raised her hand. Seema stopped speaking and looked down at the floor.

'Look Alka, I am sending you to the same school as Tanvi. Am I not?' Mrs Shetty asked.

'Yes, madam.'

'Do you know it is one of the best schools in Delhi?'

'Yes, madam.'

'Do you know how much the school fees are?'

'No, madam.'

'Let's just say it is more than what your Aayi would earn if she worked for me for two whole years. Do you understand?'

'Yes, madam.'

'If I thought your room needed a heater, you wouldn't have to ask me for one. I'd have given it to you myself. There should be a limit to your greed. Don't ever ask me for anything again. I am taking care of you well, am I not?'

'Yes, madam,' Alka said.

But Alka didn't understand what her school fees had to do with the room heater. Though she hadn't got the room heater, at least she had not apologized. That made her feel happy. She knew she hadn't done anything wrong.

That night, after Mrs Shetty and Tanvi had gone to bed, Alka and her mother sat on the kitchen floor, eating their dinner of the previous day's leftovers, dal and roti, which her mother had heated up. As they ate, Alka's mother told her never to disobey her again.

'Do you know how lucky you are that Madam sends you to the same school as her daughter and gives us a good place to stay? Just remember Alka, she took me in when you were a newborn and I had nowhere to go. She is an angel that God sent to save us. Don't think about what you don't have. You just study hard, okay? If she throws us out, you and I will be on the streets. And you have no idea what that is like, so just be grateful. Please.' There were tears in her mother's eyes and Alka hated to see her cry. Worse, she hated that she was the cause of it.

'Sorry, Aayi. I won't ask for anything again. I will study hard and get a job, and get you out of here, and you will never have to work again,' Alka promised her mother.

~

The following Sunday, Seema told Alka that she wanted her to accompany her somewhere. Alka knew that Aayi got just one Sunday a month off, and even then, she had to finish washing dishes and cleaning the kitchen before she went out, and she also had to be back by 6.30 p.m. to resume her duties. Alka didn't think this was fair, but Aayi never complained. She eagerly awaited these Sundays every month.

'Why do you get only one Sunday off, Aayi? We get all the Saturdays and Sundays off in school,' Alka had once asked her mother.

Seema had laughed and said, 'Housework isn't like school. There are no holidays from housework. Just because it's a Sunday doesn't mean people don't eat and dishes don't get dirty, does it? If I don't do the work, everything will pile up, and I will have to do it the next day,' she said.

Usually, Seema would go to the local market on Sundays. She almost always brought back something for Alka— sometimes she bought bangles, sometimes a pair of earrings. As a child, Alka used to accompany her mother, but over the years, she had got bored of these outings. She didn't like the dusty markets her mother visited, or waiting for the bus in the heat, and she had outgrown the cheap trinkets her mother still delighted in. So she'd stopped tagging along with her mother, preferring to stay home and do her school work.

'Are we going anywhere special today, Aayi? I really don't want to go to that market,' Alka said now.

'No, we aren't going to the market today. You've always asked me about your father, and I think you are old enough to know the truth now. Hurry up and get ready. We have to be back by the evening,' Seema said.

Alka was excited. She had no memories of her father at all. Whenever she asked, Aayi told her it was best not to speak about him. But Alka had thought about her father every time Tanvi mentioned hers. Sometimes she imagined that he was a rich man, living in another city, and he would take her mother and herself there once he knew they were struggling. Sometimes she imagined him to be a sailor who was far away on a ship, in the middle of the seas. At times she thought he might be in a different country and would soon find them. She prayed for it, but she never told Aayi any of this. She'd seen how the expression on her mother's face changed whenever she mentioned her father, and so she'd learnt to keep these thoughts to herself.

'Are we meeting him?' Alka asked, her eyes shining with hope. Perhaps her prayers were about to be answered.

Seema gave a bitter laugh. 'Hah … No. But there are other people I want you to meet.'

They waited for a long time for the bus, but when it arrived, it was packed with people. There were passengers hanging off the boarding steps, and some rode on the roof of the bus too.

A small group of people jostled each other to get in. Alka and her mother couldn't get inside, and when the bus left, they, along with a few others, got left behind.

'Shall we walk instead? It's about 30 minutes away,' Seema said.

'It's better than getting into that awful, stinky bus. Look at those people; I don't think they've even had a bath. They are so dirty, Aayi,' Alka replied.

'Not everyone has access to clean water and a bathroom, Alka.' She sounded stern.

As they walked on, Alka's feet hurt. Her throat was parched as the fierce sun beat down on them. Aayi, though, didn't seem to notice. Alka saw that there was a slight smile on her lips and she was humming as she walked with a spring in her step, so Alka didn't complain either, but she wished desperately they would reach their destination soon.

As they walked on, Alka noticed that the houses in the neighbourhood were becoming smaller and were closer together. The streets got dirtier, narrower and more crowded. Garbage cans overflowed, but they didn't seem to bother the people, who went about their daily business. Alka covered her nose—the stench from the streets made her want to puke. They turned into a very narrow street between two buildings. Dark, slimy water flowed down and Alka had to carefully watch her step. Aayi seemed to be an expert though, as she navigated the street with ease.

The street opened out to a row of tiny hutments. None of them had windows, and most of them used asbestos sheets for roofs. Stray dogs wandered the street. Young children and toddlers, some of them with no underclothes and some with snotty noses, played with each other, just outside the huts.

A woman cooked a meal on a stove with firewood and the thick smoke rising from it made Alka cough. Another group of women gathered around the community tap, taking turns to fill water in old discarded paint tins and plastic vessels of various shapes and sizes.

Suddenly, her mother stopped in front of a small mud tenement, which had a tiny bit of open space in front of it. A large peepal tree grew by its side. Someone had tied a sacred red thread around it. The ground was covered with dried cow-dung, patted down to prevent the dust from rising up. A rangoli made of white powder adorned the entrance. Surprisingly, a few well-tended plants grew in chipped old plastic buckets. Two low wooden benches faced each other in the open space. The shade from a makeshift canopy made from a discarded old canvas material, provided the area with some coolness.

'Renuka! Oye, Renuka! What are you doing?' her mother called out from the gate.

'Seema! Is that you?' a chirpy voice came from somewhere inside the house.

'Aye! It's not your mother-in-law.' Seema laughed.

A thin, sprightly woman, dressed in a bright yellow saree, rushed out from inside, shouting, 'Arey! If I had known you were coming, I'd have got sweets.'

Both women hugged each other, and there were tears in both their eyes when they pulled away. It was only then that Renuka noticed Alka.

'Oh, my god. Look at how she has grown, and how pretty she is!' Renuka said, looking at Alka.

Alka, feeling very self-conscious, retreated behind her mother.

'My, my! She is a beauty, isn't she? Don't feel shy, girl. Your mother and I are old friends. Come, sit down. It is so good to see you,' Renuka said as she took Alka's hand in hers.

'Oye, Manish! Go get some Fanta and samosas. Tell Kaka to put it on the tab,' Renuka called out to a boy who looked slightly older than Alka.

'Yes, Aayi,' said the boy as he sped off.

Renuka brought out a folding chair from inside the house.

'Sit down. Make yourselves comfortable. Your mother and I … we have so much to catch up on!' she said.

3

1981

A Different World

MANISH RETURNED WITH SAMOSAS AND AN ICE-COLD Fanta bottle. He carefully wiped the bottle with a dish cloth. Then he expertly opened it with the tip of a spoon and, putting in a straw, offered it to Alka, who took it from him gratefully. It was the best drink she had ever had in her life. Meanwhile, Renuka put the piping hot samosas on a steel plate and served them along with the bright green chutney that she poured into a small bowl.

'This is so good!' Alka said as she sipped the drink.

Her mother and Renuka both watched her expression and chuckled.

'Don't you get Fanta in Mrs Shetty's house?' Renuka asked.

'Madam doesn't like the flavour. She only keeps imported milk and things like that in the fridge, and of course they are only for them,' Seema said as she rolled her eyes.

Alka was seeing a different side of her mother now. She'd never seen her this relaxed and happy. It also was the first time in her life that she had heard her mother disapprove of Mrs Shetty's ways. There was another thing Alka noticed. Here, everyone was sitting on benches or chairs. In Mrs Shetty's house, she and her mother were never allowed to sit on the sofas or at the dining table. Their small room had no chairs and so Alka had always seen her mother sitting on the floor or standing in the kitchen.

'I am so glad you decided to visit, and more importantly, brought Alka along too. The last time I saw her was when she was four or five. Do you remember Alka?' She asked. Of course Alka didn't.

'I wanted to tell her about us—about how much you helped me, and I wanted to tell her about her father,' Seema said as she took a bite of the samosa.

'Arey, what help. I was happy to have you around. It was a difficult time in my life too. You were helping me too,' Renuka answered.

'Still—it is important that Alka knows. She is nearly ten now. She is at an age where she can understand. She needs to know about everything we went through.' Seema sighed.

Alka was all ears. But she was too overwhelmed to ask questions.

'You know, Alka, I was renting a room from Renuka when I was pregnant with you. She didn't even want to take money from me, but I insisted and she finally accepted a very nominal amount. I stayed here for seven whole months. She looked after me like a sister,' Seema told Alka.

'I had just lost my husband and Manish was a three-year-old child. Your mother helped me as much as I helped her,' Renuka said as she lit the kerosene stove, kept an aluminum vessel on it and poured water from an earthern pot, and added some tea leaves. Alka noticed that there was no space for a kitchen. One side of the tiny hutment was allotted for stacking the dishes. The stove was on the floor. The other side had rolled up mats. None of it seemed to bother her mother but Alka silently noticed all of it.

'I did not think that I was helping you at all. I was just grateful that I escaped from my husband, I will never forget your sister Manjula's kindness. I could have never got away from that useless lump of a man but for your sister. How is she doing?' Seema asked.

'She wants to quit her job at that office. She's thinking of selling meals to workers and wants to shift here. She says this area is better for business. She's even asked me to join her,' Renuka said.

'Will her husband allow her to move here? His job is in that area and so is his family.'

'Oh, her husband left her. He moved in with a younger woman.'

'I am not surprised at all. He too was a useless idiot anyway. But slightly better than my husband I would say. At least he didn't beat her up.'

The last sentence made Alka stiffen, her eyes widening. Renuka noticed it and turned to her with a sad smile.

'Alka, don't be scared. This is the world, and it is a cruel place. We all have to watch out for each other,' Renuka said as she strained the tea into two ceramic cups and handed one to Seema.

'Yes, and it's time you know my story, so you never forget,' Seema added.

She took a sip of the tea and looked away for a moment. She took a deep breath, and her eyes reflected her sadness as she started speaking.

'I was only seventeen when I got married to your father and moved to Delhi. Manjula—Renuka's sister—was also from my village in Maharashtra and this proposal had come through Manjula's aunt . Everyone back in the village thought we were both lucky women to have escaped from the village and gotten married to men in Delhi. But your father, as well as Manjula's husband, were raging alcoholics as well as drinking buddies. They drank together, every evening. I soon realized that whatever money he gave me for running the house hardly sufficed. He spent a majority of it on alcohol. He was also a violent man, who worked for a local goon. He was nice to me only for one thing—his physical needs. If I asked for any additional money for household expenditure, he would get extremely angry. So I decided to take up a job. Manjula helped me get a job and I began working as a cleaner, sweeping and mopping in a garment shop. I squirrelled away whatever I could save after spending on the household expenses. I learnt to hide my money in places he would never find. If I didn't, he would beat me up and take that money too, to buy himself more alcohol. Then I became pregnant with you. He nearly beat me to death one evening when I refused to sleep with him. It was Manjula who interfered and asked him if he even knew I was pregnant, and she took me to her house that night and bolted the door, refusing to even let her own husband in.

I realized that my life as well as my baby's life was in danger if I continued enduring this. I wanted to go back to my village. I'd had enough … But when I contacted my family back in the village, they said I had to adjust and live there. They were worried that if I left my husband and went back home, no one would marry my sisters. The villagers would gossip. I decided that day that my family was dead to me. Being the oldest, I'd looked after all of them while my parents worked in the field. But in the hour of my need, they had turned their backs on me. I didn't need such a family; I cut off all ties with them and have never spoken to them since that day.' Seema looked away, blinking back her tears. 'Manjula helped me leave my old life and I came here and stayed over with Renuka.'

Alka was shocked to hear her mother's story. She'd never spoken about it till now, and so Alka had never known of the trauma her mother had undergone.

Renuka continued where Seema left off. 'Anyway, I was working in the same building back then, where you now live. Shetty madam was looking for a live-in domestic help. Her husband had just left her. I was working for them temporarily. Her parents were insisting that she should move back to Bangalore, because she wouldn't be able to manage her two-year-old daughter Tanvi on her own. But Ranita madam refused, saying that her life was in Delhi,' Renuka said, looking at Seema and then added, 'Do you remember how we both went to her, asking her for a job?'

Seema managed a small smile at that memory.

'You were a month old when Renuka and I turned up at her doorstep. The only question Ranita madam asked was whether I would be able to manage my own baby as well as her two year old, and be able to cook and clean,' Seema said.

'Haha, yes! And I remember your answer too. You gave her such a good reply.' Renuka smiled at the memory. 'It is why she hired you.'

'Really? What did you say to her, Aayi?' Alka asked.

'I told her "Madam, in my village, I've taken care of all my six siblings. I've been cooking and managing the babies and handling all the household chores since I was twelve!" I told her that I may look frail but I was strong and that I would do a good job, and not give her any cause for complaint,' Seema replied. 'That was what got me the job. I was so glad that she took me in. I didn't bother about how small the room was. It might seem very small to you now, Alka, but I remember that it felt like heaven to me. It had its own attached bathroom too, and it was unlike any house I've lived in before.'

'She was kind enough to take you in. I must grant her that. Not everyone will take in a lady with a newborn baby. Do you know how many of my friends lost their jobs the moment their employers found out that they were pregnant? They just wanted a couple of months off for their delivery. But their employers replaced them,' Renuka said.

'Alka, listen to all of this,' Seema said. Then she turned to Renuka. 'Do you know what she did yesterday? She went and asked Madam for a heater yesterday, even though I told her not to,' Seema said.

'Heater? Wah! What luxury!' Renuka commented.

Alka looked at the floor, her face turning red.

Renuka insisted that they stay for a meal. She sent Manish out again to get chicken, even though Seema said there was no need for it.

'You've brought Alka after such a long time. It calls for a celebration,' Renuka said.

The two women chatted happily as they made rotis and chicken curry.

Renuka took out steel plates and served the food in them. The four of them—Manish, Alka, Renuka and Seema—ate together, and when they were done, Alka helped them clean up and wash the dishes.

They left after the afternoon tea, which Renuka served them.

'Please come again soon. It was so wonderful to see you,' Renuka hugged Seema and Alka as they parted.

~

Seema was happier than Alka ever remembered.

'Do you want to wait for the bus or do you want to walk back?' Seema asked Alka.

'Let's walk,' Alka replied.

They walked in silence.

'What's the matter? Why aren't you saying anything?' Seema asked her.

'I don't want to go back to that place ever again,' Alka was sullen.

'Why?'

'I have nothing to do with them, Aayi. If she is your friend, you go and see her. I don't want to visit that place again.'

'Alka! How can you say that? You saw how nice she was. I told you all this because you are old enough to know.'

'I don't want to know, alright? I hate that place. I hate these streets. I hate everything here. Let's just go back and never talk about this again, Aayi. Please,' Alka said with tears in her eyes.

'Alka, Renuka is like a sister to me. I don't know why you say you don't want to see them again. She genuinely cares for us, you know,' Seema's lips trembled as she spoke.

Alka did not know how to tell her mother that she was so ashamed of her social background and she was worried that someone from their school would see her in this area and ask her what she was doing there. The truth was she was embarrassed to be seen here. She didn't speak a word as she trudged behind her mother, determined to put this memory behind her. She would pretend this visit never happened.

From that moment on, she stopped thinking about her father. The truth was too painful for her ten-year-old mind to absorb, and so she acted like it did not matter, knowing no other way to deal with the gnawing pain inside her heart.

When they got back home that evening, Alka's heart sank when she saw the several pairs of footwear at the front door. She groaned inwardly. She had forgotten that Mrs Shetty's friends from the Inner Circle Club would be dropping by that evening.

Whenever Mrs Shetty's friends from her club came over, she'd show Alka off as her charity project. While Alka served the guests snacks and tea, Mrs Shetty would converse with her in English. When Alka replied in perfect English, the women would all exclaim about how well she spoke and what a great job she was doing. Mrs Shetty would bask in the praise and Alka felt like a circus monkey who had to perform and please its master.

Today was no different. As soon as Alka and her mother entered the house from the servants' entrance, Mrs Shetty called out from the hall. 'Ah! Alka, are you back?'

'Yes, madam. I'll make tea,' Seema answered for Alka.

'Alka, come here,' Mrs Shetty called out.

Alka gritted her teeth and went to the living room, where all of Mrs Shetty's friends were seated.

'So, how was your outing?' Mrs Shetty asked in English.

'It was lovely, madam,' Alka answered, swallowing her tears, anger and frustration.

'Where did you go?' one of the ladies asked.

'To the bazaar, madam. There were a lot of colourful shops and I enjoyed looking at all of them,' Alka replied, giving them exactly what she knew they wanted to hear. She wasn't going to tell them the truth.

The ladies asked her some more questions and Alka made up things she knew would please them.

~

That night, after work, Alka and her mother lay on their mats. Alka told Seema that she disliked following Mrs Shetty's orders.

'Alka come here, Alka press my feet, Alka dusting was not done properly,' Alka mimicked Mrs Shetty's commands.

'Shhh Alka, she might hear you,' Seema said supressing a giggle, placing a hand over Alka's mouth. Then she said, 'Remember Alka, we are survivors. We have to fight with whatever we've been given.'

'I hate it, Aayi. She treats me like I am some pet she has taught tricks to. I hate answering all her friends' questions. She is trying to show off to them that I know English, don't you see that?'

But Seema did not understand why Alka got so upset over such a trivial thing.

'They are praising you for speaking well. What is there to feel bad about?' Seema asked.

'Aayi, have you ever thought about why she doesn't ask her own daughter to speak in front of those ladies? Don't you see how unfair that is?'

But Seema's answer was a practical one. 'It's such a small thing. How does it matter? You are getting to go to such a good school,' she said.

Alka knew she'd never understand. So Alka 'performed' whenever she was asked to. The routine continued for many years, with different people who visited Mrs Shetty. At one such gathering, Alka overheard them talking about what a good thing it was that the school had a provision for taking in underprivileged children for almost no fees. She was shocked to discover this. That night, she told her mother that Mrs Shetty hadn't really paid her fees and so they weren't that indebted to her.

Her mother said, 'How does it matter Alka? If she hadn't taken us in, you would not even have discovered this school. It's a very harsh world out there. I've seen it and now you've seen it too. I don't want you to suffer the way I did.'

But the humiliation had made its way into Alka's soul, scarring her with a permanence that she would never be able to shake off. She learnt to hide it by pretending it did not matter, because there was nothing else she could do.

4

1988

The Party

WHEN ALKA ENTERED HER TEENS, SHE BECAME ACUTELY aware of the disparities between herself and her rich classmates and their families. When she was younger, she could push aside the differences and stay inside a protected cocoon. But as she grew older, she noticed how her classmates went to cafes after school, how there were so many outings and get-togethers, which she was never a part of, and how stylish their haircuts were, compared to hers.

She thought about how different the lifestyles of her classmates were, compared to her own life. She remembered how disgusted she was with the surroundings, when she visited Renuka's home. Alka became even more determined to give her mother a good life. Seema often told Alka that there was only one thing she wanted from her—to study well, so that she wouldn't have to clean other people's toilets. Alka resolved that she would never let her mother down.

She knew that in order to accomplish this, she had to work hard and top all her classes. She made sure that, after finishing all the tasks Mrs Shetty assigned her, she spent every bit of her free time buried in her books. As a result, her teachers were happy with her academic performance and so was her mother.

When she entered high school though, a new set of problems arose, which she had never anticipated. She desperately wanted to be like her rich classmates. She longed to fit in. She carefully observed Tanvi and her friends for their style and mannerisms, and imitated them closely till they became a part of her personality. Soon, she began to look and sound exactly like all the other girls at her school. But, even though she learned to act and talk like them, she could not shake off the feeling that she wasn't good enough, that she would always be an outsider, looking in.

She was grateful for the school uniform, as it meant one less thing to worry about—at least she would be dressed like them. As a child she had only worn Tanvi's hand-me-downs and it never bothered her. But as a teenager, she had become very self-conscious. Her mother bought her clothes once a year on Diwali, but even the best clothes that her mother bought were inferior to Tanvi's old clothes.

As the months passed, Alka became quieter and quieter, preferring to keep to herself, choosing books over friends. Every few days, she would borrow as many books as the librarian allowed her to. She read voraciously to escape her reality, and soon the school librarian, Ms Jalan, became Alka's friend. They would discuss the characters in the books Alka had read, and Ms Jalan always had more recommendations for the young girl. Alka, on her part, was always happy to read anything Ms Jalan suggested.

~

Alka would walk home after school every day. She was glad that their residential complex wasn't too far from school. Tanvi never walked with her. She was a senior and had her own set of friends, and there would invariably be friend's car waiting for her outside the school gates. Tanvi often went out to coffee shops, or to Connaught Place for shopping with her friends, and came home much later than Alka. Mrs Shetty did not seem to mind at all, whereas Alka's mother was very particular that Alka should come straight home after school. Alka had to help her mother with the housework, and one some days, she had extra chores Mrs Shetty would assign her.

Alka never invited anyone home. Whenever Tanvi's friends visited, Alka hid in the room she shared with her mother till they left. She never made any friends at school, always preferring to keep to herself.

~

In high school, while Alka continued to do well academically, she also became increasingly aware of the boys in her school; she had never really paid attention to them before. Harish, Alka's classmate, was a tall, thin boy with shining eyes and straight floppy hair and, recently, he had begun paying attention to her. Alka did not miss his glances. Every time he looked at her, excitement coursed through her and she turned away, blushing. She hoped it wasn't too obvious to her classmates. One evening, after school, he walked up to her.

'Hi, Alka,' he said.

'Uhh … hello,' Alka replied, struggling to get the words out.

'I'd like to invite you to a party this weekend. It's at my place. Will you come?'

'Uhhh—I don't know. I'll have to ask my mother.'

'Oh, my driver will pick everyone from their homes and drop them back too. Tell aunty she doesn't have to worry about your safety. I will see that you get home safe.'

It took a few moments for Alka to realize that Harish was referring to her mother as 'aunty'. It felt nice. She was used to Mrs Shetty and Tanvi calling her mother by shouting her name, and here was Harish, treating Seema like an equal—the same way he treated the parents of his other friends.

'I'll see,' she said.

'My friends told me you won't come. I've made a bet with them. Don't let me down,' he said as he smiled at her and walked away. She stood there for a few seconds, gaping at him. She couldn't believe what had just happened. Then her mouth broke into a wide grin. She smiled the whole way home, and found it hard to stop even as she went about her daily chores. Her mother noticed how unusually buoyant she was and asked her which boy she was thinking of.

'Aayi! It's nothing. Can't I be happy for no reason?' Alka replied.

That night Alka told her mother about the invitation to Harish's birthday party and how she felt happy that he had referred to her mother as 'aunty'.

'Aayi, Mrs Shetty doesn't really respect you, you know,' Alka said.

'Madam takes care of us. It doesn't matter whether some boy called me "aunty" or not. And I don't think it's a good idea for you to be going to this party.' Her mother's tone was firm and final, and Alka could feel her stiffening up with disapproval in the dark.

'Please Aayi, please. I want to go. It's the first time I've been invited to a party. I promise you I'll be safe.'

But Seema was unshakeable.

Alka didn't give up though, and over the next few days, she pleaded so much with her mother that Seema finally relented and said she would ask Mrs Shetty if Alka could go.

'Why should you ask her? *You* are my mother, not her,' Alka said.

'We live in their house. I have to ask her. If she agrees, you can go.'

Alka waited with bated breath for her mother to ask Mrs Shetty for permission. But as things turned out, her mother did not have to ask her employer anything after all. Mrs Shetty was leaving for Dehradun for the weekend, with her friends from the Inner Circle Club. She was taking Tanvi along as well, as the other ladies would be bringing their children too. Alka danced with joy after the mother–daughter left.

'See Aayi! Even God wanted me to go to this party,' she said, grinning.

'Be careful, child. These rich kids might be drinking. You are not to drink, okay?'

'Never, Aayi. I will remember,' she said.

～

Alka wore the best outfit she had—a pale blue satin dress which Tanvi had outgrown. She wore her hair in a loose long braid, and put on Tanvi's old earrings. She felt like a movie star. She paced about nervously at the gate of her building till Harish's car pulled up outside to pick her up, and when she spotted him waving from the car, she was so happy she thought her heart would burst.

'You look great!' His compliment made her blush, and she shyly told him that he did too. They picked up three more teens on the way who chatted among themselves but ignored Alka. Harish shot them a triumphant look when they got in, as if to say that he had won the bet. But Alka didn't care. She was with Harish, going to a party at his home that he had invited her to. That's all she cared about.

~

Harish's home was an independent bungalow at Golf Links. When they arrived at the venue, Alka discovered that the party included not only Harish's friends, but friends of his parents as well. It was a massive gathering, with professional caterers, uniformed waiters serving snacks to people, and a DJ blasting the latest party music. The lawn was covered with big round tables that had centrepieces of exotic flowers on them, and the chairs were all covered in shiny satin cloths. The outdoor dance floor sparkled under disco lights and it was hard for Alka to believe that this was someone's home. To her, it looked like a palace and she felt like Cinderella, whose story she loved as a child.

'Come, let's dance,' Harish said, but Alka shook her head. She was so much in awe of it all that she just wanted to sit down and take everything in. Besides, she'd never danced before and didn't know how to. The others joined him and she sat back, enjoying the music and enjoying looking at Harish on the dance floor. He moved well, and was a good dancer.

A waiter brought around a tray of drinks, and she knew a few glasses held alcohol, but Alka settled for an orange juice. She could see that most of the other kids were drinking alcohol, and so was Harish. He would stop dancing for a bit, come to the table, sip his drink and head back to the dance floor. Alka was beginning to feel uncomfortable with how boisterous everyone was getting. She wished Harish would stop dancing and talk to her. All the grown-ups were dancing too.

The music continued and the party showed no signs of stopping.

At last, Harish came over to Alka and said, 'Having fun?'

She heaved a sigh of relief and nodded.

'What are you having?' Harish asked, peering into her glass. 'Vodka with orange juice?'

Alka nodded again. She didn't want Harish to think of her as uncool, and she didn't want to admit to him that she had promised her mother that she wouldn't drink alcohol. She was just happy that he was standing near her.

'Nice!' Harish smiled in approval. Alka smiled back at him, and her heart leapt with happiness as he pulled a chair and sat down right next to her. He was very close to her, his shoulders touching hers. Alka's cheeks flushed as though she had stepped out into the sun. She could feel the blush creeping up her face, and she thought her heart would explode with joy when he put his arm around her.

She sat up proudly, smiling back at him as he asked her all sorts of questions—about the books she liked to read, what she'd read recently, and her favourite characters from those books. She had never discussed books with anyone except the school librarian, and she was delighted when he seemed interested. He listened intently to everything she said, and he had read some of her favourite books too.

'People who read—they are different, aren't they?' Harish asked.

'Yes, I think they understand others a bit more deeply, because they can put themselves in other people's shoes and see from their perspective,' Alka replied.

He understands me, she thought. *He truly does.*

They sat talking for a while, oblivious to the party around them. Harish had eyes only for Alka. Alka was overjoyed at how easily the conversation flowed between them. He beckoned to a waiter, who refilled his glass and asked Alka whether she wanted some more. Alka said she didn't. She didn't want to drink, and she didn't want Harish to find out that there was no vodka in her orange juice.

When he put his hand on her thigh, she didn't stop him. She had never experienced these sensations before and her heart raced in excitement. Alka looked around to see if anyone had noticed, but everyone was busy enjoying the party. The flowing table cloth hid Harish's hands, and he grew bolder and slowly moved her dress so he could feel her bare skin. Alka's cheeks were flushed as she tried to pretend nothing was happening.

'Like it?' he whispered.

Alka nodded, unable to speak.

'Your hair smells so nice,' he said as he leaned into her hair and nuzzled her neck.

Alka was so giddy with excitement and happiness that she thought she would faint. No one had paid her such compliments, no one had even noticed her, and being spoken to like this by him made her feel like a princess.

'Want me to stop?' Harish asked as his hands crept further up her dress.

Alka shook her head. She didn't want him to stop. She wanted him to go on. She was feeling things she had never known were possible to feel.

'Will you say something or do you only talk about books?' Harish asked, amused.

'Sorry,' said Alka not recognizing the hoarseness in her voice. 'Thank you,' she said, not knowing what else to say.

Harish chuckled. 'I should be the one thanking you! You're so gorgeous. Want to go somewhere else?' he asked.

Alka nodded.

'Come,' he said as he walked towards the back of the house.

Alka followed him.

5

1988

A 100 Servants

ALKA WAS SO HAPPY SHE WOULD HAVE FOLLOWED HARISH to the moon if he had asked her to. He led her to the back of the house, which had a sprawling garden. A row of large bushes hid them from view.

'Wait here,' he said, and returned with a dhurrie from a small shed at the side of the garden. Alka began feeling a little uneasy but not scared enough to ask him to stop. She knew what he wanted but she wasn't sure what to do. He, though, seemed to know exactly what he was doing. He looked into her eyes and motioned for her to lie down. Alka quietly obliged. She lay down next to him, expecting him to kiss her, and she closed her eyes. This is what had happened in all the books she had read. But Harish didn't kiss her at all. Before she knew, one of his hands found her breast and the other bunched up her dress. He was murmuring, 'Oh Alka, you're so hot ... so hot,' and Alka didn't know how to ask him to slow down. She wanted to ask him to be little gentle. She wished it didn't hurt so much, but Harish seemed oblivious to what Alka wanted. His breath came in short gasps now and she didn't like the smell of alcohol on it. She gritted her teeth, clenched her fist and stared at the stars in the sky, hoping he would finish soon. When he was done, he said 'Woooh ... God, Alka, you are great. You are so good.' He hadn't even realized that it was her first time.

Alka bit her lips. Blinking back her tears, she sat up and rummaged for her underwear, and she panicked because for a few seconds she couldn't find it. Harish thought that was hilarious and he laughed while she put in on. Alka turned away so he couldn't see the tears in her eyes.

She smoothened her dress and said 'Harish, I want to leave now. Could you drop me back please?'

Harish sat up then. 'Oh my god, Alka, I am so sorry. I wasn't laughing at you. I wasn't. I just thought—Never mind. I was just being silly. I am a bit drunk you know. I have to find my pants too. You can laugh at me while I look for them.'

But Alka had already stood up and walked back to her table at the party, leaving him on the dhurrie. She hadn't enjoyed it at all and now she wanted to go home.

When she got back to her table, the DJ was playing old numbers that the grown-ups had requested and the young people had stopped dancing.

'Alka! What the fuck?!' a familiar voice cried and Alka was shocked to see a very tipsy Tanvi standing before her.

'Oh, hello,' Alka said nervously. 'Weren't you supposed to be with your mother at Dehradun?'

Tanvi laughed. 'Oh, my poor innocent Alka. Who wants to go with oldies to Dehra when you can party here instead?' She laughed.

Her friend looked at Alka and said, 'Hey, don't you live in the same building as Tanvi? I've seen you walk home.'

Alka nodded.

'Listen, don't tell on her, okay? Tanvi feigned an upset stomach and her mother let her stay back with me. You won't tell, will you?'

'If she does, I will ensure her mother loses her job. Don't worry about it,' Tanvi said.

'What do you mean?' the friend asked, surprised.

'She lives in the same building as me because her mother is our maid. Look at her, all dolled up in my old clothes—I can get her thrown out if she dares to open her mouth,' Tanvi rolled her eyes.

'Oooooh! Who would have guessed! Then how is she here? Oye, who did you come here with?' the friend asked, her tone immediately changing.

Alka felt her face turning crimson with embarrassment. Her lips quivered but she couldn't speak. Her legs felt wobbly and she slumped down on the nearest chair, looking for her drink, which she had left on the table. But the waiter had cleared it away and she just sat there stupidly. Her stomach was sinking and she felt her throat going dry. On one side was the shame and confusion of what had just happened with Harish, and before she had even had a chance to think about it, Tanvi's words had rained upon on her. She wished she could sink into the earth and disappear.

'How did you come here? Does your mother know? And does *my* mother know?' Tanvi asked.

Harish reached the table then.

'Hey, Alka. Shall I get you another drink?' he asked. Alka shook her head.

Both Tanvi and her friend looked at Harish, and Tanvi giggled. 'She came with *you*?' She shrieked like it was the funniest thing in the world.

'Yes, what's the matter with you two? Drunk or what?' Harish asked.

'No, no. It's just that you have such fine taste in women.' Tanvi and her friend doubled up with laughter.

Alka heard nothing after that. All she could hear was their laughter ringing in her ears. She had a vague sensation of Harish asking her if she was okay. She had gone pale. She managed to say that she was not feeling too well and requested him to drop her home. But Harish said he couldn't leave the party so suddenly. He would send her back by herself, with his driver.

'He is trustworthy, don't worry. He has worked with us for over thirty years. You will be safe with him,' he said. Alka nodded blankly. She was in a daze and everything seemed like a bad dream.

The buildings whizzed by and she sat silently in the car, her ears still burning with shame. When she reached her building, she got out of the car and sped home. When her mother opened the door, Alka burst into tears and hugged her tight.

'I shouldn't have gone, Aayi … You were right,' she managed to say between large sobs.

It took Alka's mother over two hours to comfort her and find out what had happened at the party. Alka didn't tell her the part about her and Harish. She only told her about Tanvi and her friend.

'Oh, thank the Lord that nothing else happened. I was so worried when you came home like that,' her mother said.

'I can never show my face at school again. They all know ...'

'Know what?'

'That ... That ... I am a maid's ... that you are a maid!' Alka wept as she said this, knowing that she was hurting her mother.

But Seema was unfazed. She shrugged.

'It doesn't matter what others think of us, Alka. That is their opinion. You do what you have to, to get what you want,' she said. 'I did all that I could to give you a good life, a life that we would possibly not have if I did not work as a maid. If they think you are not good enough for them, then that's a reflection on them, not on you. Now let me make some Haldi milk for you. It will calm your nerves and help you sleep. Just forget about this whole thing and move on.'

As Alka watched her mother make the milk, she was filled with a new form of respect for her. She noticed the wrinkles on her hand and her frail body. Many years of hard work had taken its toll on her mother, but on the inside, she was strong as steel.

She drank the milk that Seema handed and then hugged her tight.

'Aayi, wait and see, I will buy you a house with a large garden and it will have many rooms. You will never have to work. We will have a 100 servants,' she said.

Her mother laughed and asked, '100? What work will they do? And how will we pay them? And what will I do if they do all the work?'

'Oh, you just watch TV. They will do whatever we tell them to. And don't worry about the money, Aayi, just wait and see,' Alka said, sniffling, even as her mother smiled and put her hands around her and hugged her tight.

～

It was only the next morning that it occurred to Alka that Harish hadn't used any sort of protection at all. When it occurred to her that there was a possibility that she could be pregnant, she was terrified. She went about her daily chores with a heavy heart. When she sat down to study, she couldn't focus at all. The anxiety gnawed at her insides. Her mother repeatedly told her not to be upset if her classmates knew her reality, but Alka couldn't possibly tell her mother the real reason for her worry.

On Monday, when she went to school, she put on a brave smile and waved at Harish. Harish gave her an embarrassed half-smile and turned away. Alka didn't know what to make of it. Was that a brush-off? Had he approached her only to win a bet with his friends? Was whatever they shared at the party all an act that he had put on? Or was he ashamed of her background? She had to know. She also had to tell him that she was worried if she was pregnant. Surely he had to take some responsibility.

She was so distracted that the teacher noticed and asked if she was unwell. Alka replied that she was fine, but the truth was that she was so consumed with worry that she hadn't slept properly for two nights.

During lunch break, she gathered up all her strength and walked up to Harish. He was with his friends.

'Listen, we have to talk,' she said, her tone blunt and abrupt.

His friends sniggered, but Alka did not budge.

'What is it?' The annoyance was evident on his face.

'Could we talk in private, please?' Alka asked.

He stepped aside, a little distance away from his friends. But not far enough to be out of earshot.

'Listen,' he said. 'Please don't act like you're my girlfriend just because we spoke for a little while at the party, alright? We were both drunk. Let's pretend it never happened.'

Alka opened her mouth to speak but no words came. She felt as though she had been slapped. Shame, fury, shock, outrage—all of it consumed her at once.

'Okay,' she managed to whisper. Then she turned and walked away. She wouldn't cry in front of them. She fled, not knowing where she was going or what she was doing. She found herself at the library. It was her sanctuary, her safe space. She needed to think about things.

Ms Jalan knew right away that she was upset.

'What happened, Alka? You seem pale. Are you okay?' she asked.

Up to that point Alka had managed to hold in her emotions. But she now burst into tears at Ms Jalan's kindness.

'It's okay. It's okay. Come, let's go to my room and talk,' Ms Jalan said, leading her to the room at the back of the library.

Alka had never been to this room. She didn't even know it existed. It had a very comfortable-looking couch, a desk and a two chairs.

'Sit,' Ms Jalan said. 'What class do you have next?' she asked, handing Alka some tissues, as Alka sank into the couch.

'English and PE,' Alka answered between sobs.

'I'll call both your English teacher and PE sir on the school intercom and tell them I want you here in the library, and you are assisting me with something, okay?' Ms Jalan sat at her desk and picked up the phone.

'Thank you,' Alka said as she wiped her tears and blew her nose.

When Ms Jalan was done with her calls to Alka's teachers, she poured out two cups of tea from a flask she had on her desk, and handed one to Alka.

'Have some tea, and you can tell me what happened whenever you are ready, if you want to. If you don't want to, tea always makes things better,' she smiled.

Alka sipped her tea, grateful for Ms Jalan. She didn't know how she would go back to class and face Harish or her other classmates, or her mother later. She wished she could stay in the library forever.

'I am sorry about this,' Alka said.

'Oh, no need to be sorry. I know what it's like to be your age. Every single thing seems to hit us like a tornado. We give far too much importance to things that don't matter and we're not wise enough to tell the frogs from the princes. Guessing it's a boy problem?' Ms Jalan said.

Alka nodded. Ms Jalan had nailed it. She found herself opening up to Ms Jalan. She told her everything that had happened at the party between her and Harish. But she hid what Tanvi and her friends said. She hid that her mother was a maid. She was too ashamed to admit that to even Ms Jalan. She told her she was worried that she was pregnant. Ms Jalan asked her when she'd had her period. Then she calculated the dates and said it was highly unlikely that she'd get pregnant.

'From what you tell me, you will probably get your period in a day or so,' she said. 'And as for that boy—you haven't done anything wrong. If he is being a jerk, you don't need him in your life. Don't even give him a second glance. Hold your head high and ignore him. That's the best thing you can do for yourself,' she said.

Alka took Ms Jalan's advice to heart, and thanking her, left the library feeling lighter. Two days later, just as Ms Jalan predicted, Alka heaved a sigh of relief when she got her period. How dangerously close she had come to throwing away her dream of working hard and getting her mother out of Mrs Shetty's place. All for what? A boy who was too immature and naive to even acknowledge her. How foolish she had been. She decided she would never get close to anyone ever again. She would guard her secret and never allow anyone to put her in a position that she found herself in now. She would be strong and focus on her goals. She would ignore all the gossip, which she probably knew was going on right now. She would harden her heart and move on.

Like her mother said, she would do whatever it took to get what she wanted.

～

Harish tried to talk to her after a week.

'Listen, I am sorry alright? I was with my friends, and I didn't know what to say when you suddenly walked up to me,' he said. 'Can I take you out for coffee?'

'You know what Harish?' Alka said looking straight into his eyes.

'What?' he asked.

'Buzz off. And don't you dare approach me again,' she said as she flicked her plait back, and walked away.

6

1989–93

A New Life

AFTER HER CLASS 12, TANVI MOVED TO THE US TO BE with her father for her undergraduate studies. Mrs Shetty felt a void in her life as she adjusted to a life without her daughter. She seemed to transfer all her attention to Alka.

'You must study hard and do well, okay?' she reminded her every now and then, even though Alka needed no reminders. All her life she had been an exemplary student.

More than ever now, Mrs Shetty loved to show off Alka's progress at her club meetings. All of Alka's hard work and single-minded focus on her studies paid off. When the results of the CBSE Class 12 board exams came out, Alka was elated that she was among the top two per cent of the successful candidates in the country. All of her classmates were going out for celebration of their results. Harish tried to congratulate Alka too, but she refused to speak to him. She went to the library and told Ms Jalan her results instead.

'Wonderful! I am so proud of you,' Ms Jalan said. 'I should treat you to something nice. Let's go to the bakery and I'll buy you cupcakes,' she said.

'I would have loved that, madam, but my mother is waiting eagerly for me at home. Perhaps another time?' Alka said. Getting close to people meant getting hurt. She would keep her distance.

~

She ran all the way home and gave her mother the good news. Her mother was overjoyed. Mrs Shetty was elated as well. 'Well done, Alka!' she said. But Alka still had to do all the chores that Mrs Shetty had assigned. Doing well in the exams didn't change anything for her at Mrs Shetty's house.

~

Mrs Shetty boasted about Alka's exam results at her club meeting.

'I think we should all sponsor her education. She shows so much promise,' one of the members said. The others agreed. The club decided that Alka was a 'worthy case' and they raised funds for her education. The club members set up a trust fund.

Alka got accepted into a prestigious women's college in Delhi, and enrolled for her Bachelor's degree in sociology. She won a scholarship, which meant that she had to pay only

50 per cent of the fees. The members of the Inner Circle Club said they had made the right decision in raising funds, and said they could help a lot more children like Alka, who were deserving of it. Seema was so proud of her daughter.

'How I wish I could share this news with my family!' she said.

'Aayi, they haven't bothered about you all these years. What makes you think they will be remotely interested now? They will anyway expect me to get married instead. It is for the best that we're not taking to them. You yourself said that they are dead to you,' Alka replied.

'Yes, that is true. I will celebrate this Sunday with Renuka though. She will be so proud of you,' Seema said.

~

The college years whizzed past. For Alka, it was no different than school. She kept to herself and did not mix with the others. Most of the other students had formed 'groups' but Alka wasn't a part of any of them. She soon gained the reputation of being a loner. But since she was so good at academics, nobody dared make fun of her. In fact, they respected her.

In the third year of college, there was a career counselling programme where the students were asked of their future plans. Alka was ready to start applying for jobs as soon as she graduated as she felt she could start earning money. She dreamt of the day when she could have her own place, and move her mother out of that prison she had grown up in.

Ms Senapathy, a lecturer in the science department at Alka's college, whose daughter-in-law was a member of the

Inner Circle Club, knew about Alka's background. Though she was from a different department, she took a special interest in Alka. She'd seen how bright Alka was and she mentioned to the head of the sociology department that Alka should be encouraged to apply to the Management Institute at Bangalore. The Head agreed that it was a good idea and convinced Alka to apply. Alka cleared the management entrance exam and got called for interviews. She did not think that she stood a chance of getting selected, but when she did, she was in two minds.

On the one hand, she saw the benefits that a good management education would give her. The money required for fees and living expenses was not a problem because of the trust fund that the club had created for her. But she wasn't sure that she wanted to go, as it meant being separated from her mother—something she had never thought of. Her mother urged her to go. Surprisingly, so did Mrs Shetty.

'What else will you do otherwise? You've got good marks in your graduation. You can study now and later we will fix up your marriage,' Mrs Shetty said. She even offered that Alka could stay at her parents place. 'They have a big house and am sure they will have a spare servant's room,' she said.

Alka's ears burned when she heard that. She was studying so hard so she could escape this servant's room. She definitely did not want to go to Bangalore to live with Mrs Shetty's parents.

Later, when she was alone with her mother, Alka said 'Mrs Shetty got married to that industrialist's son and then got divorced. Now she is the owner of this big house. She wants me to study, but then in the same breath she mentions my marriage later. What do you think of marriage, Aayi?'

'It all depends on what kind of a man you get married to, Alka. Mrs Shetty comes from a wealthy family and I think her marriage was more a business alliance between families. I don't think she loved her husband. I got married to your father, and look what happened,' her mother said. 'I think you should be in charge of your life. You should go to Bangalore and study if that is what will get you a good job. It will be a different world, and you will learn a lot more living on your own. It will prepare you to be independent. Forget about marriage till you complete your studies.'

'Alright, Aayi. If that's what you feel, I will go. But I definitely do not want to stay in a servant room at Mrs Shetty's parents' place. They have campus accommodation there, and I can stay there.'

Alka took the Rajdhani Express from Hazrat Nizamuddin to Bangalore, with all her belongings packed into a single suitcase. She had chosen the best of Tanvi's hand-me-downs and a few new clothes that her mother had bought. Seema went with Alka to see her off at the station. Alka was nervous about leaving.

The journey would take thirty-two hours. As soon as she boarded the train and found her seat, she chained her suitcase to the berth. Then she looked out of the train window and smiled at her mother, who was walking along the platform. They held hands through the window of the train. Alka asked her mother not to worry. On the seat opposite to hers was a family with two little girls. The burkha-clad lady smiled at the tender exchange between the mother and daughter.

'Don't worry, we will look after her,' the lady told Seema. She introduced herself as Amina. She lived in Delhi but was travelling to Bangalore to visit her parents. Her husband worked in Dubai, she said.

'Thank you,' Seema said gratefully.

The train gave out a long whistle as it got ready to pull out of the platform. Seema couldn't stop the tears from rolling down her face.

'Aayi, don't cry! I will call as soon as I reach,' Alka told her mother.

'I am crying out of happiness, not out of sorrow. Study well,' Seema said as she wiped her tears.

As the train sped on, Alka relaxed in the company of the two little girls, who were utter chatterboxes. They took a great liking to Alka and she found herself smiling at their antics and little fights. Alka soon got over her nervousness and began enjoying the journey. She was also fascinated by the world outside the train window. She had never travelled outside Delhi, or sat in a train, and she loved looking at all the stations that whizzed past. As the train meandered through the tracks running through Agra, Adilabad, Warangal and Hyderabad, Alka noticed how the accents changed, how the cuisine and landscape changed. When the train entered Raichur in Karnataka and Alka heard Kannada being spoken, she was astonished.

It was the language she'd heard growing up, as Mrs Shetty spoke only in Kannada to her parents and relatives. Alka had carefully listened to them since childhood, and she could clearly make out everything spoken in Kannada, even though to her and her mother, Mrs Shetty always spoke in Hindi. She was surprised at how she felt instantly at ease when she heard the familiar tongue.

'Karnatka at last! It is such a peaceful place,' Amina told Alka.

Alka felt exhilarated as she took an auto and reached the campus.

It was an entirely new world; a new life filled with opportunities. She couldn't wait to explore it.

7

1983–89

The Boy at the Boarding School

'PLEASE ... PLEASE ... I DON'T WANT TO LEAVE YOU BOTH. Don't send me away. Please!' the boy pleaded with his older brother and his mother.

His clothes were packed in a trunk and loaded into the jeep that stood waiting to take him to Pinewood Charter International School in Ooty.

But his mother sat still, staring vacantly ahead, unable to comfort her son.

'You know I want the best for you, right?' His older brother held him by his shoulders and looked into his eyes.

'You've seen how good the school is. You get to go horse riding, and their swimming facilities are world class. You will never get anything like this in the government school you attend. You know how proud Appa would be?'

'But Appa isn't here now, is he? Then how will he be proud? Can dead people be proud?' the boy screamed in frustration.

His brother was patient. 'I've had to give up my education to take on all these responsibilities. I don't want the same for you. I want you to have the choices that I never had. You can come back here at any time you want. But this is the only chance you get at having a good education.'

'But I want to stay here!'

'You're twelve now. You're not a baby any more. Come on now, say bye to Amma. We will drop you,' his brother said as he climbed into the front of the jeep.

'Bye, Amma,' the boy said as he threw his arms around his mother.

'Bye, Kanna. Go study hard,' his mother replied.

His brother, watching the whole exchange from the jeep called out, 'Hurry up now. It will take us six and a half hours to get there. And that is if we don't count the coffee and food breaks.'

The boy got into the back of the jeep, and took a last look at his home, blinked back his tears as the Jeep drove away.

~

'Look, we have to both do our best for Amma. She has no one except us. We have to make her happy now, okay? So study hard,' his brother said as he dropped the boy off at the school. The hostel warden Brother Frederick was there to welcome them.

'How will you manage everything there? Take me back with you please; I will help you run the estate,' the boy tried a last time to make his brother agree. But his brother was having none of it.

'You'll be fine. Don't make this harder for me,' he said as they parted.

~

With a heavy heart the boy trudged up the stairs. He couldn't bear to turn back to see his brother leaving. His eyes filled with tears. He didn't know how he would survive in this school. He was shown to his dorm and he was told that his trunk would be sent upstairs. All the rules of the school were explained to him. They had to wake up at 6.30 a.m., make their beds and attend the morning prayers. Then they had to go outside for a jog for 30 minutes. After getting back, they had to shower and get ready. Breakfast was served at 8 a.m. sharp. After that was shower time, and then they had to get ready for classes. School activities went on till 2.30 p.m. Then the students had various sports, extra-curricular activities and clubs. But the boy was too distraught to see how exciting and interesting they actually were.

In the initial days, the boy was devastated. But he saw that everyone else felt the same way too. Some of the boys had been at the boarding school since they were five. They said that no matter how much time had passed, returning from home was always painful.

'Don't worry. You'll soon adjust,' one of them said.

He made friends with another boy from Bangalore, who too was coming to a boarding school for the first time. He looked just as lost as him. Both were happy to have made a friend. The boy discovered that his new friend's parents had divorced, and his mother had moved to Bombay.

'Why didn't you go to school in Bombay?' The boy asked him.

'I think my mother's new boyfriend can't stand me. And my father says boarding schools shape our personalities,' his friend rolled his eyes.

The boy coming from a conservative background was shocked hearing this. He was surprised to know about mothers having boyfriends. His friend didn't mind the boarding school at all. He said it was better than being at home because there was nothing much to do there, and there was so much fun they could have here.

Soon both boys discovered that a favourite sport of the senior boys was to pick on the younger ones. These two being new were their favourite targets. The older boys were cruel and both boys were terrified of them. To escape the older boys, both began hiding in the school library. They both read a lot and escaped into the worlds of Tom Sawyer and Huckleberry Finn. Both boys looked out for each other, and stuck together, and somehow got through their first year. But the experience had changed the boy. It had hardened his heart and at the same time softened it. He decided no matter what anyone did to him, he would not let it affect him. His brother had sacrificed so much to send him here. He would never let him down.

Twice a month, they had to write letters home. The other classmates expressed how they felt. They wrote about their life at school, what they looked forward to, what they were studying and that they missed home, but they were fine overall. They tried to peep into each other's letters, while hiding theirs.

But the boy's letters home were all similar. He never once expressed how he truly felt. He said he was happy, he had adjusted to the life at school, and made friends. He thanked his brother for giving him a fine education. He asked him to take care of his mother.

He never talked about the bullying that he and his friend were facing. He didn't talk of how he cried himself to sleep even after nine whole months. He didn't speak of how much he missed his father and the estate, and how he longed to be back home.

The following year, the boy's friend said he was leaving the school. He had written to his parents about the bullying and both of them were horrified at what he had been through. His friend's father came to the school and the boy was heartbroken when his friend left. Though his friend had promised to write, the letters never came. The boy waited eagerly each day. But he went to bed disappointed.

The boy was deeply saddened. *Maybe whoever he got close to, would be snatched away from him*, he thought. First it was his father, then he had had to part from his mother and his brother, and now his friend had left him too. Maybe he was being punished for something. He decided he would never get too close to anybody. That way he wouldn't be hurt. He would protect his heart from pain.

After a few years, the boy adjusted to the life at boarding school. There was a girls boarding school in the same town, and on weekends when they were allowed to go into town for a few hours, the girls and boys met at cafes and ice cream parlours. The boy had now grown into a handsome young man.

'Look at how all of these girls stare at you like you are a god,' his classmate remarked .

'You're imagining it,' the boy replied, but secretly he was pleased. It felt nice to be admired by the opposite sex. He could see the effect he was having on them. At one such outing, a pretty-looking girl walked up to him and asked him if he would take her out for a movie. She said she had taken a bet with her friends who said that she would never dare do anything like this. He looked at her and smiled. He asked her which movie she wanted to see and when they could go. Then he smiled at her and winked at her friends who giggled as well as gasped in equal measures. He could never resist a bet.

Soon the girl declared his love for him. For a few weeks, they dated each other. They met at cafes, went to movies, spent time at the botanical gardens. But soon the boy grew tired of her. They broke up soon after.

The following week, there was another girl who walked up to him and asked if he'd like to date her now that he was single. He shrugged and agreed. In a few months, he got bored and broke up with her too. But during the time that he would date a girl, he treated her like a perfect gentleman. He would buy them flowers, he would make them feel happy, he would converse with them about their interests and he would do everything that a good boyfriend does. So there was never a dearth of girls wanting to be his girlfriends. The boy didn't think much of it. As far as he was concerned, the girls knew what they were getting into. He had never been dishonest with them.

As he grew older, he began taking part in every activity that the school offered. He excelled in his academics too and he also took part in the inter-school festivals. When he reached class 12, he was the obvious choice for becoming the school captain—a role he took seriously. He soon became the favourite of his peers as well as his teachers. He put an end to bullying that year. He said enough people had suffered because of this archaic and cruel tradition. There was no need for the older boys to prove they were greater than the younger ones by picking on them. He got the students together and formed 'watch groups' to report bullying. He spoke to the teachers and they came up with posters to spread anti-bullying messages. It had a positive impact on the school, and everyone talked about the wonderful changes that the new school captain was bringing to the school.

His brother and his mother said they were proud of him. But the boy felt a void within himself. He wasn't sure what it was. Even though he was surrounded by people, he always felt alone. Even though there was never a dearth of girls who were willing to date him, he never felt a deep connection with any of them.

The boy knew he was looking for something—but what it was, he couldn't tell.

Part Two

Half-Way Home

'A thousand laughing suns are in your eyes. A thousand crying stars in mine.'
—Ahmad Shamloo

8

1993

Campus

ALKA FELT EXHILARATED AS SHE TOOK AN AUTO FROM Bangalore Cantonment station and reached the college campus. After a short registration process, a woman from the administrative staff handed her a welcome kit consisting of a brochure, a map of the campus and keys to her room. She pointed to where Alka had to go. She told her about the facilities within the campus—libraries, cafeteria, a little shop just outside the back gate for essentials like toothpaste, soap and instant noodles. She also informed her about the paid phonebooths within the campus itself, if she had to make calls.

The residential buildings were walking distance from the main buildings, where the classes took place. The 75-acre campus was full of curved paths, and sprawling, lush-green lawns and innumerable trees. With their cascading terraces and pillared halls, the buildings too were pleasing to the eye, and each of them had courtyards of various sizes, where students could gather for occasions. The main buildings housed large classrooms, seminar rooms and a world-class library, and Alka noticed the coffee shop that the girl at the reception had told her about. In addition, there was even a restaurant. Alka stared in fascination at the information on the brochure. She couldn't believe her eyes. She was elated that she would get to study here. This campus was so much better than her Delhi college campus. She walked to the residential building, her suitcase rolling behind her over the natural stone-paved pathways. There was a song in her heart and a smile on her face. Suddenly, her whole world had opened up.

She found her room easily. It was on the first floor, and the room itself was pleasant, with a single bed, a side table and a desk that ran the length of the wall next to the bed, and above it were empty bookshelves, built into the wall. On the wall across from the bed was a large built-in-wardrobe. There were two chairs in the room. One was for the desk, and looked like an office chair. The other was an easy chair for relaxing.

For Alka, this sparse and ordinary room seemed like her own little palace. It was the first time in her life that she had an entire room to herself. She ran her hand along the desk. All her life, she had studied and done her homework sitting on the floor in the small room meant for her mother and her. In comparison—this was pure luxury. Alka flopped down on the bed and took out the map of the campus from the welcome kit. How she wished her mother could see this! How she wished her mother could move in with her!

Suddenly, all Alka wanted was to talk to Aayi. She headed towards the closest phonebooth. A couple of students were waiting to make calls and Alka waited patiently for her turn. On the call, she excitedly described her campus, the sprawling lawns, the well-stocked library and all the facilities she could use. Her mother, happy to hear from Alka, told her, as she always did, to study hard. Alka promised that she would make her proud.

'Just two more years, Aayi—time will fly, and once I get a job you can move in with me,' Alka said, with one eye on the phone meter, which was ticking.

'God bless and God willing,' her mother replied.

Alka paid for the phone call and walked back to her residential building. Outside the entrance, she noticed a slim girl with stylishly short hair—dressed in a short top, flared jeans and platform sandals—struggling with three heavy suitcases, trying to pull them up the stairs.

'Need a hand?' Alka asked.

'Oh, yes! Please. Thank you so much. I'm Manasi,' she introduced herself.

'I'm Alka.'

'Malka? That's a unique name.'

'No! Alka. A-L-K-A.' Alka laughed, and Manasi laughed too.

They huffed and puffed, and between them, they managed to get all the three suitcases to Manasi's room, which turned out to be on the first floor too, right next to Alka's.

'Looks like we're neighbours,' Manasi said.

'Yes, we are. May I ask what's in these suitcases? They are so heavy!' Alka said.

'Oh don't even ask!' Manasi rolled her eyes. 'My mother insisted I carry everything—kettle, induction stove, rod heater. She thinks Bangalore is Siberia.'

Alka learnt that Manasi was from Bombay, and both her parents were doctors. When Manasi asked Alka what her parents did, Alka said her father was no more, and that she and her mother lived in Delhi. Alka didn't volunteer any more information, and Manasi did not pry. Alka loved that about her. Manasi seemed to have an easy-going nature and was a chatterbox. Alka liked that, because it meant she didn't have to say much herself to keep the conversation going. Manasi was jovial, bubbly, enthusiastic and within a week, much to Alka's surprise, she, who hadn't let herself get close to anyone in school or college in Delhi, became good friends with Manasi very quickly.

Leaving Delhi and moving to Bangalore felt strangely liberating to Alka. It felt like she had been given a new identity and she could craft a new life in Bangalore, where nobody knew her. In Delhi, in the circles she was used to, most people dressed up in expensive clothes. In the campus here, people wore casual T-shirts, jeans or shorts, and flip-flops. Alka found that to be a welcome change.

The campus here had a very relaxed vibe compared to her earlier college. There were students from all over India, and there were also a couple of international students. Some of them weren't as fluent as Alka in spoken English. There was a wide variety of accents, and Alka found that she felt at home. Far away from Delhi, with all these students who were new like her, she found herself fitting in more than she did back home.

After having a few meals at the college canteens, Manasi said she was tired of hostel food, and they ventured outside to explore the city a little.

They discovered a small stall selling North Karnataka meals. It was inexpensive, and Alka surprised herself as well as Manasi when she placed an order in Kannada.

'Oh wow! You speak the language? Is your mother tongue Kannada?' Manasi asked.

'No, it's actually Marathi. But I have a friend who speaks Kannada and I spent a lot of time at her place,' Alka said.

'That's impressive! You do have an ear for languages. I've lived all my life in Bombay and I can't speak a word of Marathi. The only languages I can speak are Hindi and English,' Manasi said.

~

Alka loved everything about the campus. The infrastructure was world-class. The classrooms were spacious, shaped like mini auditoriums, and there was a feeling of excitement and competitiveness in the air. The professors were passionate about their subjects, and the students were inspired to live up to their high standards. Several business leaders, powerful government officials, and successful and famous entrepreneurs, artists and intellectuals visited the campus to deliver talks and give presentations to the students, and Alka and her classmates often got insights into the careers and life of their role models. Alka never missed a single opportunity to attend these sessions. She wanted to get as much out of this experience as was possible.

The course work kept her glued to her books. The teaching methodology was very different from her previous curriculum. In this course, they were given case studies, and Alka loved reading them, analyzing them and applying the principles they covered.

Alka still loved going to the library, and in this one, she spent a lot of time researching the topics that they covered in class, and reading extensively about them.

'How can you read such big fat books?' Manasi grumbled once when Alka came back from the library with a stack of tomes in her arms. Alka just laughed in response and retreated to her room.

Alka also never turned up late for a lecture. Like she had in Delhi, Alka would wake up at 5.30 a.m. every day here too. But while in Delhi she had to do the chores that Mrs Shetty assigned before she could focus on her schoolwork, here she was completely free! She had a lot of time on her hands and she used every second of it.

Manasi, on the other hand, seemed to be interested in everything other than the course. She secretly wondered if she had made a mistake in choosing to pursue an MBA. She couldn't understand how Alka eagerly lapped it all up. She joined the photography club, as well as a students' dance club, which had instructors coming into the campus from outside. This, Manasi loved. She began learning Salsa and ballroom dancing.

'You must come and try it! It's great fun. You meet all the seniors and it's great for networking,' Manasi tried to get Alka to join in.

'No, no. I can't dance at all. I'm really not as social as you, Manasi,' Alka replied.

At the same time, Alka realized the importance of expanding her co-curricular activities, and after some thought, joined the reading club on campus. The reading club had only six members and only three turned up for the first meeting. Alka had read all the books on their list of suggested titles. The members argued about which book they should choose to read. The next week, the number of people who turned up for the meeting had dwindled to two, and the following week, the founder told Alka that she was dissolving the club. Reading was a solitary activity anyway, she said.

The clubs that Manasi joined, though, were well established and active clubs with a lot of members. They met regularly, had various seminars and activities, and took trips to the city together.

It was in her dance club that Manasi met Krishna Shekhar, who was a year senior. He stood out in the crowd, with his tall frame, square jaw, broad shoulders and deep expressive brown eyes that had a constant faraway look, like he was seeking something. When he smiled at someone, which he did often, Manasi could see how they almost melted with joy. He had that effect on women and it was evident that he knew it too. There was something very different about him, and Manasi found herself drawn to him. She found that she couldn't stop staring at him whenever he was on the dance floor.

One day, while he was up on the floor and Manasi was sitting it out, a girl next to Manasi noticed her gaze and said 'Drooling over Krish?'

'Huh?' Manasi was startled.

'Join the Krish fan club.' The girl smiled. 'The guy you've been staring at—he's in my batch.'

'Oh, is he? Does he have a girlfriend?'

'Right now, no. He has a reputation for breaking up with girls though. He just broke up with his third girlfriend last week,' she shrugged.

'So, he is available?' Manasi raised an eyebrow.

'He sure is! But you've got competition,' the girl said, grinning.

'Hmmm,' Manasi said dreamily.

That evening, she told Alka about Krish and her plan to get closer to him. Alka couldn't understand her. 'You know nothing about him. How can you just decide you want him, just based on his looks?' she asked.

'Hook first, look later.' Manasi winked. 'Let me see if he notices me. Once he does, I'll get to know him gradually. You know, in my school in Bombay, I had a friend who got whichever guy she wanted. I am going to use one of her tricks.'

Alka marvelled at Manasi's self-confidence, and wished she could have some of it at least.

The next day, Manasi dragged Alka to wait with her outside the college building. They leaned against a tree in the garden, close to the exit.

'He'll be coming out any minute now. I got a hold of his schedule. He doesn't have classes for the rest of the day,' she said.

Alka was amazed. 'How in the world did you get his schedule?' she asked.

'Easy peasy. I made friends with one of the girls in his class. She is in my dance club. Where there's a will and all that …' Manasi shrugged.

When Krish emerged from the class, Manasi said, 'Watch me,' and she walked towards Krish, her stride confident.

Alka watched her from a distance as she walked towards the building, pretending she didn't know he was there. Before Alka realized what had happened, she had 'accidentally' bumped into him and dropped all her papers, which scattered in all directions. She acted embarrassed and apologized profusely. Krish bent down to pick up the papers and Manasi thanked him, gathered all the papers and instead of entering the building, fled towards Alka, leaving him puzzled. He shook his head and walked away.

A happy Manasi told Alka, 'Step one is successful. Now he knows who I am. It might be corny but it works every time. Tomorrow I will seek him out and apologize for fleeing. I will tell him that I was too embarrassed and then introduce myself.' Alka was too dumbfounded to speak.

But Manasi clearly knew what she was doing. She carried out her plan and it worked like a charm. She kept running into Krish under different pretexts. She sought him out at the dance club. She asked him if she could dance with him. She asked him out for coffee. She complimented him on how smart he was. When she found out that he was fond of reading, she asked him to recommend to her his favourite books. She knew exactly how much attention to give him without seeming too desperate, and she knew exactly when she had to be 'unavailable'. It was a game she was good at. Within six weeks, Manasi and Krish were an item.

'He is so handsome yaar—just look at him. He can have any girl on the campus and he chose me. Or rather, I chose him and worked to get him, and of course, he couldn't resist me,' Manasi told Alka as they lay under their favourite tree.

'I think there's more to a relationship than just looks,' Alka said gravely.

'Are you twenty or fifty? Where is all this wisdom coming from? I've set up a double date this weekend. Don't say no!'

'What!? I don't want any dates, Manasi. You know—'

'Yes, yes, I know you have to study … But this one time, please. You know Rohan? He's in Krish's batch.

'Rohan? No, I don't know him,' Alka said.

'He's also a part of the dance club. I promise, you will like him. He told Krish that he has been mustering up the courage to ask you out. But you never give him the chance to. You always rush out after class and spend full days in that dreary library.'

'Please, Manasi. I don't want to meet this person.'

'Give him a chance. Don't be such a party pooper. It's bad enough that you don't even notice any of the boys in the campus! Do you want me to set up a date with a girl then?' Manasi teased.

In the end, Alka relented.

'Great! We'll all go in Krish's car. We'll go to Peco's. It's the most popular pub right now!' Manasi said.

'Are you sure Krish doesn't mind that you are dragging along two more people on this date?' Alka asked.

'You've met him a few times and you've seen what a nice guy he is.'

'That's why I am wondering if he hates the idea and if he is just being polite.'

'Oh no, he would tell me if that was the case. And he isn't so polite when we … you know.' Manasi giggled. Alka felt embarrassed and turned away.

~

That weekend, Krish drove them to the pub.

Manasi loved it, but Alka hated every moment of it. Rohan didn't read at all. He came from a family that had its own garment business in Indore, and he was into movies. He named all his favourite movies one by one and asked Alka if she had watched them. Some of them were book adaptations and Alka said that while she'd not watched the movies, she had read the books they were based on.

Krish smiled when he heard that.

'I've read the books too,' he said.

'I didn't even know these movies were made from books. You must watch the movies,' Rohan told her.

He and Alka had nothing in common, and Alka was bored within fifteen minutes. But she was good-natured about it. She nodded, made conversation and was polite.

By the end of the evening, Rohan had asked her out for another date. Manasi overheard this, and clapping her hands in delight, said that they could go on a double date again. Between Rohan and Manasi, they'd already decided on the place too.

All Alka could think of on the way back home was the excuses she could give to get out of this next date. She did not want to spend another evening with Rohan.

~

When they got back to the hostel, it was past midnight and a couple of a girls were waiting at the entrance of the building. Alka didn't know their names but she had seen them around and knew they were her seniors.

'Are you Alka Divekar, first year?' one of them asked.

When Alka nodded, she said, 'You had an urgent phone call from Delhi. A Mrs Shetty asked you to get in touch with her immediately.'

Alka knew from the girl's expression and the grave tone of her voice that there was something she wasn't telling her. Her palms went cold and she walked towards the phone, already dreading the news that awaited her.

9

1993

Loss and Longing

IT WAS THE FIRST TIME IN HER LIFE THAT ALKA WAS TAKING a flight. Manasi, Krish and Rohan accompanied her to the airport, helped her with the tickets, and waited with her till she was inside. The airline staff helped her board the flight. The fright of getting into a plane for the first time, the check-in procedure, the fumbling with the seat-belt—all of it gave Alka no time to process the shock. It felt like she was far away, observing her body going through the motions.

With that single phone call, her world had changed forever. 'Sorry, Alka. Seema collapsed suddenly. The hospital said it was a massive cardiac arrest. She seemed fine, really. She'd even finished washing the dishes and was waiting up for me. I'd just returned from the Inner Circle Club party. I asked her to fetch me a glass of water and she went to the kitchen and collapsed,' Mrs Shetty had rambled to Alka over the phone.

A thousand thoughts ran through Alka's mind as she heard the other woman's voice, but not a single word escaped her lips. Her mother was overworked. She hadn't had a health check-up for years. She didn't sleep well. She was always at Mrs Shetty's beck and call. But she was too devastated to say anything.

~

In every funeral scene in a movie that Alka had watched, there would be a group of people gathered to pay their final respects. But when Alka reached Mrs Shetty's house, she saw that there was nobody.

A few maids in the building whom Seema knew, had come earlier, and paid their respects, Mrs Shetty informed her. She also said all the right things to Alka. 'At least she did not suffer. She went in a good way. She was like our family member.'

'Bullshit,' Alka thought. 'If she was like a family member, why were my mother and I always cooped up in the dark, ill ventilated 10 x 8 feet room that was attached to your sprawling house?'

What hurt Alka most was that her mother's body was kept in that very room till Alka arrived from Bangalore. Alka sat like a rock next to her mother's body till four men came to take away the body to the crematorium. She wanted to accompany them, but they told her that women were not allowed. They told her she could come with them up to the ambulance if she wished to, but Alka shook her head and watched them take her mother's body away.

*It must not have been pleasant for you to have a dead
househelp in your living room, and so it was better for the body
to be tucked away in the servant's room*, Alka thought bitterly.

Twenty-two years of faithfully working for Mrs Shetty,
cleaning her toilets, taking care of her home, even cleaning up
her vomit when she was unwell and changing her daughter's
diapers when she was a baby, what hadn't her mother done
for them? She deserved better than her body being sent off
in an ambulance to the crematorium where Alka wasn't even
allowed to go.

No one mourned her mother's death. At least not too
deeply. Alka was certain that if Mrs Shetty was sad, it was
about the inconvenience of having to find a new maid. She
had already put out the word in her circles for a replacement
who would be joining them soon. She now asked Alka
whether she would clear her mother's belongings from the
room, as it was needed for the replacement.

The same windowless room that had been their home
for many years now, the room that had all the memories of
her childhood and her Aayi, felt like an empty coffin to Alka
now. Alka hadn't shed a single tear when they had taken away
her mother's body, but now, sitting alone in this room, she
howled, clutching her mother's thin straw mattress and her
blanket, not recognizing the high-pitched wails coming from
her throat.

'Look, Aayi! You treated her like a goddess just because
she sent me to the same school as her daughter and gave me
an education. But look at how she treated you even in death.
She didn't perform any last rites for you. She didn't ask me if I
wanted to. She threw you out like garbage. She didn't respect
you when you were alive, and she doesn't respect you even

in death. You deserved more than this, Aayi. You deserved more.' Alka swallowed the words that rose to her throat. There was no one to listen.

Her grand plan, her lifelong dream had been to get her mother out of here as soon as she got a job and could afford her own house. But now that plan was going to turn into a dream that could never come true.

Alka's sobs subsided eventually and she began to clear out her mother's sparse belongings, putting them all into a bag, that she threw into the garbage dump at the end of the lane. Her mother had taught her to lock away her sentiments. She only kept with her mother's thin gold chain and earrings. Like her Aayi always said, there was no point in looking back. She remembered the countless conversations she'd had with her Aayi, who had repeatedly told her that life was cruel and she had to be prepared to do whatever it took to keep going. Alka clung to those words and somehow mustered the strength to return to her life in Bangalore.

'Flying back today itself?' Mrs Shetty asked, when she got back to the house and began packing her own bag.

'Yes. Anyway, your new help is arriving and there's no place for me as well as for her in the servant's room,' Alka replied, hoping Mrs Shetty would get the jibe, but she didn't.

~

When she got back to the campus, Alka's heart was so heavy with grief that she couldn't drag herself out of her room. Submerged in agony, she couldn't make herself return to her life as it had been before. Manasi kept a watch on her.

She came to her room every single day, and brought her all her meals. She sat on Alka's bed and told her about the day's lectures. Alka listened politely, but she was far, far away. When she managed to fall asleep, she would dream of Aayi. In all her dreams, Aayi was alive and well, and was telling her how proud she was of her. She dreamt that Aayi was in her room, with her, admiring her campus. For those brief moments, Alka was happy, but when she woke up, the pain came back with double the intensity. She wished she could sleep forever.

After two weeks, Krish and Rohan knocked on her door along with Manasi.

'Alka, you *have* to get out of the room at some point. You're missing a lot of classes,' Rohan said.

'I can't … I … had only my mother. All of this—it is all meaningless to me now, because I don't have her. None of this makes sense anymore.'

'Do you think she'd want to see you like this?' Krish asked.

They insisted that Alka should get ready and go out with them. They took her to the tea stall across the street from the college. Alka could barely drink the tea they ordered for her. A little boy served it to them, and when he spilled some tea, he apologized profusely, fear on his face.

'It's okay, it's okay,' Alka consoled him. 'It's only tea, not gold.' His reaction had brought back a memory from her childhood for Alka, when Mrs Shetty had scolded her *so* badly for spilling tea that she'd gone to her room and wept.

Tears rose to Alka's eyes now, and she started crying even though she hadn't meant to.

'It's okay, Alka, it's okay,' Manasi said, handing her a tissue.

'Listen, I understand what it is like. I lost my mother too when I was five. My father remarried and I was raised by my stepmother,' Rohan said.

'I lost my father when I was eleven,' Krish said.

Alka wanted to tell them that it was different for her. They all had their families, someone to call their own. But Alka was alone now—all alone in this world. Even so, while she said nothing, she was strangely touched by Rohan and Krish's attempts to console her.

~

After that, when Manasi made plans with Alka that involved Rohan and Krish, Alka did not protest. She was too lonely, too grief-stricken and too broken to even protest. Soon, these small outings that Manasi planned began distracting her, and she also started attending classes again. Before she even realized it, six months had passed since Aayi's death. Alka did not even know when or how she and Rohan had become a couple. It had happened gradually, partly due to Manasi's efforts and party because Alka was too grief-stricken to think, and being around her friends made her forget her sorrow for a brief while.

Alka went on dates with Rohan, but she didn't feel any connection or deep love for him. Anytime he wanted to put his arm around her, or if he tried to kiss her after a date, she stopped him. She didn't even let him hold hands.

'I don't feel anything special for him, Manasi. I don't even know why I go on these dates with him,' she confessed to Manasi one day.

'I think you're still recovering from your grief. Give it more time,' Manasi advised.

While this was true, Alka also realized that, deep down, she was terrified of getting too close to Rohan, because if she did, he might discover something about her background. After the incident with Harish in school, she had been careful to hide everything about her past. Whenever Rohan asked her about her home or family, she gave him evasive answers. She wished he was more like Manasi, who had accepted that she was a very private person who did not like to talk about herself. Manasi respected that and had never once asked her questions about her childhood or her life in Delhi.

One evening, Alka walked to the men's hostel to return a book on marketing to Rohan. There was an assignment due the next day, and Alka had finished working on it. She had made detailed notes for it, and Rohan said he could use the notes, so she'd brought them along.

When she knocked on his door, she found him with a girl—one of their batchmates. It wasn't hard to fathom that they had been sleeping together. She handed him the book and walked out without a word. Though she was shocked, she was also strangely relieved. It meant that she now had a reason to break off things with him. She didn't hesitate to call it off with him. At first he was angry. He tried to blame her for what had happened. He told her how closed off she was, and how much he had tried to make it work. But it didn't affect Alka at all. She had built a wall around her heart, and nothing could get past it. 'Listen I wish you well with whoever that girl is, and I am happy you found someone,' Alka said.

'Look, that was nothing. I'm sorry, Alka. Please forgive me,' Rohan pleaded.

But Alka didn't want to get back with him. She had decided all those years ago that she would never allow herself to be put in that position again. She knew she would never give her heart fully to anyone. She'd learned that when you got too attached to people, it only brought you pain and sorrow, and she had to shield herself from it. So Alka told him she would not change her mind.

'You deserve to be with someone who can commit to you completely, Rohan. I can't give you what you want. I am sorry,' she said as she walked away.

~

After the break up with Rohan, Manasi became even more protective about Alka. Anytime that she was with Krish, she insisted that Alka should come along as well. Krish didn't mind. He felt that Alka had been through a lot in the brief amount of time that he had known her. The three of them spent many evenings together and life returned to the normal routine of lectures, classes and assignments.

'Let's go to Sakleshpur for the weekend that is coming up. We will have no classes on Monday because it is Founder's Day. It's just a five-hour drive,' Krish suggested on one Thursday evening.

'I don't want to be the third wheel,' Alka protested. 'And how do I know this isn't a pity-invite?'

'What the hell is a pity-invite? Did you just make that up?' Krish's eyes twinkled with amusement.

'No, we're not inviting you out of pity or anything. Come on, you know me better than that. And anyway, I know you can take care of yourself. You have already demonstrated that to us more than once. We just want your company!' Manasi cajoled.

'I just thought we could go because it would be an easy drive. I have already spoken to my brother and my mother. They are expecting us. And knowing my mother, she would have gotten a feast ready for us. She loves to feed people,' Krish added.

'I've never been to a coffee plantation. I am excited to see it. What about you, Alka? Ever been to one?' Manasi asked.

Alka hadn't.

'Then say yes na! We can explore it together.'

'Let me think about it? I'll let you know,' Alka said.

'You've been through too much this year, Alka. I think a break will do you good. Your mother—and then the break up …' Manasi trailed off, not wanting to mention Rohan's name.

'I'll let you know,' Alka said again.

She wanted time to think about it. She was done going along with whatever people suggested, just because she didn't want to say no. She was going to be in total control of her life from now on. She would make each decision after giving careful thought to it.

That evening she made a pros and cons list. She'd submitted all her projects and assignments, so she didn't have much to do. The grief of losing her mother still hung around like a dark cloud. It hadn't allowed her to experience any joy in anything she did.

Alka also realized that over this long weekend, the college would be nearly empty. Most students were going to their hometown or to nearby places. She had nowhere to go. It would be a nice, refreshing break. Manasi was right and exploring a coffee plantation might do her good.

She felt a tiny frission of excitement at the thought of doing something different. Perhaps, the only way to live now, would be to squeeze life for all the joy it could offer her. After all, nothing in this world was certain. So she accepted Manasi and Krish's invitation.

10

Anandi and Subbu

'SUBRAMANIYA ... SUBRAMANIYA!' ANANDI CALLED OUT to Subbu from the verandah. She always used his full name when she wanted his complete attention. 'Krishna's friends will be here any minute now. Go, change! Look at how you are dressed.'

He glanced down at himself. He was drenched in sweat. With a green cloth wrapped in a coil, around his head, and dressed in a bright blue lungi and a sleeveless white vest, which was wet with perspiration and clinging to him, he looked more like one of the plantation workers and less like its owner.

'You know there is work to be done here. Krish will take care of his friends. I don't have time to socialize,' Subbu said as he continued to carry the firewood to the shed behind the house.

'You know what your Appa used to say? Greet your guests in the proper manner. Not like this,' she gestured at Subbu. 'Your Appa would take the time out, no matter how busy he was, and he would properly welcome whoever came to our doorstep. He would always greet them like a true gentleman— well dressed in his coat and polished shoes. Isn't that what he taught you too?'

Subbu grimaced. Though it had been over a decade since his father had passed away, any reference to him still felt like an arrow to his heart. Subbu had to drop out of school and take charge of the estate along with his mother. His grandfather had been a financier to many of the coffee plantations nearby and as a child, Subbu had always accompanied him and his father on their travels, visiting the different plantations. He'd learned about how each region and each planation had a different method of cultivation, as the plants and the topography in each region were different. Though Subbu had grown up learning the ropes and had a fair idea of production and other things—still, being in charge of the entire estate when he was still in his teens, had been downright terrifying for him.

On one side was the shock and grief of his father's sudden death, and on the other side were the practical matters of running a coffee estate. Anandi expected Subbu to step right into his father's shoes. And soon, one of the ways that Subbu discovered he could cope with his grief and stress was to throw himself into hard manual labour. He worked alongside his workers from dawn to dusk, tiring himself out and falling into his bed exhausted at the end of every day. Over the years, he learnt to cope with the grief better. As he got more and more involved in managing the estate, he found that he no longer needed to push his body to the extreme with laborious physical work as much as he used to. But every now and then, he would chop firewood, fix compound walls and do minor repairs. The physical labour made him feel happy. Anandi though, had never understood her son's need for it.

'Hurry now. Go have a bath and change into decent clothes. Let one of the workers do this instead. Also, tell them to put the dogs in the enclosure. We don't want them jumping on our guests. Go on now—I don't know why you insist on doing all this yourself,' Anandi part-reprimanded and part-chivvied him.

'Okay, okay! I'm going.' Subbu sighed as he dropped the firewood inside the shed and headed upstairs.

When Subbu emerged from the shower, having changed into a freshly pressed, full-sleeved shirt and dark blue well-fitted trousers, with his dark hair neatly slicked back, he did not expect to find two young women seated in the verandah along with Krish. Since Anandi hadn't mentioned anything about the guests, he had assumed that Krish was bringing over a gang of boys, like he used to when he was at boarding school.

'Ah, there you are, Anna! These are my friends. This is Manasi and this is her best friend Alka. We're all together at the Management Institute. Girls, meet my big brother, Subbu,' said Krish as he introduced them.

Manasi was seated next to Krish, and Alka was next to his mother. Manasi had an angelic face, large, bright eyes and very short hair. She was dressed in a blue, flowing, printed dress that fell to her knees. Subbu could immediately see how bubbly and enthusiastic she was. Manasi held out her hand over the snacks and coffee that were laid on the table in front of them, offering it to Subbu, and said 'Ah, hello! I've heard so much about you, Subbu.'

'Hello, Manasi,' said Subbu as he awkwardly shook her hand.

Alka was less ebullient compared to Manasi. Her long hair was wild and tousled, reflecting the sunlight. Her eyes were a deep, dark brown, like the soil after the rains. Her face was delicate, with sharp cheekbones, smooth skin and lips like a cupid's bow. She was dressed in a simple white T-shirt and faded blue jeans. There was an aura about her that held Subbu captive for a few seconds. It was as though she radiated wisdom and sadness, simplicity and sophistication, anger and calm, all at the same time.

'Hello,' she said, but she did not hold out her hand.

'Hello, Alka,' Subbu replied, and for a second, when their eyes connected, Subbu felt like she was assessing him, studying him, like she was looking into his soul. Then the moment passed.

Alka was surprised to see that Subbu looked nothing like Krish. He was much shorter than Krish and had none of the suave charm that Krish exhibited. He had worry lines on his forehead that were visible when he smiled. And she could tell by his tanned skin that he was clearly someone who spent a lot of time outdoors. His wavy black hair was cut short. He seemed to be a practical, no-nonsense kind of a guy. Krish had a polished neutral accent, but Subbu spoke like a local.

It was Manasi who dominated the conversation. Anandi seemed to genuinely enjoy her company and kept asking Manasi questions about her life and family, which Manasi was happy to answer.

'Where did you do your schooling? What do your parents do? Anandi asked.

'I grew up in Bombay. Both my parents are doctors, aunty. They have a small hospital. They had me when they were in their late forties. In fact, my father was in his fifties. So you can imagine how it must have been for me at home. They have high expectations from me. They very badly wanted me to go into medicine. But I am not interested in working in their hospital for the rest of my life. I've had enough. So here I am, doing my MBA, hoping to take up a corporate job,' she said.

'Bangalore or Bombay—which one do you like better? ' Anandi asked.

'Amma, stop grilling her!' Krish rolled his eyes at his mother. He knew what his mother was doing—she was assessing Manasi to see if she was marriage material. Krish had specifically told her not to do that when he had called to tell her that he would be coming over with them. He had been happy that Alka was coming along, as he didn't want it to be a 'meet-my-mother' scenario. He has been hoping to keep it causal but his mother was turning it into precisely what he dreaded.

'Oh come on Krish—she isn't grilling me, and I don't mind answering her questions,' Manasi said. 'Well, to be honest, Bangalore is so green. And the houses in Bangalore are so huge compared to the ones in Bombay. But I think Bombay is where the big opportunities are—especially in the corporate world. I like the fast-paced life there and I guess I am more of a city girl.'

'Hmmm,' said Anandi and then she turned to Alka. 'What about you Alka? What do your parents do? Where are you from?'

Alka hesitated only for a fraction of a second. 'I lost my mother recently. And my father when I was very young. My father was a prominent industrialist. My mother did a lot of work for charities. She was the chairperson of the Inner Circle Club,' Alka said, looking at Anandi.

'Oh, I am so sorry,' Anandi said as she touched Alka's hand. Then she couldn't help herself. 'How did she pass away?' she asked.

'Maaaa! I am sure Alka doesn't want to talk about it. It's too soon,' Krish said, trying to protect Alka from his mother's nosey questions.

'It's fine, Krish.' Alka said. 'She died of a heart attack. It was too sudden. Everyone was shocked. The number of people who turned up for her last journey—I had no idea she touched so many lives,' Alka said.

She took a sip of the coffee and closed her eyes—'And this coffee—it is exactly like she used to brew. Reminds me of home. Tastes divine.'

'You have fine taste. It is our special in-house blend,' Anandi beamed.

She was quiet for a few seconds after that, and then she took a sip of the coffee and said, 'You know, I lost my husband the same way you lost your mother. All of a sudden, without warning. Life changes in a second.'

'It does. It must have been so hard for you,' Alka said.

'I think it was harder for Subbu. He had to drop out of school. But he took complete charge, put Krish through boarding school and he manages everything so well. It was only when my husband died that I was glad I had two sons.'

'Why aunty? Daughters are no less than sons!' Manasi couldn't help remarking.

'Oh, some things at the estate require a man. Women won't be able to do this kind of work. It is very hard,' Subbu said.

Then Subbu asked them if they were scared of dogs. Manasi said that as long as they stayed at a distance she was fine. Alka said she wasn't scared at all, as a lot of people had dogs in the residential complex that she had grown up in.

'Ha—but these are not like those city dogs. They roam the entire estate. We only put them in an enclosure when we have guests,' Subbu said.

'How many dogs do you have?' Alka asked.

'Seven now!' Subbu said 'So is it okay if I release them?'

Both Alka and Manasi said they were fine, and Alka watched as the dogs happy to be let out, bounded off into the estate.

~

At lunch, Anandi had laid out a feast fit for kings. She'd supervised the cooks and hovered over them to ensure they followed her recipes exactly. The table was groaning under plates of food—steaming hot rice Kadubus accompanied by a spicy Koli Saaru, the pungent fragrance of Menthya sasve mingled with the aroma of fresh seasonal fruits, and musambi, guava, jackfruit and bananas had been laid out in a neat row at one end of the table.

'All the produce used is grown right here on our land,' Anandi said proudly.

Manasi was vegetarian and she barely touched any of the dishes. Alka, on the other hand, genuinely enjoyed the food, with its intense flavour and tangy, spicy taste. She finished every single thing on her plate, and much to Anandi's delight, took second helpings of everything. She asked Anandi questions about how it was made, and Anandi was even more pleased. She answered all of Alka's questions and explained in detail the finer points of Malnad cuisine. For Alka, the cherry on the cake was the dessert—Halasina Hannina Mukka, a local dish made with jackfruit, rice, jaggery and coconut. Anandi told her that it was all made using firewood on traditional stoves.

'No wonder it has the flavour of unspoilt nature, mountains and waterfall. I can taste it all in this food. All of this—it is the best thing I have ever eaten. Heavenly,' Alka said quietly.

Subbu smiled. He could see that Alka had achieved the impossible. She had won his mother over. Ever since he turned twenty-six—an age his mother considered 'the right age' for marriage, Anandi had turned matchmaker, even though Subbu had told her he had no intentions of getting married.

'How long are you going to mourn for her? It's time you moved on. *She* has moved on. Let me know and I shall put out the word and there will be so many proposals coming in for you,' Anandi had told him repeatedly.

But Subbu, busy with his coffee plantation, had no time for romance. He had, on his mother's insistence, gone on a few dates with prospective brides, all whetted by his mother, and none of them had worked out. His mother had said, 'Look, whoever you marry, it is important she comes from a good family and fits in with this culture that we have here. We do not want namby-pamby girls who are afraid of living on a coffee plantation.'

'So why don't you include a questionnaire in their assessment interview? Do you like nature? Are you afraid of the dark? Will you be okay being cut off from humanity on a 400-acre coffee estate? Will you be okay with not being a working woman and only a coffee-grower's wife?' Subbu smiled wryly.

'I think that is a good idea,' Anandi had fetched her notebook and begun scribbling in it.

'Amma, I was being sarcastic!'

'But whatever you said—they are all valid points. The girl who will ultimately be your wife must be worthy of this estate. She must consider all this and make it her home. This life—it's not easy and it's not for everybody,' Anandi said. A sikra cried in the distance as though agreeing with her.

~

Later that evening, as the sky darkened and night fell, they had a bonfire. Subbu set it up with the wood he had chopped earlier in the day. The helpers served spicy roasted wood-smoked chicken that they grilled on a barbecue, roasted organic farm-grown bell peppers, imported whisky and home-brewed wine. Everyone including Anandi sat around talking. The warmth of the fire and the alcohol loosened their inhibitions, the dancing flames creating a strange intimacy. Even the irrepressible Manasi revelled in the silence under the canopy of a million stars. The chirping crickets, the chattering cicadas and the gently blowing wind—all of them were in perfect harmony, adding their gentle magic to the night.

Subbu wasn't sure if it was the atmosphere or the alcohol that made him ask Alka more about her family. He felt drawn to her, like she was a powerful magnet and he wanted to know everything about her. He'd never felt like this for years now.

Not since his break up with the one girl he thought was 'the one'. But that was years ago.

'So what about your family? Do you have close relatives? Siblings?' he asked her.

'I am an only child, and there are no close relatives. So, well, right now I'm all alone,' Alka looked into his eyes as she said this and held his gaze. He felt like he could dissolve into her eyes.

Was she flirting with him? Were her words a hint that she was attracted to him? Subbu didn't know. Since she didn't take her eyes off him, he fidgeted and looked away.

Alka had honed this look over the years. She knew it made people slightly uncomfortable. It was a defence mechanism that came from years of practice. She hated questions about her family. So to avoid answering, she always asked the person about themselves.

'What about you? Any girlfriends?' she asked.

'The last girlfriend I had was a few years back,' Subbu said.

'What happened then?'

'Let's just say it didn't work out,' Subbu gazed at the dancing flames as he said this.

'Some things are just not meant to be. We think we control things. We think we can conquer the world. Then life comes along and screws us over, doesn't it?' Alka was staring into the flames too as she spoke. She was thinking about her mother. Subbu, lost in his own world, didn't notice her blinking back her tears.

But he knew what she meant.

'Yes, it does,' he said. 'It certainly does.'

～

The next morning, Subbu gave them a tour of the coffee estate in his jeep. Alka sat in the front with Subbu while Krish and Manasi sat at the back. He drove expertly through the well-marked mud trail.

'Wow! This is fun. And so, so bumpy,' Manasi shrieked, holding on tightly to the safety handles that hung from the roof of the jeep.

'The only vehicle that you can drive here are these jeeps. And even then, in the rains, the wheels often get stuck,' Subbu said as he manoeuvred the vehicle down a narrow path.

He first took them to the sorting sheds, where there were many women at work. He explained how the day's harvest was sorted manually by hand before they were sent to be weighed. The harvest season was typically from December to March and it was during this time that the estate was abuzz with activity. He took them to the pulping rooms and explained how the ripe cherries were immediately processed to ensure quality and freshness.

He noticed Manasi stifling a yawn. Krish, having heard all of this whenever they had visitors, had wandered off and was talking to some of the labourers. Alka was the only one who was all ears, listening intently and asking questions.

When he drove them to a stream that ran through the estate, with paddy fields on one side and the estate on the other side, he noticed Alka's pure joyance in the place. She kicked off her sandals and squealed as she entered the cold water, splashing it on her face and laughing in delight.

'How lucky are you guys to have your own stream!' she said. 'Come Manasi—take off your shoes and get in!'

But Manasi was scared of the leeches, which Krish had warned her about.

'No way—I am fine,' she said and she refused to get down from the Jeep.

Krish walked back towards the stream and got into the water. He began splashing water on Alka playfully, and laughing, Alka splashed the water right back at him. When Alka slipped over a rock in the cool water, Krish reached out for her waist and steadied her. 'Ooooh, careful! These rocks can be treacherous,' he said.

Alka held on to his hand, 'Oh my god! Thanks,' she said, momentarily disoriented. She was close enough for her to inhale the masculine woody scent he wore and she felt a little jolt of energy pass through her and at the same time felt a little explosion in her stomach. His arms were strong, muscular. Alka froze for a moment and then instantly dismissed it. She attributed it to just being caught off-guard.

Subbu watched the whole exchange and turned away.

Manasi, blissfully unaware of any of it, chattered away happily as they drove back to Anandi estate. Subbu was quiet throughout the journey.

Krish's heart was pounding in his ear. He had felt it too. He had been with enough women and he recognized this feeling. This wasn't just sexual chemistry. Or was it?

He had been observing Alka over the past weeks, and he'd grown increasingly fond of her. At first he thought it was because Manasi spoke so highly of her. Then he told himself that it was to do with how much he admired her for the diligence in her work and her love for books. But his little moment they'd had confirmed his suspicion—it wasn't mere fondness. It was something more.

He didn't know though what this new feeling between them was. He couldn't name it, but it scared him.

11

Feelings

ALKA HAD FALLEN IN LOVE WITH THE COFFEE ESTATE. Every day, she woke up before the others and took a walk through the mud trail, enjoying the dense greenery, the silence and the tranquillity. Completely cut off from the cacophony of a busy world, Alka found herself relaxing completely. She felt at home among these mammoth oak trees and the coffee shrubs. She admired the colonial mansion with its white walls, antique British furniture and the sloping tiled roofs. She wondered how Subbu and Krish felt about it being their home. What a magnificent house to grow up in! Did they even know how fortunate they were? She compared it to the only home she had known—the tiny room in Mrs Shetty's home with an even tinier bathroom. While Alka knew how luxurious living spaces could be—after all, she had seen opulence closely in Mrs Shetty's house—she never knew how elegant a historic property like this could be. She'd never experienced anything remotely close to this in her life.

As she walked along the path, into the dense greenery, a bright blue kingfisher swooped past her and she gasped in delight.

'Hello. Up early?' a voice said and she turned around, startled.

Subbu waved at her. He had been further ahead, deep inside the plantation.

'Hello, yes. This is ... beautiful,' Alka replied.

'It is also a lot of work,' Subbu smiled shyly, as he walked down the path and joined her.

'I am sure it must be. I can't even imagine how you manage it all,' Alka replied.

'Have been doing it for a long time now,' Subbu replied.

He asked her if she wanted to walk to a waterfall. She nodded eagerly and Subbu led her further into the forest.

'Careful now, this grass here can cut. Actually you must wear rubber boots when you venture into the estate. Like these,' he said pointing to his own galoshes.

'Next time,' Alka smiled as she carefully stepped over the grass.

When they reached the waterfall, Alka stood speechless in awe and reverence, looking at the water, a brilliant white, rushing and tumbling down the perpendicular rocks and cascading into the dark clear spring. The sound of the water rushing down felt like a balm to her bruised soul. Having never experienced a waterfall so closely, she inhaled deeply, closing her eyes, savouring the moment as a few droplets splashed on her face. A hornbill swooped over their heads and Alka's eyes shone as she said, 'Did you see? It had a fish in its mouth.'

Subbu smiled and nodded, 'Do you know they do not build their own nests? They nest in the cavities of large trees?'

Alka had no idea about the nesting habits of any bird. She hadn't given much thought to it. Now she mulled over it and said, 'How nice it must be to just go and make a home in any hole you find. They don't complain about size, they don't need windows and they are happy with whatever they get,' Alka said.

Subbu had never thought of it that away and he found Alka's thoughts to be interesting and original.

'Yes, that's true!' he agreed.

When they got back to the bungalow, Krish was sitting on the steps, sipping his coffee, and Manasi was clicking pictures of him. It looked like a proper photoshoot, with Manasi snapping away and Krish posing like a model. The sun fell on Krish's face, lighting up his deep brown eyes, and Alka couldn't be oblivious to how good-looking he was. No wonder all the women, including Manasi, thought he was a great catch.

~

'Where had you both gone off to, leaving us here?' Manasi asked. She'd stopped clicking when she spotted them walking up the steps.

'Subbu took me to a waterfall deep inside the estate. Oh Manasi, it was magical,' Alka replied.

'Let's check your legs and see if there are any leeches. You won't feel them at all. They suck as much blood as they can, and become fat round globules. When they can't suck anymore, they fall off,' Krish said.

'Eeeks! I am out of here,' Manasi yelled as she bounded up the steps, towards the house. Both Krish and Subbu laughed and Alka giggled nervously.

'Let's see,' she said, and rolled up her jeans.

Subbu was mesmerised. Her bare legs were shapely, feminine and so beautiful. For a few seconds, he stood staring. He couldn't look away. Unknown to Subbu, Krish was feeling the same way.

'Oh, you do have a leech there,' Krish pointed to a thin black leech on her left ankle.

'Oh yes! This is the first time I've seen something like this. It doesn't even hurt!' Alka said, staring intently at it, sitting very still. After having spotted it, she wasn't scared or repulsed. She was simply fascinated.

Krish carefully pulled the leech off. Alka felt a shiver run up her spine. It was a strangely intimate action. There was a thin trail of blood where the leech had been.

Subbu turned away then, trying to control his arousal, jealousy and a strange feeling that he couldn't define. He had to do something. He couldn't let his feelings show. So he went into the house and emerged with something in a little steel bowl, some cotton and a safety pin.

'What's that?' asked Alka.

'This is turmeric paste mixed with some hot water. It's an excellent antiseptic. Wipe off the blood with this cotton, and apply some of the mixture,' said Subbu as he handed over the items he had just got to Alka.

'Let me do it for you,' Krish offered.

'Oh—no. No, it is fine, I can manage,' Alka replied.

Subbu was secretly pleased about her refusal.

Alka did as she was instructed, carefully wiping off the blood with the cotton and gently applying the mixture with the safety pin.

'It might itch for a few days, but do not, under any circumstances, itch it. Just apply a calamine lotion or some moisturising cream,' Subbu instructed her.

Manasi sat with her feet up on the chair and her face covered with her palms.

'Is it over? Alka, are you sure you have no more leeches on you? Will they spread?' she asked warily.

Subbu laughed. 'They don't "spread" like that Manasi. They are leeches, not head lice. When we were kids we used to sprinkle salt on them to get them off us,' he said.

'YUCK! Why would you want to tell me that? You've ruined my appetite now!' Manasi said to Subbu.

'How will that ruin your appetite? We aren't serving you leeches,' Subbu countered.

'Let's please stop talking about leeches. The very topic is disgusting,' Manasi crinkled her nose.

'You should wear rubber boots when you wander through the estate,' Krish told Alka.

'I know. Subbu said the same thing. I am glad I'm getting the coffee plantation 101 rules,' she replied.

'We always keep extra shoes for guests. Next time you visit you can just borrow those,' Subbu said.

~

Anandi came out from the Bungalow just then and told them that breakfast was ready. They were leaving for Bangalore after breakfast. She called out to her maid, 'Gowramma, please set the tables.'

Alka felt a sharp pang of pain shoot through her. Anandi's tone was exactly like the one Mrs Shetty used to summon her mother. It took Alka a few seconds to compose herself, and then she looked around to see if the others had noticed, but everyone was busy admiring the food.

Gowramma laid out a scrumptious spread of Akki roti, Jwala roti, Huli avalakki and Halbai—a kind of rice halwa. Anandi explained to Alka what each dish was made of and Alka took it all in, rapt.

'You must teach all these recipes to me. This food is so, so good. Thank you, Gowramma,' Alka said as she savoured each bite.

Gowramma, unused to anyone thanking her, broke into a wide grin.

'Come and spend some time here, and you can learn all these traditional recipes,' Anandi was pleased at Alka's interest in the food. 'You know, all these things—they are so healthy, prepared with fresh, local ingredients. My grandmother or my mother never fell ill. And even me, for that matter—the only time I have been in a hospital is to deliver these two boys.'

'It must also be this fresh mountain air. And thank you aunty, I would love to learn all these recipes,' Alka replied.

'I wish you kids were staying longer. I really enjoyed having you around. You must come again,' Anandi told them.

'I'll bring them again, Amma. We have placements coming up. I also have my final year internship. I am on the placement committee too. So perhaps after that. Placements are so stressful,' Krish said.

'What do you have to do for it? What are your responsibilities?' Anandi asked.

'We have to coordinate all the activities leading to placement for all our students. Unlike other management institutes, we do our internships in the final year. If we perform well, we are straight away absorbed. But still the companies like to come to campus and interview candidates. So right from making a schedule of interviews, overseeing the registration process, pre-placement talks, helping the students with their CVs, displaying the welcome posters for the companies, allocation of the rooms for interviews, arranging everything for recruiters—we do it all,' he said with a hint of pride in his voice.

'That sounds like a lot of work,' Subbu remarked. Since he had never been to college, he listened eagerly whenever Krish shared anything about his courses. Whenever he thought about it, Subbu was filled with regrets about missing out on all these college experiences. He was proud of Krish, but every time his younger brother spoke about his college life, Subbu felt a prick of pain at what he had lost.

'It is a lot of work, and only if we do our jobs properly will our batchmates get placed. Once I get placed, I can see that these two here also get good internships,' Krish said, nodding at Alka and Manasi.

'Enough! Enough. Don't throw your weight around just because you are a senior,' Manasi said.

'Ah, don't mess with me young lady. I can decide your fate,' Krish narrowed his eyes and pointed at her with a fork.

Manasi stuck out her tongue at him and everyone smiled.

~

It was with reluctance that Alka bid goodbye to Anandi and Subbu, as they left for Bangalore from Sakleshpur. Manasi, on the other hand, was glad.

'You know, the estate is beautiful. But looking after the planation is so hard. It is not for everyone, Maybe Aunty was right about it being a man's job,' she declared as Krish made his way out of the estate and they joined the highway traffic.

'I don't know about that. And anyway, for me, the estate is home, but for my mother and brother, it is life itself. They can't imagine any other way of living,' Krish shrugged.

'What about you? Would you prefer living at the estate or in a city?' Manasi asked.

'After my father passed away, my mother and Anna decided to send me to one of the finest boarding schools in the country. I haven't really spent much time at the estate. I visited only for my holidays. I am more used to city life now,' Krish said.

'Did you miss home when you were at boarding school?' Manasi probed.

'Let's just say I coped. Subbu had to take charge after my father's death. I felt helpless that I couldn't do much. Subbu told me that I had to do well in my studies—and he would do everything he could to ensure that things at the estate run smoothly.'

His eyes were on Alka as he spoke. He was glancing at her from time to time through the rear view mirror.

Alka was aware of it. She fidgeted uneasily each time their eyes met. She felt the same familiar sharp jolt of electric current like she had felt when he'd held her waist at the stream. She was taken aback by the intensity of her feelings. She told herself that it was only because she was at a strange point in her life. Perhaps it was all the grief that she was carrying inside her, combined with the visit to the coffee estate and the last few days where she'd felt, for the first time, completely at peace—all of it together was messing up her head. *I shouldn't encourage this*, she thought.

So she moved to the other side of the car, where Krish couldn't see her unless he adjusted the mirror.

Manasi, oblivious to what was happening, was busy looking at the scenery outside. She was chatting about what a fun time they'd had but how she was also glad to be getting back to the city, and how it was 'too much wilderness' for her.

Alka nodded but she was barely listening. Her face displayed no emotion but she felt uneasy. Whatever her feelings were towards Krish, she simply had to keep them in check.

A few seconds later, Krish adjusted the mirror so he could see her again. Though she told herself that she shouldn't look into the mirror and meet his eyes, she couldn't help it. For the rest of the journey, they kept stealing glances at each other in the rear-view mirror.

Alka couldn't look away, and neither could Krish.

12

1994–95

White Blossoms

ONCE THEY WERE BACK AT CAMPUS, IT BECAME increasingly harder for Krish to suppress what he had begun feeling towards Alka. The fact that she had visited the coffee estate, met his brother, conversed excitedly with his mother about the local food, all of it further endeared her to him.

While he'd always had relationships, he hadn't been this powerfully drawn to anyone before. Also, while he was in a relationship with one woman, he'd never been attracted to another. So he couldn't understand this. But feelings were something that happened to you—it wasn't something you controlled. All he knew was that he was strangely excited, and adrenaline squished his insides into jelly each time Alka was around. And she was around often. They had become a trio and Manasi asked her along on almost all their outings and plans.

'Listen, you used up all your alone time when you locked yourself up in the room for weeks. Enough now, don't sit and brood, come along,' she would insist.

Sometimes, Alka had genuine excuses—an assignment to be submitted, a paper to be turned in, a test, a project. But Manasi knew exactly how much work each one required and she called her out on the excuses that she felt were clearly not valid. So, Alka went along, thankful that she had a real friend who was looking out for her.

But she was also aware of the explosive chemistry growing between her and Krish, and began avoiding looking at Krish when the three were together. She would address Manasi, and pretend Krish wasn't there till he asked her something directly. Then she would be forced to reply, and as soon as she answered, she would look away, her heart beating loudly. But her face revealed nothing. Alka was used to keeping secrets. All her life she'd done that. She was an expert at concealing what she truly felt deep down.

The placements were approaching and Krish threw himself into work. He was glad to have something to distract him. He worked extremely hard, and Manasi and Alka hardly saw him.

Eventually, the senior batch, including Krish, graduated and everyone in the batch got good placements. Krish felt rather proud about it, as he had spearheaded the placement committee. His efforts had paid off. The director of the institute commended them on a job well done and Krish was proud. He himself landed a job at a multinational FMCG where he would join as a management trainee. He would move to Bombay soon for six months of probation and training. After this, Krish would be posted in a city of his choice, if an opening was available there.

Alka was glad when this happened, not just because he had landed his dream job, but also because it meant she did not have to be on guard and fight her feelings when he was around. *Six months was plenty of time*, Alka thought, and by then she would be completing her last semester, which was an internship at a corporate organization, after which they would graduate.

~

It had been months since Alka left, but Subbu couldn't stop thinking of her. He had a spring in his step as he went about his daily routine at the estate. He wanted to see her again. The dry season was over and the first showers of the rainy season had just started. The coffee estate would soon bloom. It was the most magical time to be at the estate—the entire place burst into splatters of white, as though an artist had carelessly toppled a can of silken white paint over it. As far as the eye could see, the estate would be filled with the most beautiful jasmine-like flowers that formed garlands over the coffee plantation. The air would be perfumed with a heady aroma. The burgeoning bushes would sway gently in the misty cool breeze, as though waving to you. Framed by the Nilgiri mountains, the bumblebees buzzing around and the honeybees thronging to the bushes, each bush would be laden with thousands of white flowers, like a thick blanket of snow. The sight transported even the most cynical to a magical fairyland, where anything was possible. This would last for just three or four days after which the delicate white petals would drop off, making way for the cheery red berries.

Subbu wanted Alka to witness this incredible, ethereal sight. He knew how much she would appreciate it. He called up Krish at the men's residential building and left a message with the student who picked up, asking him to tell Krishna to call him back. Calling Krish was something he rarely did, mainly because it was difficult to get him on the line. He was always busy. Krish called him back as soon as he got the message, worried that there was something amiss.

'Is everything okay, Anna? Why did you call?' Krish asked.

'Yes, yes. Amma wanted to know if you will bring your friends over to see the coffee blooms. It will bloom in ten days,' Subbu said, not wanting to tell Krish that he wanted Alka to see the blooms.

'Ummm, I am not sure, I will check with Manasi. She isn't exactly a nature person,' Krish replied.

'But Alka would love it. It has to be seen to be believed,' Subbu said a bit too quickly.

'Yes, it is. And you know how much I love being at the estate during this time too. Okay, I will ask them and let you know,' Krish said. He'd enjoyed the last trip immensely, and the idea of going back appealed to him.

Krish waited till he, Alka and Manasi were together to broach the topic of another visit to Sakleshspur, knowing that he had a higher chance of success with Alka around. He described the coffee blossoms and how it would be a magnificent sight. Alka hesitated. While what Krish described sounded magnificent, it would mean more time with him, which she didn't want. *But then, I might not get this chance again later*, she thought.

'I would love to visit again; I really liked it the last time. I also want to learn the recipes of those delicious stuff that Aunty makes,' Alka said.

This time it was Manasi who was reluctant.

'But Alka, our classes? Krish's placements are over, but we still have our classes.'

'Show me your schedule?' Krish said.

Alka fished out the schedule from her bag and gave it to him. He looked at the course calendar.

'Look, if you miss one lecture on Thursday, you practically get four whole days. I can see that your submission isn't due until the following week,' Krish pointed out.

'Ummm—that's true. We haven't missed too many classes this term,' Manasi said. 'I guess we can make it.'

'I think it will be a perfect way to celebrate my placement,' Krish said. 'Also imagine the photos you would be able to take of the white coffee blossoms. I bet no one in your photography club would have seen such stunning pictures,' he added and that was enough to convince Manasi.

~

Alka's second visit to Saklehspur was even better than the last one. She felt as though she was in an enchanted forest. She couldn't believe her eyes when she saw the coffee blossoms.

'Oh my goodness, this is heaven!' she exclaimed as Krish took the steep turn that swerved into the estate and drove up the winding path that lead to the colonial bungalow.

This time Subbu was waiting right at the bottom of the steps, dressed impeccably in a pristine white shirt tucked into a smart pair of light blue jeans, with brown suede leather boots. Anandi hugged Alka like she was a long-lost friend as she welcomed them. Never had Alka felt or experienced this kind of warmth, except from her mother.

After a scrumptious meal, Subbu took them deeper into the estate, his jeep expertly winding its way through the tall towering trees, passing the perky green peppers and Alka stared at the expansive shaded Arabica plants laden with the white flowers. When they stopped, Manasi got busy clicking photos, capturing the magic of the white flowers.

'These blossoms don't last long. So I am glad you could make it,' Subbu said. He was looking at Alka.

'Me too,' Alka said softly as though afraid that if she spoke any louder, it would break the spell.

Subbu held a flower in his hand without snapping it from the bush and explained the difference between an Arabica flower and a Robusta flower.

'Look—this is an Arabica flower. The corolla will divide itself into five. If it is a Robusta, it will divide itself into seven short-stalked petals. Robusta flowers are also slightly bigger.'

When they went ahead to another side of the plantation, he pointed out the Robusta flowers.

To Alka and to Manasi, they all looked the same.

They heard a loud noise in the distance then.

'What's that?' Alka asked.

'Elephants—we have electric fences to ward them off, but every now and then, they uproot trees and put them on the fences and then cross over. They are extremely smart animals,' Subbu said.

'Oh wow! I never knew estates can have elephants.'

'Oh, we have elephants, bisons, chitals or deers, foxes—all sorts of animals. It's a proper forest area,' Krish said.

'Last year we lost two of our workers in elephant attacks. These animals are extremely agile and dangerous,' Subbu added.

~

When they returned to the house, they found Anandi stretched out on the easy chair on the verandah. A young girl who looked like she was in her teens was applying oil to her legs and massaging them.

'Ah, there you are—do any of you girls want a foot massage? Selvi is so good at it. This is a special oil that wards off arthritis,' Anandi said.

'No. No ... I don't want it,' Alka was quick to reply. She had to look away as she couldn't bear to watch Selvi massaging Anandi's feet. She'd noticed a bookshelf in the hall and she went over and looked at the books with great interest.

Krish, Manasi and Subbu sat on the verandah and chatted with Anandi about various things at the estate, the city life, their course work. It was only when Selvi finished and went inside that Alka joined them.

~

'I can't thank you enough for hosting us, aunty,' Alka later told Anandi.

'Ah, I am happy you all made the time to witness this,' Anandi said.

'We're lucky we got the chance. And aunty, this time I am determined to learn all the recipes. See, I brought a notebook along and I will write it all down as I watch you cook,' Alka said as she showed Anandi a notebook she had brought along.

'Oh, I don't cook myself. I supervise the staff. But you have to be very careful about the exact quantities and proportions, and also about when to add the spices, how much time to roast for and a lot of other things. You can write all that down in your notebook.'

The next few days went by in the blink of an eye. Whenever Anandi was in the kitchen, Alka was there too, carefully making notes. Anandi told her that Gowramma and her husband Manikantan were excellent cooks and they had migrated to the estate from near the Tamil Nadu border many years ago. Their daughter Selvi was born and raised on the estate. They spoke Kannada. Since Alka had grown up hearing the language, it felt strangely like home. Years of watching and carefully listening to Tanvi and Mrs Shetty meant that Alka could easily understand it though the dialect was different from the one she had grown up hearing.

Alka, being good with languages, observed keenly the way they spoke, the way they pronounced words and the way in which Anandi communicated with them. Anandi was astonished when Alka began picking up the phrases and repeating them with perfect pronunciation within two days.

'Oh, you have picked up Kannada so well! Anyone would think you are a native. North Indians generally don't get our language so easily,' Anandi remarked.

Alka loved every moment of her time at the planation. Any time she wasn't in the kitchen with Anandi, she went for long treks with Subbu and Krish. Manasi came along sometimes, and at other times she found fascinating subjects within the bungalow itself to photograph.

At the end of their holiday, when it was time for them to leave, Anandi packed a jar of pickle for Alka.

'It's grown in our estates; eat it with rice or chapati,' she said.

'Aunty, I can't tell you how much all of this has meant to me. I am so grateful,' Alka blinked back her tears. She missed her mother so much, and she felt as though she saw her mother in Anandi's kindness.

Anandi sensed this too. Overcome with emotion, she hugged Alka and asked her to come again.

'I will, aunty, I will,' Alka said.

~

Krish watching this whole scene knew that Alka had found a way not only into his mother's heart but also into his own. He was definitely falling in love with her. She had stirred inside him feelings he never knew existed.

Once they were back at the campus, he tried hard to ignore how he felt. He was acutely aware of how ridiculous this whole situation was, considering he was dating Manasi. He wondered if he could he even call it 'love'.

How could he be in love with her when he and Manasi were in a relationship? What did he feel for Manasi? Of late his feelings towards her were more like what one felt for a dear friend. As far as Manasi was concerned she considered them to be a couple. But Krish was increasingly feeling stifled with Manasi. She never did anything to offend him. On the contrary, she was thoughtful and considerate. She was such a nice person. He could not pinpoint what it was that was lacking in their relationship. But he knew—like he did with all the other girls before her—the relationship had lost its fizz. With any other woman, this would have been the time he would have ended it, told them it was over and he would have parted ways. Yet he hesitated to break things off with Manasi. He knew how close Manasi was with Alka, and what if Alka decided never to speak to him if he ended it with Manasi?

Trying to ignore his feelings for Alka only made things worse. They rose inside him like a storm that threatened to spill out and he couldn't keep them within him anymore. The more he tried to pretend that there was nothing between them, the more his attraction to her grew, digging its claws deep into his heart.

He was glad that Manasi wasn't a jealous person. Other guys had told him about their girlfriends and how they kept their boyfriends on a tight leash. Manasi, on the other hand, trusted both him and Alka completely. This only made him feel worse.

He felt like a complete jerk for being so wildly drawn towards Alka. The intensity of his feelings puzzled him. He had always presumed that when it came to women, he was in control. He understood them, knew what to say and mostly took charge. But Alka unravelled all of that.

If Alka was aware of the effect she was having on him, she never once showed it. Surely, she must feel *something*. How could she be this oblivious, he wondered. Alka's indifference only strengthened Krish's feelings for her. He was used to women pursuing him for attention, but Alka did none of that.

～

One morning, when Manasi was attending a seminar organized by the photography club and Alka was in the library, Krish saw a window of opportunity and decided to grab it. He simply *had* to speak to Alka before he exploded.

'Hey,' he said, drawing up a chair and sitting down next to her without asking.

'Hi,' said Alka, without taking her eyes off the book she was making notes from. She'd seen him coming in and glancing around. She felt as though her world was about to spin out of control. She wanted to hide, but since there was nowhere to go, she sat very still, pretending to be engrossed in her work.

'Kotler, eh?' Krish asked.

Alka nodded, not trusting herself to speak.

'Porter's *Competitive Strategy* is good too. I can lend it to you if you like,' Krish said.

Krish knew that he hadn't come here to talk of Kotler or Porter, and yet that was what he was doing, unable to say what he really wanted to.

'Thanks. You can give it to Manasi, and she will pass it to me,' Alka replied, her face unreadable.

'Why? Will it hurt you if you take the book from me?' Krish's pride was bruised at this slight brush-off.

'No, but it might hurt Manasi,' Alka replied, meeting his eyes at last.

'Err ... what do you mean?'

'You know what I mean, Krish. You don't strike me as a dumb guy.'

Krish wasn't expecting this and he was stumped.

'I actually came to talk about your internship,' he improvised.

'What about it? And why are you seeking me out privately? Why not speak to me along with others?' Alka had a small smile now and her eyes sparkled with mischief.

'Alka, don't make this so difficult please … I … you know—'

'I know, and that is why we should nip this in the bud. It's not fair on Manasi,' she cut in before he could finish.

'Yes. I agree. I am considering telling her how I feel about you.'

'What? No! Are you crazy? There's nothing that has happened between us. If you tell her, what do you think will happen?' Alka's outrage was evident in her voice.

'I don't know,' Krish shrugged.

'Look Krish—there's nothing to be done. These things— they happen. Whatever we pay attention to, grows. So let's just pretend nothing exists between us, and nothing will. It will die on its own once you move to Bombay for your job. I suggest we do nothing about it. Telling Manasi will mean that I lose the only friend I have on this campus.'

'You have me,' Krish said.

'Let's just say I prefer Manasi as a friend,' Alka said trying to lighten the mood.

They did not realize it then, but with this little exchange, they had already crossed a line. They had left the safe shores of friendship and waded into the capricious waters of a relationship, even though both had agreed that they wouldn't take it further. Despite their best intentions, the seeds of something more had already been sown, but it would be a while before they sprouted, in the most unexpected way.

13

1994-95

Alone, yet Not Alone

AFTER ALKA'S VISITS TO THE ESTATE ANANDI WAS FULL
of praise for her—something she rarely did.

'She was really interested in our cuisine unlike the girls of today. She is studying in such a big institute and yet interested in cooking,' Anandi remarked one evening as she and Subbu sat on the verandah sipping their home-grown coffee.

'Yes, she seemed very interested in all the coffee production too. She was asking me a lot of questions,' Subbu replied.

'Do you like her, son?'

'What do you mean by "like her"? She is a good girl but I hardly know her,' Subbu was evasive.

'I think *I* know her, Subbu. I am a good judge of character. She spent so many days here. I've been observing her. There is something special about her. I've never met anyone so eager to learn. She is interested in everything, and she soaks up knowledge like a sponge. She even learnt Kannada in two days. She is very smart.'

'She didn't even flinch when that leech was on her leg. So, I don't think she is a namby-pamby either,' Subbu smiled, throwing back at Anandi a term she had used once.

'Haha! That is for sure. What say Subbu? Shall I broach the topic of your marriage with her relatives? It's a pity that her parents are no more, I would have loved to meet them,' Anandi said.

Subbu turned away, 'I don't know if she has a boyfriend, and she barely knows me. Marriage is such a big step …' he said.

Anandi, who was a staunch believer in arranged marriages, said, 'Bah, what is this "know each other"? You have an entire lifetime for that. Your father and I met for the first time in the marriage pandal. We trusted our parents and we knew they would choose well for us. Here, you have met her, spoken to her. I will ask Krish to get me her number and I will tell her I want to speak to her relatives.'

'No, no, Amma. Please wait. Give me some time. This is too fast.'

'You should never wait for such things. In my time, the eligible girls and boys would be gone in a jiffy. If you hesitate, someone else will swoop in.'

'Amma, these are not your times. We're in the nineties now, not in the sixties. I urge you to please wait.'

'Nothing comes of waiting. We must act on this,' Anandi was not willing to give up on a potential match so easily.

'Please don't meddle in this, Amma,' Subbu pleaded. 'Anyway, the busiest season is coming up at the estate. I will not have time for all this. We will see how we feel about it after the harvest.'

'If not Alka, then someone else. You cannot keep putting off your marriage forever Subbu. I am not getting any younger.'

'Yes, Amma, I know. But this isn't the time. I promise you that after the harvest we will take a decision. You know how hectic it is right now. I don't even have time to breathe.'

'Yes, yes. I agree. I won't bring up this subject with you for now. Let this busy time be over,' Anandi conceded, agreeing to drop the topic for a while. She knew that the coffee estate consumed her older son and, during this time, it was imperative for him to stay fully focussed on it. 'But once it is over—'

'Yes, then you can go ahead and take it up; I will marry the girl you choose,' Subbu said.

~

Manasi had no idea what was going on with Krish, but she'd noticed that off late, he'd become less responsive and distracted. Alka had noticed the small changes in Krish's behaviour towards Manasi whenever they were together but there was nothing she could do about it. One evening, when Manasi and Alka were in Manasi's room, she brought it up with Alka.

'I think you must bring it up with him; it is between both of you,' Alka shrugged and changed the topic.

Manasi took Alka's advice. When she raised it with Krish, he said that it was because he would be going away to a new city.

'Come on Krish, it is *my* city! You don't have to be worried about being alone. I have already told my parents that you will be there. Do go and meet them and you can count on them for anything you need,' Manasi said.

'I don't think I will need anything, Manasi. The company is taking care of our accommodation and everything else. Also, aren't your parents always busy?' Krish asked. He didn't want to meet Manasi's parents.

'They have an off on Sundays and I have told them to invite you for a meal. Once you go there and give me your new phone number, I will pass it on to them,' Manasi said.

'I think it will be better if we meet them together,' Krish stalled. 'Anyway, there's plenty of time to decide all of that. Let me go and join the new company first.'

~

Alka heaved a sigh of relief when Krish left for Bombay. It meant that she didn't have to tiptoe around her emotions when they were together.

Krish himself fell in love with Bombay. He loved how vibrant the city was. He settled down in a flat in Bandra which the company had assigned to the new employees. He shared it with three other trainees and they walked to office together every day. Krish loved his work and his colleagues, and he was delighted with this new phase of his life.

Away from Manasi, engrossed in his work, Krish discovered that he didn't miss her at all, but he did miss Alka. Manasi, on the other hand, missed Krish terribly. She called him almost every other day, but Krish found himself avoiding her calls. She would call four or five times and leave messages before he called back. He'd apologize, saying that he was caught up with work, but deep down, he knew that his feelings towards Manasi had changed.

~

Mansi sensed this. She spoke about it with Alka.

'He seems so distant and aloof.'

'He must be busy with his work,' Alka replied, hoping that this was true.

'I miss him terribly. I think I will fly to Bombay and spend a bit of time with him. We have a long weekend coming up. If I take two days off, I'll get almost a week, He has spent over five months there, and not once has he gone to see my parents, even though I've asked him to.'

'Maybe he feels awkward to go on his own. You will feel better then when you see him and introduce him to your parents,' Alka said.

When Manasi came back from her trip to Bombay, she thanked Alka.

'You were right. He was just so caught up in his work, but it was so wonderful to spend time with him. I did make sure to take him to my place for dinner, and my parents loved him.'

'That's great,' Alka said. She was happy for Manasi, yet felt terribly sad. Introducing someone to her mother would be something she would never be able to do.

~

Manasi called Krish every other day. She got him on the phone sometimes, and at other times she left messages for him to call back. He never did.

One evening when Manasi and Alka were entering the girls residential building, the phone at the reception rang and Manasi picked it up. She was so excited that it was Krish. She mouthed his name to Alka and gestured for her to stay.

Alka felt awkward as she did not want to listen to the conversation between Krish and Manasi.

'Holy moly! That is fantastic, Krish. Just great! Yes, in fact she is right here, you can speak right now and tell her yourself,' Alka heard Manasi saying as she handed her the phone.

Alka looked at Manasi questioningly, and then reluctantly took the phone from her.

'You have to hear this, Alka,' said Manasi as she handed over the receiver to Alka and did a jig.

'Hi, Krish,' said Alka.

'Hey there,' said Krish, his voice low. Dreamy. Alka turned her back to Manasi so she wouldn't see her flaming cheeks. The moment she heard his voice, she knew.

So much time apart and nothing had changed. She could tell by the way her heart raced. She'd hoped that whatever it was that was there between them would wither and die when he left. But it hadn't. It was still very much there, alive and kicking, twisting her insides in knots.

'I had hoped … I … I wanted …' Krish was trying to find the right words and failing miserably.

'What?' Alka asked.

'Three of us—it is highly possible that we're going to be working for the same company,'

'What? How?' Alka couldn't believe what she was hearing.

'I've finished my probation now and I just got confirmed as an assistant manager, and when they asked my preferred place to work, I told them I wanted Bangalore. They also asked me to recommend some names for the summer internships. I recommended both of you along with a few more names. I have put in a good word and I am pretty sure you both will be taken in for the internships. This is a great opportunity, Alka, and it will look really good on your resume when the placements happen. Just do well in the interviews.'

'Oh … Okay. Errr … Thank you,' Alka said trying to soak in what Krish had just told her. Manasi snatched the receiver from her.

'Isn't it great? Yayyy! Alka, how can you be so calm? Krish, I am dancing, really dancing! I can't wait for you to come back here,' she said.

Alka had to hurry away to her room, leaving Manasi to finish her conversation with Krish.

One part of her was angry. How could Krish just take charge of their internships and do this? Yet another part of her was immensely happy. The company that Krish was working for was among the leading FMCG multinationals in the world. Most people in their batch would give an arm and a leg to get in. If they were both getting in on Krish's recommendation, Krish must have really impressed them.

She entered her room and lay sprawled on the bed, her arms spread out. She wished her mother was alive. She was just a step away from fulfilling her lifelong dream of getting her mother out of Mrs Shetty's house—the dream that had fuelled her all these years. But now she didn't have her mother. She had nobody. What in the world would she do after her internship, when she had to face the big world alone? The thought of being on her own, once she graduated frightened her. Here, inside the campus, she had Manasi, her daily routine, her lectures, her assignments, her professors and her other batchmates with whom she felt safe. She knew what she was supposed to do. But once she left this campus, she would be like a baby in a jungle. How would she manage?

There was a knock on her door.

'Come in,' Alka called out.

'Isn't it great news? We can all be together again!' Manasi bounced into the room with a huge grin plastered on her face. She dropped down on the bed, lying next to Alka.

'It is ... I suppose ... but it is also scary,' Alka replied.

'Why scary? We will be on our own! Working, darling! Living it up! What is scary about that?'

Alka didn't know how to explain to Manasi that it was different for her. The rest of them—Krish, Manasi—they had their families. They had supportive parents. They had financial security. All Alka had was her mother's lifelong savings and her depleting trust fund, which amounted to a couple of lakhs. She also was the sole beneficiary of her mother's LIC policy, which was a few more lakhs. She was yet to receive it, but she had made an application for it and they had written back to her saying everything was in order and it would soon be credited into her bank account. She remembered how diligently her mother used to pay the premium every year with Mrs Shetty's help. She missed her mother terribly. It was unfair, so unfair that she was snatched away from her.

Manasi sensed Alka's mood, her silence giving her away.

'Hey, what happened?' she asked gently.

'Just wished my mother was around to see me graduate,' Alka's voice broke as she said it. It wasn't the whole truth, but it was the truth nonetheless.

Manasi was silent for a while.

'I know, Alka. I wish she could see you too. But you will always have me and Krish. We're going to be okay,' she said, and squeezed Alka's hand.

They lay that way, side by side, staring at the fan in Alka's room for a long time, thinking about what lay ahead in their lives, Alka full of trepidation and Manasi full of excitement at the thought of all of them being together once again.

14

1994–95

Closer

WHILE MANASI HAD BEEN OVERJOYED AT THE THOUGHT that all three of them would be working together, it hadn't turned out to be what she expected at all. Manasi had presumed that it would be like college, where all three of them would hang out, have lunch together and meet every day. Alka too had expected, and feared, this same scenario. But as it turned out, the company had hired five interns and all of them were separated and assigned different departments. They were so busy that they hardly saw each other, and after the two-day orientation programme, Manasi was sent to a different building altogether. Krish would join them soon but his department would be on a different floor.

Alka was very disappointed with the internship. She didn't like the person she was reporting to. He was brash, arrogant, hardly had time for her and he made her feel like he was doing her a massive favour by giving her even five minutes of his time. She found it hard to adjust to the work culture of the company. There were at least 150 people on her floor, all boxed up in cubicles. Each individual cubicle had little personal things that the employee working there had put up—some of them had pictures drawn by their children, some had photos of their families and some had sad-looking wilted plants. Alka's desk was in a corner. She felt suffocated looking at the large hall and all these people working, neatly slotted into identical little boxes, talking on the phone and being so busy they didn't have time to look up from their desks. The senior managers had glass cubicles, which lined up next to each other on one side. These were called 'private cabins' but Alka thought there was nothing private about them. They were made of glass and anyone could see what was happening inside. And even the 'views' they had from their windows were simply views of other buildings in the office complex. Alka felt the frustration and dread growing within her every day. They wound around her insides so tightly that she constantly felt a little sick. She couldn't wait for the day to end, so she could clock out and breathe the fresh air outside.

Manasi, surprisingly, loved it. She loved the atmosphere in the office, loved the person she was reporting to, and made a group of friends very quickly. Alka, who was still mourning the loss of her mother, found all of this meaningless. She couldn't imagine a life where she would be doing this for years and years. After a week, she spoke to her college professor at length. He advised her that the best option was to complete her internship as it formed an important part of the semester. Her grades had been excellent so far, and it was imperative that she completed the internship with the same degree of diligence that she had displayed in her academics.

'The very atmosphere stifles me. How can I work where I just feel like a cog in the wheel? It feels like I can't breathe,' Alka said.

'Welcome to the corporate world, Alka. This prepares you for what lies ahead. You'll soon get used to it,' her professor replied.

But Alka knew her professor was wrong. With her mother gone, there was no motivation for her anymore. Having invested two years of her life in getting this management degree, she thought she would somehow stick with it, and complete it. But she was growing more and more disillusioned every day.

Nobody genuinely cared about anyone within the organization. It felt like they were all a part of some invisible race where the winner would be rewarded with more work. Since Alka needed the internship to graduate, she put her head down like the others, and did the dreary projects she was assigned by her boss. For the first time in her life, she waited for the weekend where she could simply lie in her room and not go to work. Before the internship, she was always busy on weekends with her coursework. But now she had nothing to do. So she hung out with Manasi, who insisted on going to every new restaurant and pub that was being talked about. Alka wasn't comfortable going out often and told Manasi that she didn't want to spend too much money.

'Oh, don't worry about it. This is on me. I can do this much for my friend,' Manasi offered. But Alka didn't want that. All her life, she had grown up with reminders of how grateful she had to be for other people's kindness. She didn't want to be Manasi's charity project, even though she knew that Manasi had no idea at all about Alka's background or the demons that haunted her. She was simply trying to cheer Alka up.

~

Krish was arriving in three days and Alka, tired of her job, tired of life, tired of having nothing to look forward to found herself awaiting his arrival as eagerly as Manasi, although she took great care to not express it or reveal what she felt. Manasi invited Alka to accompany her to the airport, but Alka refused.

'No way! Let the lovers have their alone time,' she said and she was glad when Manasi, for once, didn't insist.

'Alright, I'll pick him up from the airport and spend time with him, but we will drop by in the evening and then all of us *have* to go out together. Now don't say no to that,' Manasi said, before Alka could even begin protesting.

Krish was staying in the company guest house for two weeks. After that, he would be renting his own place. His company had several options from which he could choose. Manasi was excited about accompanying him on the house hunt.

'It'll be so good once he has his own place. Think about the parties we can have there,' Manasi said.

'I don't think I'd want to party. After putting in a whole week of work, I would rather spend some quiet time, alone,' Alka replied.

'Quiet time? Don't act like you are sixty years old! Krish and I will come and pick you up this evening, okay?' Manasi said.

Though Alka had told Manasi she didn't want to party, she also knew she would've died of loneliness if she didn't have Manasi, so she said she would be ready.

That evening, Alka took great care in choosing her dress and her accessories. She finally decided on a simple black sleeveless dress—her favourite, and paired it up with mother's delicate gold earrings. She wore her expensive perfume, the one she saved for special occasions. She brushed her hair till it was shining and left it loose, tumbling down in waves to her waist. She even put on make-up—something she never did, choosing a light pink lipstick, a swipe of mascara and carefully applied eyeliner. All the while, she tried to avoid acknowledging the reason she was dressing up.

Manasi and Krish arrived together in the evening. When Alka opened the door, Manasi looked at her for a few seconds and then whistled.

'Wow! You know how to really dress up, Alka. Why have you kept this from us all this while? All the boys in our batch would have lined up for you.'

'That's precisely why I don't dress up. I hate the attention,' Alka replied.

'Well, don't be surprised tonight if you get a lot of it,' Manasi said.

Krish was silent, but he couldn't stop looking at Alka. She was even more beautiful than he remembered.

'Hello, Alka,' he said finally.

'Doesn't she look ravishing?' Manasi said proudly, as though she had dressed up Alka herself.

'Uhhh … yeah, I guess,' Krish replied.

Manasi did not see it but Alka noticed the blush that had crept up on his face.

Krish said he was taking them to a new pub that had recently opened and that it was his treat. Though Alka had told Manasi that she preferred a quiet evening, she found that she was enjoying it now. Manasi sat in the front seat of the car and chattered away, nineteen to the dozen. Alka smiled at how chirpy she was. Her enthusiasm was infectious and she put everyone in a great mood.

They drove to Millers Road. By the time they arrived at their destination, Alka was excited as well. From the outside, the building Krish drove them to looked like a warehouse. But from the inside, it was something else. A narrow staircase led them into the pub, a very upmarket lounge bar with dim lighting, packed with people.

Pink Floyd, Grateful Dead, Ugly Kid Joe—all the latest popular songs were being blasted through hidden speakers. They had to shout to talk to each other. A group of young men in T-shirts sporting names of popular bands stared at them and Krish put his hands protectively around Manasi as they made their way to the bar. Alka said she did not want to drink, but Manasi asked her not to be a spoilsport. So she reluctantly agreed to have a cocktail. Krish managed to find them a place to sit—two sofas opposite each other with a low table in the middle. Krish and Manasi sat next to each other, while Alka sat across from them, feeling awkward and self-conscious. Manasi, though, was in her element, and swaying to the music. She was talking about how happy she was and how this night called for a grand celebration.

She ordered a rum-based cocktail. The waiter informed them that there was a special deal going on that day, where they would get two drinks for the price of one. Manasi asked Alka if she would have another drink, but Alka shook her head firmly. She said she was fine. Krish said he was limiting his drink to just a beer, as he had to drive. So Manasi decided to have the complimentary drink.

Krish's eyes kept coming back to Alka. He was smiling at her, assuring her that he was around, telling her it was okay and she wasn't alone. It was strange how much he could communicate with his eyes, and the effect it almost instantly had on Alka. Alka revelled in his attention and sat quietly, soaking in the atmosphere, listening to the music, enjoying the evening. They spent a few hours there, and left only when it was time for the pub to close. Manasi kept telling them how happy she was to have two good friends by her side and what a fine celebration this was!

By the time they left the pub and drove to the girls residential building, the effect of the alcohol had hit Manasi. She had leaned against the widow and passed out. It was well past 2 a.m., and there was no one in sight. Alka opened Manasi's handbag and rummaged for the keys to her room and between them, they managed to get Manasi up the stairs, and into her room. They laid her down on her bed. Alka removed her heels and covered her with her blanket. And then they tiptoed out of her room, shutting the door gently behind them.

'I have never seen her drink like this. She always keeps it in check,' Alka said. 'I guess she was really happy today.'

'I guess she was,' Krish said. 'Want to go for a walk?' he asked.

He was so happy to be with Alka and couldn't help himself from wanting a little more time with her. Neither was he ready to go home just yet and end the night.

The corridor was dimly lit, and from the balcony, Krish gazed up at the sky. It was dotted with a million stars and the crescent moon hung low, like a happy smile.

'I would have ordinarily said yes, but I don't think it's a good idea, Krish,' Alka said, trying to sound normal. Krish looked so handsome, standing there in his navy blue T-shirt that fit him perfectly. He was looking at her so earnestly and with so much tenderness in his eyes, that Alka's heart was beating hard, just being near him. They had been communicating with their eyes all evening, and now that they were alone, Alka was nervous.

'Why? I am just asking you to go for a walk. What are you scared about?' Krish challenged her, looking into her eyes.

'Sacred? Ha!' Alka stared back. 'No way!' she said. She didn't want Krish to know how excited she was.

They looked at each other for a few seconds, like prizefighters sizing up their opponent. Then Alka did something she hadn't planned on doing at all. She leaned forward and kissed Krish on the lips. Perhaps it was the alcohol, or perhaps it was his challenge and the way he looked at her. Perhaps it was the tension that had been building up all this while.

It took a moment for Krish to recover, and when he did, it was as though everything that he had been carefully controlling exploded inside him.

'Oh, Alka,' he said as he leaned forward and pulled her towards him. She gasped as his hands went around her waist and his mouth found hers. Alka felt a shock go through her and desire coursed through her veins. His lips were demanding yet tender, fierce yet gentle, firm yet insistent. She closed her eyes, as he pressed his body against hers and he was now kissing her neck, his stubble brushing against her skin, softly murmuring her name. Alka felt safe in his embrace. She hugged him back tightly and trembled as a million sensations ran through her. It was as if every nerve-ending, every cell in her body had suddenly come to life.

'Let's go into my room,' she managed to whisper, her flesh blazing under his touch. She was surprised at the intensity of her longing for him, and how he seemed to reciprocate it with equal fervour.

He took his own time to make love to her. He stroked her cheeks, ran his fingers down her shoulder blades, made circles around her breast, teasing, rousing, till she couldn't stand it anymore. Alka found herself relaxing completely with him, as though she was under a spell. His eyes were misty and a small smile played on his lips when she took his hands and placed them on her breasts, impatient for him to make the next move. She wanted him so badly, and she pulled him into her, her hands going around his back. When he finally entered her, she shuddered, drowning in waves of pleasure.

Krish was treating her like a delicate piece of china and he seemed to worship her. They were both lost in each other, Alka dissolving into him as he held her afterwards, cupping her face in his hands, and telling her she was beautiful. For the first time in a long time, Alka felt like she was no longer alone in the world.

After their breathing returned to normal, she lay in his arms, her head against his chest, listening to his heart beat. A million thoughts swirled in her head—happiness, satisfaction, contentment and then, overwhelming guilt.

'What have we done, Krish?' she said. 'How could we do this to Manasi? This is so wrong.'

'I don't know. I don't know what this is, Alka. If it is so wrong, how can it feel so right? We're perfect for each other,' Krish asked, running his hands through her hair.

'But this—this is just sex.' Alka's guard was up now. She had an invisible armour she wore which was her defence against the world and now it was back in place, reminding her of who she was.

'No, it isn't just sex Alka, at least not for me. It's ... It's never been like this before.'

Alka was quiet for a few minutes. They lay in silence, wrapped in each other, shutting out the world.

Then Alka said, 'But there's so much about me you don't know.'

'So tell me, darling, I am listening,' Krish replied, playing with her hair.

But Alka couldn't bring herself to tell him about her past. She had lied to everyone and pretended to be someone she was not. She had buried it for so long, so deep within her that it had frozen, turned to ice. She couldn't bear to dredge it up. She couldn't tell him what her dream had been and how it had died with her mother. She couldn't tell him about Mrs Shetty, Tanvi and her life before she left that small servants' room in Delhi. She couldn't tell him about the party where she had been humiliated. She couldn't tell him about the years of housework she'd done, and how she didn't want anything to do with Mrs Shetty or that life any more.

She couldn't even tell him how she felt accepted and loved in his arms, and how much this—whatever it was—meant to her. What if it had just been about the sex for him? What if he shrank away when he knew her true story? That would break her heart and she would never recover. Besides, how could they take this forward anyway, without hurting Manasi?

So she just lay next to him and kissed him, and thanked him.

Then she told him that this, whatever it was, should never happen again.

15

1994–95

Under an Orange Sky

ALKA DIDN'T KNOW HOW TO FACE MANASI THE NEXT DAY, so she stayed in her room, thinking about what she and Krish could do. Before he'd left earlier that morning, he'd once again told her that it simply was not about the sex for him. What did he mean? Did it mean he was in love with her? What could they do about it? The questions swirled around in Alka's head and she sat gazing out of the window, not knowing what to do. All she knew was when she was with him, she felt accepted, *adored*—something she had never felt in her life. On the one hand, she felt elated to have experienced this connection with him and on the other, she felt a deep sense of loss from having to put an end to it even before it had begun.

When Manasi woke up, she had only a vague recollection of the events that happened the previous night. She knocked on Alka's door.

'Hey, thank you for last evening. I think I made an ass of myself,' Manasi said as she came into Alka's room.

'Hey! Good morning. You had fun, that's what is important,' said Alka, not meeting her eyes. She began tidying her already spotless desk.

Manasi sprawled on Alka's neatly made bed.

'My head is hurting. I have a mother of a hangover.'

'Let me get you something for that hangover,' Alka said as she walked to her wardrobe and rummaged in a small plastic first-aid box.

'You organize everything so well, Alka. I have never met anyone who keeps their room this tidy. How do you do it?' Manasi asked. Her own room always had clothes thrown on chairs, books and bags strewn on her bed, overflowing dustbin, a desk full of papers and pens and a pile of laundry waiting to be done. In comparison, Alka's room was spotless, with not a thing out of place and not a speck of dust.

'You always say this whenever you come to my room.'

'And you never tell me how you manage to do it. What is the magic you use?'

Alka shrugged, 'No magic at all. I guess when you value something you try and make the most of it.'

'Come on! What is to value? This ordinary tiny room?' Manasi asked.

Alka didn't know what to say. How could she tell her it was bigger than the room she had stayed in all her life and that she had been so excited to get it? So she said nothing and handed Manasi the medicine she had found, along with a glass of water, which she poured from the jug that she kept next to her bed.

'Are you mad at me? You seem subdued—different,' Manasi said as she took the pill gratefully.

'No, Manasi, why should I be mad at you?' Alka avoided her eyes, putting away the medical kit.

'Was I terrible last night? Oh god. I don't remember anything at all. I don't even remember how I got to my room.'

'You passed out in the car. Krish and I helped you to your room, and I tucked you in,' Alka said, avoiding her eyes.

'I'm glad you guys were there to take care of me. Thanks, Alka. We'll see you later. Don't forget we're all going out again today,' Manasi reminded Alka as she got up to leave.

Alka groaned. She had forgotten that she had agreed to Manasi's suggestion in the pub last evening that they would go out again today. Now things were very different, and she didn't know if she could bear seeing Krish again so soon.

'Listen, please Manasi, I hated the pub yesterday. You both carry on, I honestly would prefer a quiet evening.'

'Is it because you think you are interrupting my time with Krish?'

'I guess something like that,' Alka said giving away nothing of the turmoil that was going on inside.

'You aren't! I don't want you sitting alone here, Alka, and Krish enjoys your company too. We can go to some place quieter than yesterday, and no excuses now. I am going to the guest house now to meet him and we will pick you up in the evening.'

An hour later, Alka was still thinking of excuses she could make to get out of it, when there was a knock on her door.

'Phone call for you,' one of the girls shouted and hurried away. Alka went to the reception area, wondering who on earth would call her here. Apart from her mother, there was nobody else who would get in touch with her.

When she answered her hands went cold when the voice at the other end said, 'Have you forgotten us already? You haven't bothered to even call.'

'Hello, ma'am,' Alka said standing up a little straighter automatically as she recognized the voice. She hated the way she sounded—subservient, timid and terrified. It was as though she had become an eight-year-old again and Mrs Shetty was ordering her to press her feet. Alka had not spoken to the Shettys after her mother had passed away and she'd never thought that she'd hear from her. The trust fund that the Inner Circle Club members had set up was almost depleted, and since Alka was in the final year, she didn't think she would need it anymore. Her mother's insurance money had come through as well. She wondered what this phone call was about.

'Ha, so you still remember us, eh Alka? You haven't called at all. At least you should call us once in a while to let us know how you are.'

'Of course. Sorry, I have been busy,' Alka said. She had no idea why she was apologizing. She bit back the 'ma'am' though, making a conscious effort to stop using it with Mrs Shetty. That was in the past. *She has no hold over you now*, she told herself.

'Oh, that's perfectly okay. The reason I called is that my mother had called this morning from Bangalore. Do you remember Chandrakala, who works for her?'

'Yes, I remember,' Alka said wondering what this was about.

'Oh good. Well, her son is twenty-six now and they are looking for a good match for him. He has just started his own business in Bangalore—in Chickpet. He is a smart boy, and he is a graduate too. He wants an educated girl and so I suggested your profile. You can go and meet them this evening.'

Alka gripped the receiver tightly, her knuckles turning white. At first she was shocked, but then her shock turned into rage.

'Hello?'

'Yes, I am here,' she said in a cold voice.

'I think it will be a good match. Your course must be finishing soon. And you will anyway have to get married. I would have suggested this to your mother, had she been alive, but now—I have to tell you directly.'

Alka's anger boiled over when she heard that. How dare she? How could Mrs Shetty call her up and suggest this? All her life she had served her, obeyed her. With her mother's death, she thought that she had finally broken free of the shackles. Yet, here she was, suggesting this alliance like it was the most normal thing in the world. Was there a rule book that said house helps had to marry within their own kind?

Alka wasn't sure what hurt more—whether it was the fact that Mrs Shetty hadn't even enquired how Alka was coping after her mother's death or whether it was that she presumed Alka would be free in the evening and would instantly do as she commanded.

'Mrs Shetty,' Alka spoke slowly. She was so angry she had trouble getting the words out. Her heart was hammering inside her. With slow deliberation, she said, 'If he is such a good boy, why don't you look at his profile for Tanvi? She is older than me and closer to his age. Oh, and I have a boyfriend and he is taking me this evening to the Taj.'

Then she hung up and walked back to her room, her head spinning, her fists clenched, her heart pounding and her throat dry. When she entered her room, she covered her face with her pillow and screamed into it. Then she threw it against the wall, and sobbed, lying on her bed. She sobbed for everything that had been snatched from her. She wept for the little girl who had meekly accepted that she had to do everything Mrs Shetty asked her to. She cried because she felt a deep unbearable loss chewing up her insides—a void that would never be filled. After a while, she stopped when she heard another knock on her door.

'Phone call for you,' said a voice.

'Tell them I am not here,' Alka wiped her tears and called out. She never wanted to speak to Mrs Shetty again.

'It's Manasi's father. When I said she wasn't here, he asked for you.'

That made Alka jump out of bed and hurry to the phone.

'Hello, uncle? This is Alka, Manasi's friend.'

'Beta, where is Manasi?'

'Uncle, she is with a friend of ours.'

'Do you have their number? I need to reach her urgently. Her mother is in the ICU.'

'Oh no, uncle! What happened? I can find out the number.'

'She's had a medical emergency. Please call Manasi urgently. I need her to travel back to Bombay.'

~

Alka didn't know how to reach Krish. She didn't know where his guest house was. She called up her company and asked for the guest house contact details. Alka waited as they asked her to hold on. In less than three minutes, she had the address and phone number. Alka tried the number, but it wasn't going through. It was probably an incorrect number. There was no time. Manasi's father had said it was urgent. She knew the area. It was less than fifteen minutes from their campus. She grabbed her purse, jumped into an auto, without even bothering to comb her hair, and she sped towards Krish's guest house, hoping they had given her the address of the right guest house. The company had many guest houses scattered across the city.

When she rang the bell, an attendant opened the door, and she said she was looking for Krish. He gave her a strange look, and Alka caught her reflection in the mirror on the foyer wall. Her eyeliner had run from all the crying she had done, her hair was a wild mess and her eyes were bloodshot. Her clothes—an ordinary oversized black T-shirt and light grey printed pyjamas, looked strange. She had even forgotten to change her footwear—on her feet were the Hawaii chappals she wore around in her room. But she couldn't make herself care about how she looked. All she could think about was finding Manasi.

Krish was there the next moment, and his eyebrows rose in surprise when he saw her. He wondered for a second if this was about last night, but then Manasi stepped out from behind him. She took one look at Alka and knew something was wrong straight away. Alka too, looked past Krish and at Manasi, her eyes tearing up again.

'Your mother, Manasi—she is in the hospital. You need to leave for Bombay. Your dad called,' Alka blurted out as soon as she saw her.

~

Krish drove both of them to the girls residential building, and he waited while Alka helped Manasi pack. She scrubbed her face, brushed back her hair and swapped her pyjamas for track pants.

'Don't worry, Manasi, your mother is going to be fine,' Alka consoled her as Krish drove them to the airport and helped Manasi get a ticket at the airport counter.

The next flight was in two hours, and they sipped tea at a tea stall near the airport while they waited.

'I can't tell you how terrified I am,' Manasi said.

'She is going to pull through, Manasi. Don't worry,' Krish assured her with a conviction he wasn't feeling.

'Call me after you see her,' Alka said.

'Yes, I will update both of you as soon as I can.'

~

After Manasi boarded the flight, Krish and Alka were alone once more, this time thrown together by circumstances, which neither of them had foreseen.

'I hope she will be okay,' Alka said, trying to push back the tears that were threatening to spill over. This visit to the airport had brought back so many bad memories when Alka had boarded the flight when her mother had died. Krish noticed.

'I hope so too. Are you okay, Alka?'

'No, Krish, not really.'

'Do you want me to drive you around a bit?'

'Yes, please.'

'Okay, I will take you to a spot where you can see the planes take off, and go overhead. It's a beautiful sight.'

They drove in silence to a spot at the far end of Wind Tunnel Road. The sun was setting. The skies were a majestic red-orange, tinged with a magnificent lavender around the edges. Alka got out of the car and as Krish had promised, the planes were taking off almost overhead. They were massive and their engines roared as they soared into the skies, zooming over their heads and then becoming smaller and smaller, before turning into a speck and disappearing.

'Oh my! What a sight!' Alka said.

'You bet,' Krish replied. But he wasn't looking at the planes at all. He was looking at Alka.

'How did you even know of this spot?' Alka asked engrossed in staring at the planes whizzing overhead.

'My cousin lives close by. Whenever I visited him, he would bring us to this spot. Look! That might be Manasi's plane,' Krish pointed to one that had just taken off.

'How do you know?'

'I can tell by the take-off time.'

They stood there for a while looking at the planes.

Then Krish edged closer and put his arms around Alka, and she didn't resist. They stood in silence for a few minutes.

'Think about this, Alka. How many times in life do you get to experience a connection like this? I know you can feel it too,' Krish said softly .

Alka knew he was right, but she said nothing. She got a whiff of his irresistible musky perfume and she inhaled deeply, thinking about the previous night and the way it seemed so natural and good to be around him. She felt comforted by his strong hands, by his presence and his words.

Was this love? She didn't know. But if this is what love was, it felt wonderful.

16

1994-95

A Tangled Web

It was only three days later that Manasi called Alka. She said she had been in no state to speak till she knew something for sure, one way or the other. Her mother had been in the ICU and it was only a few minutes ago that she had been shifted out of the ICU. She seemed to be doing okay now but had to be kept under observation for two weeks, as she had developed arrhythmia. After two weeks, they would decide on the next course of action.

'I am glad my father is a doctor. I can be sure she is getting the best of care,' she said.

'I am happy she is out of the ICU and I hope she recovers soon,' Alka replied earnestly. Deep down, she couldn't help wondering if her own mother would have lived longer had she got timely medical care too. The two times she had fallen ill, she'd just taken some over-the-counter medication that Mrs Shetty had got. When it came to healthcare, there was a world of difference between what the privileged got and what the poor got.

She was relieved when Manasi hung up. The guilt was weighing heavily on her because she and Krish hadn't been able to stay away from each other, despite Alka's resolve.

Krish's office was a few floors above Alka's. The thought that he was in the same building made her working days bearable. Since Manasi left, Krish and Alka had been eating lunch together in the office cafeteria, and met after work nearly every day.

When they met that evening, Alka told Krish that she had spoken to Manasi. And that her mother was out of the ICU.

'I know, I spoke to her earlier today,' he said.

'I felt so guilty speaking to her. We meet every day while—'

'I know. It's hard for me as well. I'm afraid I will blurt out that I don't want to be with her anymore, if I speak to her. But now is not the time to have that conversation.'

'Please warn me before you decide to have the talk with her. I will be facing the brunt of the backlash.'

'I will. But she would be lashing out at me too, Krish said. 'I need to move out of the guest house soon. Will you help me look for houses and choose one?'

'I'd be more than happy to.'

~

All her life Alka had been in the shadows. She'd never been loved or cherished. Krish changed all of that. He gave her something she'd lacked all her life. He treated her like a queen, he didn't push her for any information about herself, and he was so happy when he was with her. She couldn't have enough of it. This was so different from her last relationship. What she had with Rohan paled in comparison to this.

Krish noticed everything about her, and he was interested in what made her mind work. He didn't think of her as an oddball—something that every person she had interacted with had seemed to, at some point. Instead, Krish found her fascinating and unique. He studied her like she was an exotic creature from an enchanted land. He asked her questions about her philosophy, her views and interests, the books she read, and didn't push her to talk about things she wasn't ready to talk about. This made Alka relax around him. With everyone else, she was guarded, but with Krish, she found that she was laughing more, and had something to look forward to every day. She greedily devoured every moment of the attention he lavished on her.

Sometimes Krish would be busy with work and wouldn't be able to join Alka at the corner table at the cafeteria, which had become "their table". On those days, Alka felt the old emptiness coming back. Krish had managed to fill that void within her, and she waited impatiently for him.

She felt extremely guilty about stealing Krish away from Manasi. She was torn between wanting to spend time with him, and staying away from him, because of her loyalty towards Manasi. But in the end, her own needs won and she couldn't stay away. Krish, on the other hand, was very sure of what he felt for Alka.

She mentioned it to Krish several times—that she was betraying her closest friend. But she couldn't stop meeting

Krish. Krish too couldn't stay away from Alka. Whenever the topic of Manasi came up, Krish was certain that he and Manasi would not have lasted, even if he had never met Alka. He said the relationship was anyway on its last legs and things weren't really that great between them.

'How do you know things won't degenerate between us the same way?' Alka asked him one evening as she took a bite of the thick slice of buttered bread. He'd suggested a cafe near their office, which was known for the fresh bread they baked, and chai they served, and they sat there, across each other, sipping excellent tea and enjoying their food.

'We just know some things, Alka. It's a gut feel. I do not have an explanation. I've seen the way you interact with people. You certainly are different from others and I mean that in a really good way. It's almost as if you are wary of them and yet I see compassion in your eyes. I don't know what you've been through, but you sure as hell don't deserve whatever happened to you.'

That made Alka look away, because his words had found a mark in her heart. He seemed to have looked into her very soul. Nobody had ever bothered to before. She felt like other people told her things they thought were the right things to say. They lacked sincerity. But she could tell Krish was genuinely in love with her by the way he cared about every single thing about her.

'You know something, I was about to tell Manasi that day how I felt about you, when you turned up at the guest house. I was about to break up with her,' he confessed.

'What?! But I'd specifically told you not to!' Alka said.

'I knew you would never be okay with it, so I had decided to go ahead anyway. Your timing was so uncanny, it was eerie.'

'Maybe it was what was destined to be. You weren't supposed to tell her. And you can't tell her now—with her mother being unwell, she is already going through a lot.'

'I definitely can't tell her right now, but I will wait for the right time.'

'It will break up my friendship with her. She will never forgive me,' Alka's voice was tinged with sadness.

'I feel really bad about that, Alka. I know how you feel towards her. But think about it, after we start working, life will take you and her in different directions anyway. It's not like you will spend the rest of your life with her. You will have me all your life, Alka. This may sound harsh or it might seem like I am uncaring. But I'm not. I've never felt for anyone like I feel for you. I am merely pointing out the practicalities in such things,' Krish said gently, taking her hands in his.

'How are you so sure of what you feel for me, without even knowing my story?' Alka whispered.

'Alka, you have to remember that whatever happened to you, you couldn't stop it. I don't know what happened. There's nothing we can do that will change the past. If you ever want to talk about it, I am willing to listen. But if you don't want to talk about it, that's fine too. You have no idea just how much I care about you, Alka. Not just care ... I love you.' Krish's eyes met hers.

'Haven't you said the same thing to Manasi?'

It wasn't the response he was expecting. It took him a few seconds to compose himself. Then he said, 'Can you believe that I haven't?'

'What? I thought you must have, considering that you two were together for a long time,' Alka said, disbelieving. She wanted to be certain about Krish's feelings for her.

'I don't know how to explain it, but I am going to try. I am hoping you will understand me. The truth is, I never felt a need to say it to her, because I never had these deeply intense feelings for her or any of the girls I've dated before her. What I have for you, it's very different. I've been in a lot of relationships. But they were all alike. It never felt like this with anyone else.'

'That's not the impression Manasi gave me.'

'I know. She has that habit where she always speaks for both of us and takes decisions on my behalf. I know she sincerely loves me. She has told it to me so many times. And one of her biggest complaints is that I don't express myself with her. I never told her I love her because the words mean something to me and I didn't want to lie. When she came to Bombay and dragged me to her parents' house, it was very awkward for me. She felt that we were growing distant. She was very upset. In the end, I said that I would go if it meant that much to her. I didn't even tell her I loved her when we … you know … were doing it. She thought sex would fix things between us, but it didn't and now I know why.' Krish was looking at the ground as he spoke, wondering if he was making any sense to Alka or whether she would think he was rambling. 'And as crazy as that sounds—because after all we're going behind her back—this is the truth. You can choose what you want to believe. I've had many relationships. None of those were the real thing. This is,' he said, raising his head to meet her eyes with the final words.

Alka could see that his eyes were shining with sincerity. She knew that he meant every word. He was speaking from his heart.

Overwhelmed with emotions, she didn't know what to say, and so she said nothing.

Krish mistook her silence for cynicism.

'Still sceptical, Alka? I do love you. I mean it,' Krish said studying her expressions with a pained look.

She smiled then, placed her hand on his and whispered 'Thank you.' She couldn't say anything more. She needed time to think about everything Krish had just said. He understood and held her hand as they walked back to the car, across the park, which was between their office and the cafe.

The world outside went about its business, not knowing how much had changed between them in the last hour. Alka carried her precious secret in her heart, all the while knowing well that things between her and Manasi would never be the same again.

~

Alka and Krish went house hunting together. The company had lined up five or six houses in different areas, which they had leased for their employees. Krish was eligible for a one bedroom apartment with a study.

The apartments were all in pleasant residential areas, and Alka found that finding a house together was a very intimate thing to do. It was like they were a 'proper couple'. The person who was showing them the houses addressed Alka like she was his wife.

'Ma'am will have nice space for gardening on these balconies. All homes have balconies here,' he said as she showed them a home on the ninth floor, which overlooked a park.

Later they laughed about it, and Krish teased Alka, 'Does madam approve? Does madam like the gardening space?'

Alka loved it. So did Krish, and he ended up choosing that one. It was a semi-furnished apartment, which meant that it came with wardrobes and a few other essential fittings.

'You'll have to help me buy a bed and a sofa,' Krish smiled.

'I will,' Alka smiled back and slipped her hands into his.

~

The next morning when they met, Krish told Alka that Manasi had called last evening.

'What happened? Did you tell her?' Alka asked, dreading what was inevitable.

'No, I couldn't. She was crying on the phone. Her mother has developed further complications. She might need a pacemaker. After that she needs to rest for at least 2–3 months. She isn't supposed to exert herself and has to be in a stress-free environment. Manasi was very worried about completing the internship. She spoke to her professor, who spoke to the company. They are speaking to their Bombay branch, and it looks like she will be able to transfer there to complete the rest of the internship, as these are special circumstances. She asked me to tell you, as she couldn't reach you.'

Though she felt bad to hear about Manasi's mother, she selfishly felt relieved as well that Krish hadn't yet told her what was going on between them. She didn't want to face Manasi's wrath. Alka felt like she was in a cocoon with Krish. It intensified and magnified her feelings for him. It was as though they were making the best of things, before an explosion, when they would tell Manasi the truth. Whenever

Manasi called, which was about once in a week, she had updates about her mother's health—she was recovering well and Alka was happy about that—or she spoke about her work and asked Alka about hers. Alka felt very guilty on these calls, but she couldn't bring herself to tell Manasi about her growing relationship with Krish. How could she? She felt terribly guilty and she didn't want to add to Manasi's woes.

~

Krish soon moved into the flat. Every evening, he took Alka to the best of restaurants—to quiet, classy discreet places, where they could talk. Then they returned back to the flat where they sometimes made slow, passionate love and at other times it was hurried as though they couldn't wait. They simply couldn't get enough of each other. Afterwards, they lay in bed and talked. Alka found herself sharing a lot of things about herself with Krish. He had unlocked a secret part of her, which she hadn't opened to anyone. She still couldn't tell him her big secret, though. Krish, in turn, shared with her things about his childhood, his terrifying boarding school experiences where he was bullied by older boys. He showed her a burn mark when one of the boys had kept a hot iron on his stomach when he refused to do the older boy's laundry. He showed her another scar near his shoulder blade, where a boy had threatened him with a knife. He hadn't meant to hurt him, but only to scare him. But the cut was deep enough to leave a scar. He told her about the times he had cried himself to sleep, and about how abandoned and frightened he felt when his only friend at school had written to his parents about the bullying and they had immediately taken him out of boarding. Krish said he felt like he was the loneliest person in the world. Alka was horrified as she listened to what he'd been through.

'Why didn't you tell your brother or your mother too, like your friend?'

'My brother was dealing with a lot already, and he didn't go to college so he could handle the estate and sent me to a fine boarding school. How could I tell him and increase his burden? Also, if the boys knew I had complained, they would bully me more.'

'I can't imagine how terrified you must have been,' Alka said as she kissed him.

'Oh, you have no idea,' Krish said.

They snuggled, speaking about many things. They discovered they had common taste when it came to music. They discovered they both loved the rains. They talked about the movies they loved, the books that they had read. They talked about how painful it was to lose a parent.

One day, Alka admired how well Krish drove, and she said she wished she had someone who'd taught her to drive. Krish immediately offered to teach her. Alka was a great student and Krish smiled when she screamed in excitement when she drove on her own for the first time.

Their bond was growing stronger each day, and Alka felt hear heart would explode with joy.

A tiny part of her dreaded facing Manasi but Krish assured her that they were both in this together, and would face it together, whatever it was.

17

1994-95

Undone

ONE OF THE BUSIEST TIME IN THE ESTATE WAS JUST AFTER the blooms. Subbu had to be extremely careful about monitoring the berries. If he slipped up, it could mean a failed crop, which meant huge financial losses. After the initial showers, the rains weren't as expected that year. So he tried his hardest to strengthen the estate's irrigation system. He constructed water harvesting structures like farm ponds. He had pits dug between rows of plants so that the run-off water could enrich the soil. He paid special attention to the pepper crops that were in danger of getting destroyed. Subbu would be at the estate with his workers before sunrise and he would return home only after sunset, exhausted. Anandi, seeing how stressed Subbu already was, glad that she had agreed to let the topic of his marriage rest for a while.

After the rainy season ceased, the bustling activity of the coffee estate eased a bit. The contractual pickers went back to their villages, and only the resident labour was on the estate. Subbu supervised the 'Yertha' activities, where they cleaned the base of the coffee bushes from mulch and other decaying plant material. Though running a coffee estate kept one busy the whole year round, this was the time when Subbu had a little more time on his hands than usual. It was a chance that Anandi pounced on to rake up the issue of his marriage once again.

'Subbu, Mrs Chinappa called me yesterday. She is sending the photographs of her niece today. Someone from their estate will bring it along. The girl has done her MA from Chennai, and is working at a college. She is very pretty and the family owns acres of coffee estates not far from here,' Anandi told him. They were both having a drink together in the informal living room that overlooked the courtyard, something they did once every few weeks when they talked about everything that needed to plan for the estate. From experience, Anandi knew that this was the time when Subbu would be most relaxed and therefore most receptive to her ideas.

'Amma, what will a photograph really tell me? You can see I am already struggling to manage our own estates. Things haven't been going too well. How does it matter to me if her family has coffee estates? That is not something that impresses me in anyway,' Subbu replied, taking a sip of his homemade betel leaf wine.

'Listen Subbu, you're not getting any younger. We have such a big house, and we have all the modern conveniences.

I am growing old and would like to enjoy my grandchildren before I go.'

'Amma, please don't go all emotional on me by bringing up your age. I never said no to marriage. It is just that the right person has yet to come along.'

'You had also promised that you would get married to any girl I chose. What about Alka? You seemed to be impressed with her and you asked me to wait. Now we have waited long enough. Shall I contact Krish and get her phone number?'

'Alka seems to be a nice girl, but I don't know if she already has someone. I don't even know if she will want me.'

'How will we know unless we ask? I'll put things in motion,' Anandi said and this time Subbu didn't protest.

~

Every evening, Krish would call Alka on the internal extension of the company phone to ask if she was ready to leave. That evening, as soon as Alka heard his voice, she knew there was something wrong. But she didn't say anything. She was waiting for him to tell her himself.

He didn't. Alka could see though that he was unusually subdued.

'Want to talk about it?' she asked

Krish looked startled. 'You know?'

'I know what?'

'What did you mean when you asked if I wanted to talk about it?'

'Krish, it's just that you look so troubled,' Alka said, placing her hand on his hand resting on the gear.

'I'll tell you about it. I just need time to process it. Give me some time please,' Krish said.

Alka didn't press him after that. He never forced her to share more than she wanted to, and she felt she had to afford him the same courtesy. She wondered if it was something at work that had disturbed him so much. She wished she could make whatever was bothering him vanish. They drove in silence for the rest of the journey, which was very unlike Krish. Usually he played her favourite songs, but today he was focussing on the road. It took all of Alka's self-control to not ask for a second time what the problem was.

Once they let themselves into the apartment, Krish hugged Alka tightly.

'I love you, Alka. Whatever happens, I want you to remember that.'

Alka was taken aback by the tightness of his hug, the urgency of his voice and his unusual behaviour. 'I know you do. You make me feel cherished,' she said.

'You are,' he replied, kissing the top of her head.

He didn't notice that Alka had never said it back to him. She had never declared that she loved him.

Alka had thought about it. She wasn't sure what she felt towards Krish. All she knew was it was very different from all her previous relationships. But the guilt of betraying Manasi weighed down heavily on her. She was also carrying the baggage of what had happened in her teens with Harish, and so a part of her was emotionally closed off.

She did love being around Krish, but whether she was in love with him or whether it was the novelty of being wooed like this that fascinated her, she couldn't be sure. She decided that when she told Krish she loved him, she had to be as certain as he was. She didn't want to have any doubts in her mind. So she decided to hold off on saying those words, and he didn't mind that at all.

Krish asked her if she was hungry and Alka said she was ravenous. Krish had a cook who let himself into the apartment and cooked while Krish was at work. Today he had made Krish's favourite chicken curry and rotis.

After they finished their meal, Alka expected Krish to tell her what was bothering him, but he didn't. He kissed her passionately and when they got into bed, both Alka and Krish forgot all about anything that was troubling him. They made love for hours, tenderly, gently.

'You know this—what we have—I agree with you, it is magical,' Alka whispered as he held her afterwards.

'It is Alka … It is. I never ever want to hurt you,' he said. Alka thought that it was an odd thing to say, but too exhausted to ponder over it, she fell asleep in his arms, with him holding her.

Krish couldn't sleep for a long time. Instead, he buried his face in her hair and inhaled deeply—her hair smelled of vanilla and lemon, a familiar scent, which brought him so much comfort. He sat for hours, thinking, contemplating. Curled up next to her, with his arm around her waist, he lay there, wide awake. It was only around 4.30 a.m. that he fell into a disturbed sleep.

~

The telephone rang shrilly the next morning at 7 a.m. Krish slept soundly and he didn't hear the ringing at all. It was Alka who nudged him awake gently.

'Hey sleepyhead, the phone is ringing,' she said.

'Let it,' he mumbled, burying his head deep into the pillows and pulling Alka towards him.

After an hour, the phone rang again.

'The phone, Krish, answer it. What if it's urgent?' Alka whispered into his ear.

They looked at each other.

'Go on—pick it up,' Alka said.

Krish rubbed his eyes and looked for his boxers. Then he trudged to his desk, flopped down in his chair and answered it reluctantly.

Surprisingly, it was Anandi.

'Amma?' he said, still rubbing his eyes.

Anandi brought up the topic of Subbu's marriage, without beating around the bush.

'Ha! Finally you pick up. Listen, Kanna, I've been thinking about Subbu's marriage. I think Alka will be a perfect match for him. I want to get in touch with her family. Could you please give me her number?' she asked.

Krish sat up bolt upright. He was stunned and couldn't speak for a few moments.

'Hello, are you there? Can you hear me?' Anandi asked.

'For ... Anna? Alka?' he managed to say, wondering if he had heard correctly or if he was dreaming.

Alka had propped herself up, pulled the bedsheet to cover her naked body and sat upright as she heard Krish speak. She was trying to make sense of it, her brain furiously working, connecting the dots.

Krish was fully awake now. He didn't know what to say. Stalling for time, he said, 'Amma, I've just woken up. I have my own new place and you talk about Subbu's marriage? Don't you want to know how I am doing?' He hoped he sounded normal and casual, even though his insides were churning and his heart began beating wildly.

'I know you are fine, Kanna. I am happy, really happy you have settled there well. But you know how we have been searching for a girl for a long time for your Anna. And you know how he is. Hence I thought ...'

'Look, Anna can very well speak to her himself. I will give him the number,' Krish said. He was now irritated with his mother.

'Okay, okay. Take care of yourself, how is the food there? Who is cooking for you?' Anandi asked, trying to pacify him.

'It is all good, Amma. I have a cook here who comes daily.'

'Okay, Kanna. Do your work well, and check with Alka and connect her with me or with Subbu. I want to proceed with this matter and it is urgent,' Anandi was determined.

Krish knew there was no point in arguing with his mother in the mood that she was in. So he simply said that he would.

When he hung up, he walked back to the bed, and sat on the edge, with his head in his hands. Alka moved closer to him and hugged him from the back.

'Hey, what happened? Are you okay?' she asked squeezing him tightly.

'No, I am not,' he said quietly.

Then he got up and walked to the window, and stood staring outside. Alka looked at him and thought he looked so vulnerable, his shoulders stooped, like there was a great burden on him. When he turned to face her, there were tears in his eyes.

'Manasi is pregnant. She is very keen to have the baby,' he said, his voice flat, broken. 'I'm sorry ... so so sorry,' he said hoarsely.

Alka sat very still for a few minutes, not believing what she heard.

'What are you saying?'

'Alka. I feel terrible. What a mess ...'

'But the phone call just now—it wasn't from Manasi, was it?'

'No, Manasi called me last evening at work. The phone call was from my mother. She wants to get in touch with you—for a marriage proposal. For ... for Subbu,' he said, his voice breaking.

Alka said nothing. She sat on Krish's bed with her arms around her folded legs, her chin resting between them. She looked like a little girl.

Krish came and sat next to her. They sat in silence.

Outside the window the world slowly came alive. Birds chirped. The newspaper boy came on a bicycle, and began delivering the papers. A distant horn sounded, indicating that the traffic had already begun.

'I am so so sorry, Alka. I wanted to tell you last evening but I simply couldn't bring myself to ... and now this,' Krish said.

Alka still said nothing.

'Say something, Alka. Please,' Krish sounded like a little boy.

'What is left to say? I knew this was too good to have lasted,' Alka replied at last.

Her heart had turned to stone.

She got up, got dressed and left without a word.

Krish didn't stop her.

Part Three

The Homecoming

'Your heart and my heart are very, very
old friends.'
—Hafez

18

2005

The Ones We've Loved and the Ones We've Lost

IN SEPTEMBER 2005, SUBBU ORGANIZED A GRAND MEMORIAL at the Minto Club to commemorate the first death anniversary of his mother. He invited almost everyone from his social circles. Alka had not wanted such a grand event. She felt that Anandi would not have liked it.

'She would have wanted something small, a quiet prayer meeting with the family,' she told Subbu. They were both lying in bed, their backs turned to each other. Outside, it was a moonless night, and the large trees around their bungalow cast dark shadows around them, like long, black cloaks. Rain fell softly and Alka lay in bed listening to the small plops of the raindrops hitting the soil. Subbu and Alka were both grieving deeply, but each had completely different ways of dealing with the loss. Subbu had immersed himself in work, while Alka brooded silently, replaying in her head every memory she had with Anandi.

Alka missed Anandi terribly. After her wedding, she'd formed a strong bond with her mother-in-law, and the two did everything together. They had, over the years, grown so close that they could sit in silence, sipping coffee on the verandah, not saying a word and yet read each other's minds. There was a special connection Alka felt with Anandi, and without her around, she felt completely abandoned. It was like losing her mother all over again. She wondered if she was cursed, and whether everyone she formed a close bond with would die.

'I don't think she would have liked a prayer meeting or anything. Do you think you knew my mother better than me?'

Subbu knew he was being unfair, snapping at Alka like that. He hadn't intended to, but the words slipped out before he could control himself.

The deep sorrow of losing Anandi mingled with his helplessness and anger, and he found himself drowning. It was hard to come to terms with losing his mother and unfortunately, it was Alka who bore the brunt of his emotions. These days, his tone towards her was sharp, his words, acerbic.

'We did grow very close,' Alka's voice was pained, withdrawn.

'What family prayer meeting are you talking about anyway? It's not like Krish or Manasi will attend. He didn't even come when she died.'

'That's being a bit unfair, Subbu. He was in Paris, on that leadership program his company had sent him for. Weren't you the one who told him not to come?'

'Still, I expected him to come later, after he returned to India. Has he visited the estate even once after his marriage?'

'That he hasn't ...'

'He has become a slave to Manasi's whims. That's what it is. Look, at the very least I expected Manasi to come down, out of courtesy. How can anyone *not* turn up when they know a family member has passed?'

'Manasi has her own problems. You know how hard it is for her with Sanal.' Alka didn't know why she was defending Manasi. The friendship between them was almost non-existent now as they had gradually lost touch with each other after their respective weddings. Alka had dutifully written letters to Manasi in the first year of her marriage. She would travel to the post office from the estate and diligently post them. But Manasi, caught up with her own problems, wrote back only once, that too after a few months. Any time Alka called her, she would be busy with the baby. Twice, she'd even sounded annoyed at being woken up. Gradually Alka stopped calling and writing, and when she got pregnant, motherhood consumed her. After that, the only common link between them for the last few years had been Anandi, and it was through her that Alka got all the news about Krish and Manasi.

'That's the excuse both Krish and Manasi always make,' Subbu's disapproving tone echoed in the dark.

'I don't think it is an excuse. It's not easy, having an autistic child. Your mother mentioned several times about how they struggle with him. It's hard enough raising our two. I can only imagine how much harder it must be to raise one with special needs. Your mother had experienced it first-hand too.'

'Yes, I've seen that too. But for me it is still inexcusable. Your family dies, you turn up.'

Alka had never met Sanal, even though he was soon turning ten. Subbu had visited Krish just once in all these years because there was always something to be taken care of at the estate. One year, Anandi had insisted that Subbu accompany her and he'd done so reluctantly. Alka always had a ready excuse to not go—she had said the girls couldn't miss school and had stayed back. But Subbu hated Mumbai. Having lived in the estate all his life, amidst greenery and nature, he had felt so stifled in Krish's two bedroom apartment that he had returned to the estate in just two days. He couldn't take any more of it.

Any time Subbu invited Krish and Manasi to the estate, Krish would either make an excuse about how busy he was or how the journey and the new surroundings might upset Sanal. Subbu couldn't comprehend how much of a distance there now was between Krish and him. Things had changed so much in a few years. Deep down, he blamed Manasi for this rift and he was resentful towards her.

Anandi would visit Krish and Manasi every year in Mumbai, and after every visit, she would tell Subbu and Alka about how much Manasi was struggling with Sanal. Subbu had heard all the stories. One time, right in front of Anandi's watchful eyes, Sanal had climbed on a chair and tried to grab on to the ceiling fan, bending the wings. Sanal was extremely creative and intelligent. Buildings fascinated him, and he could name every prominent building in the world and knew all the facts about them, like the name of the architect, the year in which it was constructed, the number of floors and all other details. Anandi was amazed at how smart he was.

Yet when she tried to have conversations with him, she rarely succeeded.

Sanal was unusually strong and prone to violent temper and tantrums as apart from being autistic, he had also been diagnosed with a behavioural issue that Anandi or the others in the family understood nothing about—oppositional defiant disorder. So Sanal listened to nobody. He did his own thing. Only Manasi could get through to him. With others, no amount of gentle corrections worked. Sanal simply couldn't understand them, and they in turn couldn't see the world through Sanal's eyes.

Alka said nothing to Subbu. She lay in the dark, curled up like a child, wishing a hundred times that things could have been different and she could rewind time to change things.

She wondered how things had come to this; She and Subbu barely spoke to each other these days. From the start their marriage hadn't been ideal, but at least they would talk to each other. She remembered the time they had travelled on their honeymoon to Siliguri. It was the first time that Subbu had taken a vacation from the estate ever since he took charge. He entrusted everything to the estate manager Muthu, and gave him many instructions, till Muthu said, 'Sir, I was taking care of the estate even before you were born, alongside your father. Please enjoy your honeymoon and do not worry about it.'

For their honeymoon, Subbu had chosen a tea estate in Assam. He asked Alka if she was fine with the destination or whether she wanted to visit the usual touristy places like Goa. Alka had said she was okay with whatever made Subbu happy.

Alka recalled how jovial he had been during the honeymoon. He had been very excited to see the process involved in manufacturing tea, comparing notes with the manager. In the evening, he and Alka would sit and have long conversations over wine. Subbu told Alka many stories about their childhood at the estate before their father had passed away. Most of the stories involved Krish, and for Alka it was bittersweet. She was trying to get over Krish, and while any mention of him hurt, she also laughed at stories of some of the mischief that the brothers had got into.

Once they got back to the estate, this playful relaxed side of Subbu vanished. Gradually, over the course of many years, communication between Alka and Subbu became more business-like. They rarely had lengthy conversations, as Subbu was busy with the estate, and Alka barely had any time, after the girls were born. These days, Subbu and she only seemed to snap at each other. Alka felt that it was also because neither had gotten over the sudden shock of Anandi passing away.

One part of Alka also felt irrationally that she could have prevented Anandi's death. She should have never let Anandi go that day. On that fateful day, Anandi was on the way to the hospital with their trusted driver Venkatesh, for her dialysis, which she had to undergo regularly. Her kidneys were failing, and the doctors had said that regular dialysis was the only option. Alka accompanied her on her hospital visits, but on that day, Tulika was running a fever and she begged her mother not to leave her. Alka asked Anandi to postpone her appointment by a day.

'I will go with you tomorrow, as soon as Tulika is better. Don't go today,' Alka had told Anandi.

'Let it be. Children need their mothers during this time. Don't worry. I will go with Venkatesh and come back soon. Supervise Gowramma while she's making dinner—especially the Koli Saar. She always overboils it and it makes the chicken rubbery.'

Those were the last words that Anandi had said to Alka. Both Venkatesh—their family driver who had been with the family for over twenty-five years—as well as Anandi had died instantly when a tipper lorry that skid off its course because of the treacherous rain, collided with their car on the way to the hospital. It sent the car crashing down into the ravines of the thickly forested Western Ghats. The lorry driver escaped unhurt with only a few minor injuries. It had taken over eleven hours to rescue the wreckage with the help of cranes that had to arrive from Chickmaglur. The sight of the mangled bodies, the blood, the bones protruding at odd angles—all of it still haunted Subbu in his nightmares. Alka had to stay back with Tulika and Nisha, and Subbu was glad that his daughters and Alka had been spared the gruesome sight of his mother's disfigured, unrecognizable body. It was ghastly.

The shock had been so great that there had been no rituals or no ceremonies. The bodies had been taken straight to the crematorium, after the mandatory post-mortem at the hospital. Hence, the first death anniversary was extremely important to Subbu, because he saw it as a chance for people to pay their last respects to Anandi. He wasn't able to give her a grand funeral, and he hoped to make up for it with this memorial event he was hosting.

'Ensure that Nisha and Tulika are well-dressed tomorrow, and they behave properly. All the business associates from coffee advisory board, people from the Coffee Research Institute and some special invitees from Bangalore will all be there.'

'If you are so worried about how they may behave, I can leave them at home with Selvi.'

'No, the others might be bringing their kids.'

'Okay. They have never behaved badly anyway on social occasions.'

'Except for the time when Nisha stuffed her face with cake and insisted on eating the whole thing, not letting the other kids have even a slice.'

'She was two then, Subbu,' Alka rolled her eyes in the dark.

'I know. My mother laughed a lot that day.'

'She did, she did enjoy that party,' Alka said recalling that incident, her demeanour softening a little at the memory.

'She loved having guests over. And I think the best thing to do is to celebrate her spirit.'

'Maybe you are right. The reason I mentioned a prayer meeting is because one evening when we were talking, the topic had turned towards what is to be done after her death. She said she wanted all her family together and she mentioned something about a family prayer meeting.'

'How many drinks had she had?'

'Maybe three or four. She loved that homemade wine. I miss her so much.' Alka started crying softly.

'I miss her too,' Subbu said, but he didn't turn towards Alka and he made no effort to comfort her.

Alka sobbed softly into her pillow, and she was just drifting off to sleep, when Subbu's phone buzzed.

She heard Subbu reaching out for his phone, and the soft glow that illuminated his face was reflected in the window pane opposite Alka.

'Krish. He says he will be here tomorrow. He is coming by himself.'

Alka wondered if she had heard right.

'What?'

'That's what he says. After all these years, it is about time,' Subbu said as he typed out a reply. Then he went back to bed. Within minutes he was snoring gently, as he always did.

Alka lay very still, wide awake, her heart racing, the news of Krish's arrival the next day slowly sinking in. She and Krish had not spoken since she had walked out of his room a decade ago. On that very day, Anandi had reached out to Alka with a marriage proposal for Subbu, Alka had asked for some time to think about it, and she had thought about it—long and hard. She would *have* to get married someday. She did not think she could be single all her life. Krish couldn't walk away from a pregnant Manasi; he had to do the right thing by her. Alka had also thought about the proposal Mrs Shetty had brought to her. She considered her social standing. She examined the choices before her in a removed, practical manner, just the way her mother had taught her to. She weighed the pros and cons. She really liked Anandi, and she absolutely loved the coffee estate. She had no one in this world to call her own. Her only good friend was Manasi, and if the truth about her and Krish came out, she would lose Manasi too.

On the one hand was this 'thing' between her and Krish. She wasn't even sure if she could call it love. Wasn't it too soon? Didn't people have to be together for many years before they could call it love? They had been together just for a brief period of time, after Manasi left for Bombay. If she accepted Anandi's proposal, Krish would have to do the right thing and marry Manasi. At least she wouldn't have the guilt of breaking them up. She would lose Krish, she knew that. But was he even hers in the first place? She also knew that if she refused this proposal, it would mean that she would be all alone, working away at a corporate job. She'd hated that life anyway.

The prospect of being all by herself, out in the world without her mother, terrified her. If she agreed to marry Subbu, she would be getting a 'readymade' family.

She didn't make a decision immediately though. For the next few days and nights, she thought carefully about it, and the more she thought about it, the more certain she became. After three weeks, she came to a decision—she would accept Anandi's proposal. She would learn to love Subbu. Wasn't that what all the women who had arranged marriages did?

Anandi said she wanted to speak to her relatives. Alka told her that she had lost touch with her father's side of the family when she was a child and her mother had been a single child.

'I have nobody left, aunty ... no family to call my own. I am sorry, but there's no one from my side you can speak to. If you want any character references, you can speak to my college professor who'll —'

'Shhhh ... don't say you have nobody. From now on, you have us,' Anandi had said.

~

When Krish had broken the news of Manasi's pregnancy to Anandi, she said he had to do the right thing and marry her immediately. She also said that since Krish was younger, it would be only right if his older brother got married before him, and proposed to have a grand double wedding for both her sons. Krish, however, wouldn't hear of it. Manasi's parents, when they learnt that Manasi was pregnant, had insisted that they get married immediately.

In the end, Krish and Manasi had a simple court marriage in Bombay, just before Subbu and Alka had a grand wedding at Sakleshpur. It was torturous for Krish to attend his brother's wedding. He'd tried telling Anandi that Manasi needed him.

'Oh come on—you cannot miss the wedding. You can fly down, attend it and fly back the next morning,' Anandi said.

Just before her wedding Alka was a bundle of nerves. She had never felt so alone in her entire life. From Subbu's and Anandi's side, there were numerous guests.

'I am sorry, Alka, I can't believe I am missing your wedding, but I am sending Krish as my representative,' Manasi told Alka over the phone. Manasi apologized a hundred times, telling Alka that because of some complications the doctors had said that she couldn't fly in her condition. Also her mother still needed care.

'Manasi, I missed your wedding too. So you don't have to apologize.'

'Well, mine wasn't even a wedding. Just a hasty signing at the crowded registrar's office. You have a thousand things to do with Anandi Aunty.'

'I know. I am grateful to her. She is taking me everywhere, introducing me to so many people from their side. She is so happy about this grand wedding. But I just feel so alone, Manasi,' Alka said.

'Don't worry about it. You will have a big crowd from your side', Manasi assured her over the phone.

'How?'

'Our classmates. Will you invite them or should I?'

Alka invited their entire MBA class even though she hadn't interacted much with them. She also invited all her professors and everyone in her office who she even vaguely knew. She was sceptical as to whether they would actually come, but they did. Alka was overjoyed when a large number of them turned up. Unknown to Alka, Manasi had made phone calls to all of them, and confirmed that they would attend. Alka was happy to see them, thanked each of them, feeling relieved that at least there were some people from her side.

Krish couldn't bear to look at Alka in her bridal attire. Alka hardened her heart and pretended she was happy. The truth was, she was dying inside, and she wept in the bathroom, after the ceremonies, and then dried her tears and greeted the guests. Seeing Krish hurt was something she couldn't bear, but she had made her decision and she would go through with it.

~

For a few years after her marriage, Alka kept expecting to run into Krish. She had braced herself for it, certain that she would meet him at family events. She had resolved that she would pretend that nothing had ever happened between them. That day, though, never came. When he didn't turn up even for Anandi's cremation, Alka thought that maybe she would never see him again. She felt that Krish was staying away from the estate, from her and Subbu, deliberately. It had been a decade now.

She thought she had put whatever had happened between them behind her. But now, a wound she thought healed had been slashed open. She didn't know how to face him. Why had he decided to turn up now? What would it be like to face him again? What would he say? What would she say?

She lay in her bed, tossing and turning, unable to sleep, her heart pounding in her ears with the same excitement that she had experienced when she was with Krish all those years ago.

19

2005

Coming Home

KRISH WAS EXHAUSTED. HE HAD BEEN TRYING AS HARD AS he could for all these years, but whatever he did, it was never enough. Sanal had just had yet another meltdown and the living room lay in a mess with overturned armchairs, an overturned centre table and a shattered pale blue ceramic flower vase, the water from which had dripped all over, soaking the hand-tufted woollen rug. The pink lilies, scattered all over the wet rug, lay lifeless. Their help, Anita, hadn't turned up that morning, and her absence was the spark that had ignited this rage.

It started when Krish, instead of Anita, made Sanal his sandwich for breakfast. Manasi was in the shower and had told Krish to watch Sanal. Sanal insisted on eating exactly at 8.00 a.m., and he said he wanted Anita Didi to make the sandwich. But when Anita didn't turn up, Krish had made his son's breakfast. When Sanal saw the sandwich Krish had prepared, he became upset. Krish had put the ingredients inside the sandwich in the wrong order. The tomatoes always went under the cucumbers and both slices had to be buttered after being toasted for precisely a minute. Krish had followed none of these directives, and to top it all off, he had also cut the bread the wrong way, so that the sandwiches were triangular instead of the rectangular ones that Sanal liked. Despite Sanal's protest, Krish asked him to give the sandwich a try and assured him that it would taste the same.

In response, Sanal had flung the plate across the room. Usually, Krish tried hard to be patient, but that morning, irritated by a deadline he had to meet at work and a fight with Manasi the previous night, he'd had enough. He raised his voice and told Sanal that it was not okay to throw a plate of food. This was a trigger for Sanal, who went around the room screaming hysterically and turning the furniture upside down.

Manasi came running out of the shower, yelling at Krish.

'Come on Krish—you ought to know by now how to handle him. Can't you see how you've triggered his anxiety by forcing him to do something he doesn't want to?'

'I didn't force him, Manasi. I merely told him to try it.'

'Krish, really? You are an adult. You should know by now how his brain works. His brain is wired differently, What part of that don't you get? How could you do this?' Manasi yelled at Krish. She was exhausted too.

It took Manasi over half-an-hour to calm him down. Once Sanal had quietened a little, she shot a murderous look at Krish, shook her head and marched out of the house with Sanal, to his school without a word, making Krish feel like a failure, a fool.

Krish grit his teeth and marched to the balcony. With his clenched fist, he hit his other palm, trying to control his rising frustration. He wished he could smash a few things like Sanal had done earlier.

As the salty sea breeze hit his face, he inhaled deeply. Sanal's shrill screams were still echoing in his ears and he took deep breaths, trying to tune them out. The silence and the city sounds far below him felt welcome. As he sat on his balcony on the twenty-first floor of the sea-facing apartment in Bandra, staring at the ocean, he wished he hadn't urged Sanal to try the sandwich. He felt miserable about triggering Sanal. Manasi was right. He ought to have known better. He'd somehow thought that if Sanal ate the sandwich, he could leave with Manasi and get to the centre on time. But now, because of him, Sanal had left home hungry. Manasi was furious as well. No matter how much he tried, he was never able to do the right thing. He thought about how hard the last decade had been for him. Usually, watching the waves calmed him down, but today, even that didn't help. The sea was calm and placid, the sunlight reflecting off the cerulean blue waters. The sky was the brightest blue with white fluffy clouds floating peacefully—but Krish didn't notice any of it. He had a client presentation in an hour and his head was throbbing. He couldn't focus.

He and Manasi had been up all night, arguing. Manasi felt Krish was never involved in their lives. Krish said he tried but Manasi was never satisfied. One thing had led to another, and everything spiralled wildly out of control, with Manasi saying that she wished she had never married him and Krish retorting that perhaps, if she was not pregnant, he would not have. The bad feelings from the fight had spilled over to the morning, resulting in the meltdown that happened a few minutes ago.

To Krish, it seemed like Sanal was getting more and more upset even with the smallest of things these days. Krish felt lost, not knowing what to do anymore. He'd hoped that with all the behavioural therapy sessions that Sanal had been taking, he would make progress as he grew up. But even after all of it, Krish didn't see much progress, which irked Manasi. To Krish, he still remained the same cranky stubborn kid, only physically stronger.

Even as a baby Sanal was difficult. He had been born with club feet and they had started physical therapy for him early on, putting his feet in casts to correct it. He was a very finicky baby and till Sanal was seven, Manasi rarely slept for more than three hours at a time, often staying awake the entire nights. Krish had been extremely worried when Sanal was born with club feet. After that was corrected, Krish and Manasi had both thought that the worst was behind him and had heaved a sigh of relief. But then they realized how soon they had rejoiced.

When Sanal was about three and began school, the teachers started noticing other things like how he never made eye contact with anyone. While other kids played with toy cars by making up a game, Sanal would line them up according to size and colour. He would never follow instructions.

'Ha! He takes after you,' Krish would chuckle and tell Manasi.

'Rubbish. I think it's because he is smart,' Manasi would retort.

When complaints from teachers about how uncontrollable Sanal was, increased as he grew older, they finally accepted that it was not something to treat lightly. There was something different about their child. Krish remembered that day when Sanal was about four when they had a neuropsychological evaluation done. Manasi had refused to accept it.

'Manasi, the doctors say it is ODD—Oppositonal Defiant Disorder. He can't help the way he is. The doctors say there's no cure for it. If he is under pressure, he is likely to have an explosive tantrum. We have to accept it,' Krish said.

'I don't think there's anything like that. I think it's just because the teachers simply don't get him. I'll work with him,' Manasi declared.

She threw herself into Sanal's care, giving up her original plan of going back to work. Dealing with severe meltdowns, sometimes cleaning up urine, being on the constant lookout to prevent self-injurious behaviour, not knowing what might be the next trigger—all of it took its toll on them as well as on their marriage.

Krish recalled the time when Sanal was six, and had to be hospitalized as he had pushed the television down from the stand and it had crashed on his feet. Manasi and Krish could never be at peace, as they didn't know what would happen next with him.

Manasi had then enrolled at a centre which had training programmes for parents with autistic kids, which would help them to cope with Sanal's condition. She insisted Krish accompany her to each session. In the initial years Krish had attended each one. Soon, he began to find it hard to balance his work and these sessions, and when he missed a couple, Manasi got frustrated.

'You would think I am asking a stranger for help. He is your *son*, Krish. I am sorry he isn't the child you expected him to be,' she would cry, worn down by the amount of effort she was putting in trying to help Sanal.

'I am trying, Manasi. I really am. But you can afford to spend time on him. You don't have to go to work the next day,' Krish would fire back, guilt making him speak more sharply.

Krish wondered if he was a bad father for feeling worn out by Sanal. On some days when he got back from work, all he wanted to do was escape into his room, and not face Sanal. He felt terrible about it. But he needed that escape. If he didn't, he would probably explode with frustration, if he faced Sanal. He was struggling to cope with it all. He wished he could be more like Manasi. She was relentless. She never gave up, no matter how hard it was, staying infinitely patient when it came to Sanal. She gave up all her interests, all her aspirations, to tend to Sanal full time.

When Sanal was born, it had been the pre-Internet era, and Manasi spoke to every specialist that she could, using her father and mother's contacts. Once she had the Internet, she read up every morsel of information on various kinds of autisms and the best way to deal with the kind Sanal had. Manasi was a walking-talking encyclopaedia and could probably have written a thesis on Sanal's condition. While the experts had all kinds of diagnoses for Sanal's conditions, the actual handling and dealing with it was something that Krish or Manasi had never anticipated.

Manasi had become a mere shadow of her former self. She lost her enthusiasm for life, rarely smiled and had bags under her eyes. Krish urged her to get trained help. He urged her to have a life outside Sanal. But Manasi was stubborn.

Krish tried hard to do all the right things. But sometimes, no matter what he did, Sanal would get triggered. Manasi would then get annoyed with Krish, and his way of dealing with this was to immerse himself in more work. He excelled at his career and rose to the position of vice president—something unprecedented for someone so young. His personal life, though, was slowly falling apart.

Krish sighed as he went into the living room and began cleaning up the mess that Sanal had made. He got a mop and soaked up the water. He threw the flowers into the bin. He dragged the rug out and hung it on the balcony so it would dry. He turned all the chairs back upright. He took a pill for his headache and left for work.

When he had been in Paris, doing his accelerated leadership diploma program, Subbu had called him up and told him about Anandi's death. Numb with shock and disbelief, alone in a foreign country, helplessness engulfed him.

'Anna—I am taking the next flight,' he'd said.

'By the time you come, the cremation will be over. I don't think there's any point in your coming,' Subbu's tone had been clipped. He was biting back his agony, his frustration, his anger and shock. He didn't want to tell Krish that he wanted to spare his little brother the sight of his mother's mangled body, which would have to be stored in ice at the mortuary.

Krish's organization had given him permission to return to India, but Krish had been in a dilemma as it would mean he would miss an essential component required for his leadership diploma. Krish couldn't focus on his course at all. He kept wondering what he was doing, when he should have been with his brother. He spoke to his manager, who was a practical man.

'If your brother has said that the funeral will be over by the time you get back, what is the point of your going back? You have just a week left to complete this program. I'd say you should stay back,' he said.

After much deliberation, with a heavy heart, Krish had stayed back in Paris.

Then, one afternoon, Subbu called Krish and told him about the first death anniversary function that he was organizing.

'Amma loved a good gathering. She would rejoice whenever people visited. We never had a proper ceremony when she passed away. So we will have an elaborate function now. Please come for it, along with Manasi and Sanal,' Subbu said.

'I'll speak to Manasi, and we will try and come. I don't want to miss this,' Krish said.

~

Krish had forgotten all about the morning's events when he got home, but Manasi hadn't. In the evening, after Sanal had gone to bed, she brought up the incident again.

'You really don't seem to be bothered about Sanal or me. You are only bothered about your great job.'

'Manasi, please don't start this again. I'm tired.'

'When are you ever *not* tired, Krish? I have been handling all of this on my own. I'm tired too, you know.'

'Sanal is comfortable with Anita. I have been telling you, so many times, over so many years, to take a break. Have a life outside of parenting him. Go to the gym. Go shopping. You need something in your life, other than this.'

'I can't be like you—hiding behind other things rather than facing the issue. Someone has got to be there for him, and if you can't step up, I definitely will.'

'That's being very unfair, Manasi.'

'Shut up, Krish—you would not have married me had I not been pregnant. And you talk about being unfair.'

'I am sorry. I said that in anger. People say things when they are frustrated. You've said far nastier things in the past but I haven't held it against you. Look Manasi, I am working hard so we never have a financial problem. If something were to happen to me, I've made enough arrangements, so that you and Sanal have no financial issues.'

'Stop lying to yourself, Krish. You're working hard so you don't have to face me or Sanal. Money isn't everything. There's more to life than financial security. It's not like I don't have money of my own anyway. My parents have created a trust fund just for Sanal. Sometimes I think it is better if we separate.'

Krish didn't answer. He knew this would not lead anywhere. It was a discussion they'd had a million times in the past. Every time they fought, Manasi would say things like this. They would go around in circles. The patterns repeated themselves. He needed a break from these constant fights. He needed to get away for a while.

He made up his mind then. He would attend Anandi's memorial event, even if it meant facing Alka. He had been running away for far too long.

He told Manasi that she was right. There was more to life than financial security. He said he had missed his mother's funeral and Subbu was organizing a grand ceremony. He asked if she and Sanal wanted to join him to attend Anandi's memorial event. Manasi ridiculed the very idea. She said that it was impossible to travel with Sanal. Krish decided that he would go alone.

He picked up his phone and texted Subbu that he would join them for the memorial.

20

2005

The Hornbill's Nest

As Alka washed her face and looked into the mirror, she tried to picture herself a decade ago, which was how long it had been since she last saw Krish. She had been so young, so immature. She'd also been confused, angry and insecure. She did not know it back then, but now, when she reflected on her decision of getting married to Subbu, she realized that she had been trying to hurt Krish. She knew now that her actions had been spurred, at least partly, by vengefulness.

She remembered the hornbill that Subbu had pointed out to her all those years ago, when she'd visited the estate with Manasi. He'd told her about how a hornbill never built it's nest but simply occupied a cavity and made its home there.

Wasn't what she had done by getting married to Subbu and moving into the bungalow which was now her home something similar?

She had, though, struck up an instant bond with Anandi. Anandi had asked Alka to call her 'Amma', just like Subbu did, and loved that Alka had readily complied. 'You aren't my daughter-in-law, you are the daughter I never had,' she'd said.

Alka had adjusted easily to life in the estate. Her Kannada improved dramatically as she spoke to Gowramma and her teenage daughter Selvi, who often helped her mother. Looking at Gowramma and her daughter, Alka thought about her mother and herself, slaving away in Mrs Shetty's house. She was determined to treat them well. She chatted with them, asked after them and struck up a friendship with them.

'You are so kind, Alka Amma,' Gowramma often told her.

'Don't pamper the servants too much. They take advantage of you,' Anandi advised her, but Alka knew how it was to be treated badly, and she never wanted that for any of her staff. So she continued to be kind, getting them gifts without Anandi's knowledge.

It wasn't so easy, though, to make the same real and genuine connection with Subbu that she had with his mother and the staff. Alka soon realized that his outlook and philosophy were completely different from hers. The differences between Subbu and Krish became obvious to Alka within the first month of their marriage.

After the honeymoon, when Alka got back, Subbu asked her when she would be taking over the kitchen.

'What do you mean by taking over the kitchen? Don't the cooks manage everything?' Alka asked.

'My mother has to supervise them, tell them what to do, instruct them and manage them. I think she can train you for two or three months, after which you can take over,' Subbu said.

Alka laughed. She thought Subbu was joking. But when he gave her a puzzled look, she realized he wasn't.

The newness of their marriage wore off quickly. Subbu made it clear through his behaviour that Alka's role was to manage the house along with Anandi and his role was to run the estate. It came as a rude shock to Alka that his worldview was steeped in patriarchy and that he was very unlike Krish, who had always seen her as his equal. This was something that Alka hadn't expected at all, or even given much thought to, when she had agreed to marry Subbu.

Alka firmly told herself that there was no question of comparing Subbu to Krish and lamenting over the life that she could have had with Krish.

Krish's chapter was over. He was in her past. He couldn't possibly have walked out on a pregnant Manasi. Alka had made her choice and she had to live with the consequences. She said this to herself over and over. She'd decided she would never think of him. But everywhere in her new home, there were reminders of Krish. His childhood pictures, the trophies he'd won, his badminton racquets, his books—all of them were reminders that this was his home too.

The mansion had seven bedrooms, and Anandi had left Krish's old room untouched. Subbu had his own room too on the ground floor, and since it was full of his stuff, there was no place for Alka's clothes. Anandi told Alka that she could choose any of the remaining rooms as their master bedroom.

Alka chose a beautiful, east-facing room on the first floor. It had large picture windows that overlooked the estate, ample wardrobe space, a huge bathroom with a bathtub. Subbu asked her if she would mind if he continued to keep his clothes in his old room on the ground floor.

'That way, I don't have to disturb you when I wake up early to go on my estate rounds,' he said. Alka did not mind at all. She joked that it just meant more wardrobes for her.

In the initial days, she had woken up at the crack of dawn, intent on accompanying Subbu on his rounds, but he told her that she needn't trouble herself. He'd done this all his life, and it was second nature to him.

'But I want to, Subbu. I want to learn what it is that you do.'

'It's not a course that you can take. You don't have to bother with all this. That's what I am here for. Anyway, it takes a lifetime.'

'I do have a lifetime now with you,' Alka smiled, but Subbu had already turned away and was looking at the crops.

Whenever Alka asked any question about the coffee process or how he knew the right time for the berries to be picked, Subbu joked about it, never giving her proper answers. The estate manager Muthu, who accompanied them, laughed at Subbu's jokes. Subbu discussed things with him and left Alka out of the conversations. Alka complained to Anandi.

'Amma, I do want to learn how to manage the estate—the roasting process, the harvesting—all of it. I want to learn,' she said.

But when it came to running the estate, Anandi's views were not very different from Subbu's.

'You know, when my husband died, Subbu was just seventeen. I let him handle everything. I never tried to learn the process of coffee production or anything. I did not go on the rounds with my husband either. The labour force at the estate is not used to women being in charge.'

'Amma, I don't want to be in charge. I merely want to know everything. Before marriage, he had given me a grand tour of the production facilities. What is wrong in wanting to know a bit more of what goes on behind the scenes?'

'Haha, you have a long way to go, my dear. That was just the tourist version he gave you. Don't worry, all in good time. You'll learn all our ways,' Anandi said.

~

Subbu's traditional views and outlook bothered Alka but she couldn't do anything about it, not without Anandi's support. She analysed her situation in a detached way. She knew she did not want a corporate job. She had chosen to be married to Subbu. She decided she would make the best of it. She would be a good wife and a good daughter-in-law. She would do everything that was expected of her. She was in love with the house and the estate, and she really felt a deep connection to Anandi. And she would try to love Subbu. This much, she thought, was enough.

~

Though Alka had made up her mind to learn to love Subbu, she discovered love wasn't something that you commanded or summoned up at will. With Krish, it had come to her naturally. She had felt at ease with him. But with Subbu, everything was forced. He didn't make it any easier for her either. He was a practical, hardworking man, set in his ways and habits. Even sex with Subbu was so different from what she had experienced with Krish. Krish had made her feel cherished, loved. Krish had treated her like she was something precious, fragile. She had enjoyed it. With Subbu, there was no foreplay, no tenderness. He did not hug her or hold her afterwards. She was aghast when the first time after they slept together, he'd turned over and gone to sleep right after.

Soon after that, Alka discovered that she was pregnant. When she told Subbu, he was overjoyed.

'Anandi Estate will have a heir! I know it will be a boy,' he said.

'You are acting like a medieval zamindar,' Alka remarked.

'Zamindar eh?' Subbu frowned. 'Well, in a way, that's what we are. We have all this land—so that makes us zamindars. And what's that word for the wife of a Zamindar? Ah! Thakurani. You, my dear, are my Thakurani,' he said, pretending to twirl his moustache and Alka did not know whether to laugh or cry.

Anandi, overjoyed that she was going to be a grandmother, pampered Alka. She got a lady from the labour colony in the estate to come every day to massage Alka's back and feet. Alka protested. She said she didn't want it and she didn't want anyone touching her feet.

'All the pregnant women in our family get pampered. Just enjoy your pregnancy,' Anandi said.

The fact that Anandi had said 'our family' moved Alka deeply, and she relented. Earlier, she had only her mother, but now she had Anandi, and she didn't feel so alone anymore.

Anandi fed Alka delicacies made specially for her. Nobody had treated Alka like this and she basked in all the attention and warmth. She slowly relaxed as she got her massages.

Anandi accompanied her to the hospital for all her monthly check-ups. On one of such visits, Alka overcome by the pregnancy hormones and the enormity of the fact that she was having her own baby, got emotional and started crying in the car saying she missed her mother, and how she wished she was there. Anandi hushed her and laid Alka's head on her shoulders, gently patting Alka's thigh. She told her not to cry as it would be bad for the baby. She held her till her sobs subsided and told her she would be there for her.

Anandi was ecstatic that both her daughters-in-law were expecting at the same time.

'I couldn't have a double wedding for my sons. But I am going to be a double grandmother! First Manasi will give me a grandchild. Then after a few months Alka will give me another grandchild. Both my daughters-in-law have made me very happy,' she proclaimed proudly to all the ladies in her circle.

A few months after Sanal was born, Alka gave birth to Nisha. Subbu was disappointed that the child was not a boy. He was envious of Krish, who'd got a son. He told Alka that if they wanted to have two children, it would be better if they had the second quickly, so that they would grow up together. Anandi too felt that this was a good idea.

'I will take care of both of them and we have enough help here; you don't have to worry about anything,' Anandi assured Alka.

Subbu had been desperately hoping that their second child would be a boy. When Alka gave birth to Tulika, he was disappointed. Alka was furious with his attitude and the rift between Subbu and Alka began then.

'I had no idea you were such a male chauvinist,' she couldn't resist telling him.

'You need a successor for these estates. It's not a woman's job.'

'Come on, Subbu! We are in the twenty-first century. How can you say things like that?'

'You've seen how hard it is to run the estate.'

'Yes, it's hard, but that doesn't make it a man's job. I've always wanted to be more involved but you've never let me.'

'It wouldn't have been possible for you. And anyway, you got pregnant almost immediately after we got married,'

Alka knew it was futile trying to reason with him. He had his convictions and he would not change.

Anandi, however, was overjoyed to have two beautiful granddaughters, and spent all her time with them, helping Alka take care of them. Alka had her hands full now, with both her daughters. Tulika often fell ill as a child, and it was Anandi and Alka who rushed her to the hospital in the city centre, along with their driver, Venkatesh.

When her girls were younger, Alka did not have any time for herself. There was always one thing or another. Once they started attending the local school, Alka found that the standard of education was simply not good enough. Having experienced the importance of a good education first hand, she knew there was so much she could do with both her girls. She took it upon herself to supplement their studies. She made trips to Bangalore, where she would go on shopping sprees to Gangarams, and spent hours browsing through all the educational books that the store had. She also bought several storybooks and read to them each night, cultivating in them the same interest she had had in books and reading.

Alka loved these trips, which gave her some time to herself while Anandi took care of the girls back at the estate.

Subbu, busy with the estate, was happy that he didn't have to accompany her and glad that Venkatesh was there to drive her around.

~

On the day of the memorial, Alka woke up early and went into the girls' bedroom. It was time to wake them up too. Gently kissing Tulika's forehead, she whispered in her ear, 'Wake up, my babies. We have to get ready.'

Tulika, who'd always been an early bird, didn't need any more cajoling. She sat upright. 'Today's the party for grandma, isn't it?'

'It's not a party, silly. We don't throw parties when someone dies,' Nisha corrected her, still lying in bed, stretching her hands lazily over her head.

'Lots of people will be coming, won't they?' Tulika asked.

'Yes, they will,' Alka confirmed.

'And we will have good food to eat?'

'Yes. Your Appa has ordered food from Mythri Hotel in the city.'

'Then it *is* a party,' Tulika declared.

'A guest is also coming to stay with us. Do you know who?' Alka asked.

'Who, who?' chimed both the girls together.

'Your chickappa.'

They giggled at the word.

'What's chickappa?' Nisha asked.

'It is your father's younger brother.'

'Ooooh, yes—our uncle from Mumbai? The one grandma used to go visit?' Tulika asked.

'The very same. Smart girl,' Alka said.

'The one with the child who doesn't behave well?' Nisha added, not to be outdone by Tulika.

'Shhh! That's not a nice thing to say. Both of you, get out of bed now, brush your teeth, have a bath and come downstairs. Gowramma has made something special for you. After that, I will help you put on your new clothes, and get ready to attend Grandma's memorial sevice, okay?' Alka said.

The girls rushed out of bed, excited about the day. They seemed to have accepted Anandi's absence a lot more easily than Alka.

After breakfast, she helped the girls to get ready. They looked like little dolls, Alka thought fondly, pleased with the outfits she had picked for them. Nisha, dressed in a plain round-necked teal dress with lace, admired herself in the mirror.

'Mummy, this is so nice!' she said much to Alka's delight.

Tulika wore a simple pale cream cotton dress. She had picked out their jewellery too and she watched fondly as the girls fussed over it, and asked her to help with the clasp of the earrings. It was in moments like this that Alka missed her mother intensely. In her childhood, Alka had worn only Tanvi's old clothes. Dressing up her girls in new clothes meant a lot to her. She missed her mother, who'd never got a puja like this one after she passed. She felt sorry that her mother had never even got to see her daughters. Anandi too would have been overjoyed to see them all dressed up, Alka thought. She sent both girls downstairs, asking them to wait for her.

Since it was a formal event, Alka decided to wear a Kanjeevaram saree. She wore her traditional jhumkis which Anandi had gifted her at the time of her wedding. She was pleating the saree to tuck it in, with a safety pin clenched between her teeth to pin the pleats, when she heard a vehicle pulling up. She glanced out of the window and saw the estate jeep pulling up. It was the one that had been sent to the airport early morning. Alka drew in a sharp breath and froze. She watched as Krish got out, looking like a movie star in his aviator glasses and a well fitted elegant charcoal grey blazer.

Alka stared at him for a few seconds, her heart thumping against her chest. Then, mentally shaking herself out of it, she tucked in her saree pleats, ran her hands through her hair, and walked down the stairs calmly, to welcome Krish into his own home.

21

2005

The Memorial Meet

WHEN ALKA GOT DOWNSTAIRS, SUBBU WAS ALREADY AT the bottom of the steps, greeting Krish with a tight warm hug. It felt like the hug would go on forever.

'Look at you—you've lost so much weight,' Subbu said, finally pulling back and holding Krish at arm's length.

'Anna! Please. At least now change your dialogues. I've been hearing this since I left for boarding school,' Krish smiled.

'It's good if some things don't change,' Subbu said.

'It sure is good,' Krish agreed.

Subbu patted Krish on the shoulders as the latter looked away. Both brothers were blinking away their tears.

'Anna, I can't tell you how sorry I am that I couldn't come for Amma's—'

'Shhh … no need for any sorry. You are here now and that's all that matters,' Subbu didn't let him finish.

'I still can't believe so many years have flown by; I wanted to come but … you know, life doesn't give us exactly what we want,' Krish said.

'I missed seeing you,' Subbu said.

'Me too, Anna, Me too. It feels so good to be back here.'

'How many years since we last met?'

'Hmm … I think six? You hated Mumbai so much you left in two days itself.'

'What can I say? I just hate city life,' Subbu shrugged.

'I can see why you say that. I've so missed this feeling of space.'

Watching them now, Alka felt almost envious at how easy the bond between them was. Being related by blood to someone made all the difference. It was something she had always felt the lack of. Growing up, when other classmates talked about their siblings, Alka would feel cheated of this chance to be bonded to someone by blood. She was glad that her girls had each other, and she hoped their bond would only grow stronger as the years went by.

Krish went to the back of the jeep to get his luggage but Shanker, the new driver who had replaced Venkatesh, wouldn't let him, insisting that he would bring it up. Krish thanked him and walked up the flight of stairs behind Subbu. His breath caught in his throat as he spotted Alka standing on the verandah. She looked resplendent in her deep yellow saree. Her hair was shorter than he remembered, her skin glowing and her eyes exactly like he remembered. She had a way of looking right into his soul. Motherhood suited her so much. She seemed to have blossomed, and she had an air of gentle calmness, contentment and a confidence, which hadn't been there before. His heart throbbed with excitement and joy on seeing her. She was even more beautiful than he remembered and he ached with longing. It took all his self-control to appear cool and unruffled as he greeted her.

'Hello, Alka,' he said formally, as though they were meeting for the first time and he was unsure of what the protocol was.

'Krish!' she said, her eyes lighting up, her face glowing with a million-watt smile. She couldn't conceal her happiness at seeing him. Intoxicated with joy, she wanted to pull him towards her and hug him tightly just as Subbu had done. Instead she stood there, her arms hanging by her sides and said stupidly, 'Welcome, welcome.'

'Good to be here,' Krish smiled, his eyes not leaving her face.

They were doing it again—just as they had done all those years ago, communicating with their eyes.

Alka looked away, and called out to her daughters, who came running down. 'Nisha, Tulika, say hello to your chickappa.'

'Hello, Chickappa,' Tulika said and chuckled.

'Hello, Chickappa,' Nisha repeated after her, joining in the laughter.

'Haha! I never thought I would answer to that,' Krish said.

Subbu told Shanker to take Krish's luggage to his room.

'Oh wait, I've got them something,' Krish said as he opened one of his bags and took out a gift wrapped package, before letting Shanker carry his suitcase inside. He handed it over to the girls who both politely thanked him and then ripped open the wrapping eagerly.

'Mummy, come and see! Chickappa has got us a game. It's called Pictionary. Can we play?' Nisha asked.

'After we come back from the function, you can. Read and understand the rules of the game till we leave,' Alka said.

'They are so well behaved,' Krish remarked.

'All the credit goes to Alka. She is great with them,' Subbu said. Alka was surprised. He'd never said that to her.

Gowramma served them all breakfast—a feast of all the traditional dishes just like Anandi used to make.

'This is delicious. Exactly like Amma used to make,' Krish said as he took a second helping of the kadubus. 'It has been so long since I ate food like this.'

'Last time we ate like this, we were all so young. How things change,' Subbu said, 'I so wish Amma was around.'

'She still is, Anna, just not in physical form. I can feel her presence everywhere. Its only when you stay away from home do you realize the value of what you have. I missed … this. All of it,' Krish replied.

'I am really glad you could come. There are going to be a lot of people, including some business associates who are coming from Bangalore. I am going to leave now, and see that all the arrangements are up to the mark. You come with Alka and the girls a bit later,' Subbu said as he got up to leave.

Alka was dreading this moment. She didn't want to face Krish alone. With Subbu and the girls around, she had felt safe.

'Around what time should we join you?' Krish asked, seemingly unruffled at the idea of being alone with her.

'Start in perhaps half an hour. We have a small puja for which Alka has to sit alongside me. I am guessing most of our guests will start arriving after that, and they will all stay for lunch.'

'Alright, we will leave after half an hour,' Krish said.

'Bring the Scorpio, I will take the jeep,' Subbu said to Alka and left.

The girls were in the verandah, busy trying to figure out the rules of the newly opened game, leaving Alka alone with Krish. He was looking at her just as he had all those years ago, dredging up emotions within her, which she was trying to fight. Flustered, she called out to Gowramma to serve two cups of coffee in the living room.

'You still take coffee, don't you?' she asked Krish.

'Of course I do. I haven't changed all that much if that's what you are asking,' Krish smiled as he followed her to the living room.

They sat opposite each other, the weight of a decade between them, and yet it felt as though time hadn't passed at all, and they were back in Krish's apartment on the day that she'd walked away from him.

'So ...?' said Krish.

'So ... here we are,' Alka replied. 'How is Manasi? It's crazy that we have lost touch.'

'She is good. Yes, how things have changed,' Krish said.

'They have. It's so unfair that Amma was snatched away so soon, I miss her so much. We were very close.'

'I am glad you had a great relationship with her, Alka. I truly am. She did speak highly of you whenever she visited us.'

'She would tell me everything that was going on there too.'

Krish was silent for a few seconds. Then he said, 'It was so strange to me that we had to hear of what was going on in each other's lives through my mother. It could have all turned out differently, you know?'

Alka looked away. She could hear the girls excitedly chattering about the game.

Alka thought she sensed some bitterness, but she wasn't sure. She didn't know what to say. She found herself stiffening, going on the defensive. She knew Krish would want an explanation as to why she had walked out on him so abruptly without giving him any choice and married his brother. Alka wasn't ready to have this conversation yet.

Gowramma arrived just then with the coffee and Alka was grateful for the interruption.

They sipped their coffee in silence.

'I think it's been half an hour, we should leave soon,' Alka said, standing up, when she finished her coffee.

'Yes, we should,' Krish said as he drained his glass.

Both of them knew there was so much they wanted to say to each other, but both didn't know where to start. They left for the club with the girls chattering away excitedly at the back. When Alka sat in the front with Krish, she suddenly remembered all the times they had driven together to his apartment after work. She glanced at his hand resting on the gear. No wedding ring. She wondered why he wasn't wearing it. She wanted to know if things were fine between him and Manasi. She had a lot of questions for him, but this was not the time to ask them.

When they arrived at the club, a large colourful tent pitched outdoors on the sprawling lawns welcomed them. Some of the guests had already arrived and were seated around the circular tables covered with white table cloth. The chairs too had white covers around them, and each one in addition to the cover, also had a red bow that ran around it. On each table stood a magnificent centrepiece—a flower arrangement with a bird of paradise flower. A massive framed photograph of Anandi decorated with her favourite flowers, lilies and jasmine, presided over the event. A traditional brass lamp with eight flickering flames shone brightly, lighting up Anandi's smiling face. Alka felt a lump in her throat. Krish stood for a few seconds in front of the photo, his hands folded in prayer.

The bricks for lighting the sacred fire for the rituals had been arranged in a rectangle at the far end of the tent. The priest was already there and Subbu was seated in front of it. Alka looked around and spotted Selvi.

'Keep an eye on Nisha and Tulika, okay? I will be sitting at the puja,' she said.

'I'll keep an eye on them too. Don't worry about the girls', Krish said as Alka joined Subbu.

'Thank you, Krish. Selvi, also remember to welcome the guests. Tell the catering staff to serve them soft drinks,' Alka instructed.

'Yes yes, I have done a fair amount of entertaining guests, I know what is to be done, madam. Go on, I will handle things here,' Krish smiled as Alka joined Subbu. Being around her made him feel less burdened, more carefree, and he found himself relaxing, like a great weight had been lifted off him. He hadn't felt like this in years.

The rituals went on for an hour. Alka had never been particularly religious. Her mother had a small framed picture of Lord Venkateshwara and as a child, she used to make Alka pray to him. Alka remembered how Mrs Shetty used to have pujas in her house occasionally, and how Alka and her mother had to serve all the guests who came. Pujas just meant extra work for them, and she used to hate that.

After Alka got married, she'd discovered that Subbu was a devout Hindu. They had pujas before the harvest, and Subbu used to visit various temples and pray for good rains and good harvest. He preferred going, with a couple of other plantation owners, to yearly pilgrimages to a few temples— Udupi, Kukke Subramania and an Anjaneya temple near Mysore. They returned home after about two or three days. Anandi had not been particularly religious. She had told Alka that Subbu took after his father, who used to carry out all these pujas before the harvest. Alka wondered if Anandi would even have wanted a puja as elaborate as this one that Subbu had arranged.

The smoke from the fire stung Alka's eyes. The priest was reciting the sacred hymns in a beautiful intonation but Alka's mind wandered. Her eyes kept seeking out Krish. He had addressed her with such familiarity, like an old friend. His initial awkwardness and hesitancy seemed to have vanished.

When it was over, Subbu thanked the priest and asked him to join them for lunch. He began mingling with the guests, greeting each one, thanking them for coming. Alka followed him. Almost everyone had a favourite memory of Anandi and they fondly remembered her cooking skills and how easily she had conversed with them. Alka knew some of the people Subbu was speaking to, as they had visited the estate at some point of time. But there were also many new faces she wasn't familiar with. Alka moved around, conversing with people, making sure that they were comfortable, and urging them to try the desserts. She was the perfect hostess. Having entertained Subbu's business associates at the estate often, she knew exactly what to do.

~

After they ate, the guests began to leave and Alka stood near the exit, bidding them farewell and thanking them for coming. Just then, an elderly lady seated at the far end of the room walked up to Alka.

'Hello, Alka,' she said.

Alka's pulse quickened. She had recognized the older woman immediately. It was Mrs Senapathy, a professor from the science department at her college in Delhi. She'd never taught Alka, but had interacted with her a few times when Alka had volunteered at cultural events at the college.

'Did you study in Delhi?' she asked.

'No—never, I've been in Bangalore throughout,' Alka said smoothly without a second's hesitation. She was so used to hiding her past that a professor from her old life suddenly turning up out of the blue before her made her instantly wary.

Confusion clouded Mrs Senapathy's face.

'Ah, I am so sorry—I used teach in Delhi and I was certain that you were one of the students I'd known,' she said. She was still staring at Alka.

'Oh—not me.' Alka gave a nervous chuckle.

'I must be mistaken. I must say, the lunch and all the arrangements were wonderful. God bless Anandi's soul.'

'Thank you so much for coming,' Alka said.

As the next guest walked up to her, Alka noticed Mrs Senapathy heading towards Subbu, who was busy talking to a tall young man in a black shirt. Mrs Senapathy waited for him and then left with him. Alka guessed she was her son, by the way she put a hand on his arm as he led her out.

When the last of the guests departed, Subbu and Krish sat on the empty chairs.

'Ah, now I feel satisfied. You've no idea how miserable I felt when we didn't have a proper funeral when she passed,' Subbu said.

'You've more than made up for it, Anna. It was a splendid ceremony. Amma would have loved having all these people here for her,' Krish replied.

~

When it was time to leave, both the girls insisted that they wanted to ride in front with Krish in the Scorpio. Alka said she would go with Subbu in his jeep. They set out for their home, and Alka could see the Scorpio in the rear-view mirror, and she could also see her girls excitedly chattering away. Krish seemed to be a big hit with them.

Subbu was humming a tune as he drove.

'I am really happy that Krish attended this one,' he said.

He didn't notice that Alka didn't say a word in reply.

22

2005

The Walk to the Waterfall

T HE NASCENT RAYS OF THE RISING SUN FELL ON THE
verandah, cutting through the greenery in thick beams,
creating a warm golden glow in front of the bungalow. The
various cries of the chirping birds mingled with each other
harmoniously like a well composed melody. Alka loved this
time of the day. She and Anandi would sit here before the day
began, chatting about various things, long after Subbu left for
his rounds of the estate. Anandi had taught Alka to pick out
the various bird sounds and now she could recognize them
all—sholakili, bulbul, lark, the crimson barbet, sikra bird and
the parakeets. This was the time Anandi would fill Alka in on
the gossip of the locality—things she learnt from her weekly
card playing sessions that she had with the other women, the

planters' wives. They met in turns at one of the houses, and Anandi's turn to host came only once in twelve weeks. Alka would help her set up the table, and take care of the snacks while the women played cards, chatting and laughing. Alka never joined in, even though Anandi had invited her many times. After Anandi's death, Alka couldn't bear to meet with them.

Today, Alka was not alone. Both Subbu and Krish had joined her and it was a pleasant change from the silence engulfing her each morning, ever since Anandi died.

'When are you leaving, Krish?' Subbu asked Krish.

'Tired of me so fast?' Krish raised his eyebrows as he sipped his coffee.

'Ha, I see you after so many years. I won't be tired in just a day,' Subbu was quick with the reply. Both brothers smiled.

'I have taken a week's leave. So I have time. I have a lot of accumulated leaves, and I never availed it.'

'Why? Love the corporate life so much?' Alka asked.

'No—I mean yes, I do love my job. But that's not the reason I never took leave.'

'Why then? I mean—it's not like a coffee estate where you have to work every single day,' Subbu said.

'It's just that there was always one thing or the other. Can you believe this is the first time I am taking off with nothing to do? I have travelled a lot, but it was just for work. It does feel good to be back home, although I miss Amma so much.'

'Yes, there's such a big hollowness without her. The house just feels empty,' Alka agreed.

'Her presence—it is everywhere though, even in this coffee you've made, Alka. It's just like how she used to brew it,' Krish's eyes met Alka's.

'She was a great teacher. I learnt from the best,' Alka replied as she looked away.

When Subbu finished his coffee, he stood up. 'Alright then. I will be off for the estate rounds. You relax and enjoy your much earned vacation. If you want to go to the town or anything, feel free to use the Scorpio, after the girls are dropped off.'

As soon as Subbu drove off in his jeep, Krish turned to Alka.

'What happened last evening?'

'What do you mean?'

'You were so quiet. Is my being here upsetting you?'

Alka was surprised at how astute he was when it came to her moods. But then she remembered how, even in the past, he always had noticed every little thing about her. The passage of time hadn't changed that.

'No—not at all. It's nice to have you here.'

'You can tell me, whatever it is. And yes, we do need to speak of what happened between us back then. It—it was unfortunate.'

'Unfortunate? That's what you call it? Please. We all made our choices.'

'Come on, Alka. *You* made your choice. You left me with no option.'

'What would your option have been? Abandoning Manasi after getting her pregnant?'

'Alka, did you even stop to think of what I might have wanted?'

'What did you want, Krish?'

'To be with you. I was certain. I was going to tell Manasi what you meant to me, I could have paid child support as she was adamant on having the baby.'

'And why didn't you?'

'I was processing things, trying to come to terms with what had happened. I wanted to discuss it with you. But you just walked out so quickly, and the next thing I know, Amma tells me that you've agreed to marry Subbu.'

Alka shrugged. 'Yes, I've had so many years to think about it. I think I was angry, hurt and upset with you. I think a part of me was also trying to get some kind of revenge. I felt so betrayed. What we had was the best thing to have happened to me, and I was in shock when you told me that Manasi was pregnant.'

'That was a real shocker to me too, Alka. But she said that life had gifted her this baby. It meant that her parents had a chance to see their grandchild grow up before it was too late. They were already in their sixties then.'

'I can understand her point of view. How I wish my mother had a chance to see my own children. Anyway, whatever has to happen, happens. We're all governed by destiny. I don't think we control anything in our lives.'

'Why do you say that, Alka?'

'First my mother was snatched away. Then your mother— so unexpectedly. And I can't tell you how much I miss her, Krish. She was like a second mother to me, and now I have lost both.'

'I agree with you about the destiny part. Manasi was so certain she would go back to work. She had hired a full time nanny. She had it all planned out, but we never expected to have a child with special needs. But giving up her job, that was her decision entirely. She wanted to be there for Sanal.'

Alka was quiet for a few seconds, trying to imagine what it was like for Krish and Manasi. Then she asked, 'Is it very hard? What is it like?'

'You know I do feel proud of Sanal. He appreciates so many tiny little things, which we fail to notice. You should see his drawings of buildings, Alka. They are incredibly detailed! And it's all from his head. If he sees a building, he will draw it with amazing accuracy, right down to the number of windows. Imagine—what a memory he has! And his honesty is so refreshing. What he feels is what he says. He has no filters. He is so creative; he comes up with things we will not even think of. His world is very black and white. There are no greys for him. But all this means I feel like a failure as a father, because I feel I am unable to express what I feel properly in a way that makes sense to him. Manasi is terrific that way. Those two— you should see them together. Their bond is incredible. I feel like an outsider most of the time.'

'Spoken to her about it? Tried to be a part of their world?'

'Countless times—including doing family therapy sessions. I feel I have failed, somehow. Manasi and I—I feel we can't connect anymore. She seems annoyed with me most of the times. I think all her love goes towards Sanal. She has changed a lot. She is no longer the person we knew.'

'I feel so bad to hear that,' Alka said recalling how cheerful and bubbly Manasi used to be.

'I feel bad too. But we're the choices we make. We have to face the consequences of our actions. I have been telling Manasi to have a life, a little bit of time that doesn't include Sanal. For her, it's unthinkable.'

'Yes, I can imagine. A large part of my life too revolves around Nisha and Tulika. Speaking of which, it is time to wake them and get them ready.'

'Does Shanker drop them to school? Is he trustworthy?'

'Yes, he is very reliable. In fact he is Venkatesh's first cousin. He drops them till the main road. They take the school bus from there.'

'You know, I feel so bad about Venkatesh too. He had been with us ever since I was a child.'

'I miss him too. I was so used to travelling with him to Bangalore', Alka sighed as she stood up. 'Excuse me,' she said as she walked to the girls' room.

~

After Nisha and Tulika left for school, Krish and Alka were by themselves again. Alka was slowly getting used to his presence. There was still electricity between them, Alka could feel it. She knew Krish could sense it too. Deep down, she also knew nothing between them had changed, even though both had become parents and had their own families. They had both lost the carefree abandon of the youth, and both of them were weighed down by life, by responsibilities and obligations to their spouses, but they were, somewhere deep down, still the same as they had been a decade ago.

Around afternoon, Alka asked Krish what he would like to eat.

'Anything, Alka. Surprise me! You are in charge here,' he said.

Alka went to the kitchen to instruct Gowramma to cook traditional food, just like Anandi would have. She immersed herself in overseeing the preparations like Anandi had taught her to. Cooking was one thing that always comforted her. While she was happy to see Krish, it was also painful, simply because it reminded her of what they could never have.

Around lunch time, Alka was surprised to see Subbu's jeep pull up. He never came home for lunch. On most days, he only returned by late evening.

'Just thought I would join you all for lunch, since Krish is here. And once he leaves, it might be years before I see him back here again.'

'Come on, Anna. I am not that bad!'

'You should take more vacations like this and relax a bit,' Subbu said.

'Look who is talking!' Alka said. 'Subbu has never taken a day off in ten years, except for the one time he fell sick. He does go to Bangalore regularly though and spends a day or two with the boys at the Bangalore Club. But a longer vacation—never! Can you believe?'

'Maybe working like maniacs runs in the family then,' Krish was now smiling.

But Subbu just shrugged. 'You know how I am—I am happiest when I am here. Anyway, there are a lot of developments happening on the coffee front. It's just a little hard right now,' Subbu said, the worry lines on his forehead deepening as he spoke.

'I'm here if you need me to pitch in for anything,' Krish offered.

'No, I've got it under control. I am meeting with some bankers tomorrow and I've to leave now as I have some finance work to do. Nice having lunch with you, Krish,' Subbu said.

Once Subbu left, Krish said he wanted to walk around the estate. He asked Alka if she wanted to join him.

'Yes, let's go,' Alka said. She had to get used to being around Krish. She had to face the regret she felt, each time she saw him, she had to calm the raging emotions stirring inside her.

'It's strange, isn't it—how ten years back we were showing you around and now this is your home as well,' Krish said as he followed Alka, walking up the trail that she was now so familiar with. She loved walking by herself. She was now adept at avoiding the leeches, knowing when the ground was slushy and when the path would be best to walk, according to the seasons.

'Yes, I fell in love with it the moment I saw it all those years ago. But I never thought that I'd end up living here. The way things took a turn ...' she said as she held up a branch of a silver oak which was obstructing the path and crossed over. Krish did the same.

They walked on in silence.

'Did you still think about me?' Alka asked after a few minutes, almost in a whisper. She had to know what it was like for him.

'All the time. At first I was angry with you. I felt very cheated. We had a good thing going, Alka.'

'We did, but it was another lifetime. We were so young.' Alka avoided looking at him as they trekked on.

'We were, but I knew what I wanted.'

'I guess I didn't know. And I never thought, even in my wildest dreams, that we would have this conversation one day,' Alka said.

Walking up the trail made it easier to talk as she didn't have to directly look at him.

'I think it is ten years too late,' he said.

Alka said nothing. They stopped when they arrived at the waterfall that Subbu had brought Alka to all those years ago. There was now a clearing where the ground had flattened out. A fallen log served as a bench.

'Your mother loved this spot. It was she who made them put this tree and had them flatten the top, for a seat, when it fell after a storm,' Alka said.

'Come, let's sit here for a while, then,' Krish said.

Alka hesitated, feeling both excited, terrified and guilty all at the same time. Krish knew what she was thinking.

'We need to talk Alka and I think we better sit down. We aren't doing anything wrong,' he said gently. He was filled with a tenderness towards her that he couldn't explain. She looked so vulnerable, and yet so strong, like she always did.

Alka sat next to him.

'What do you want to talk about?' she asked quietly.

'Don't you ever wonder about how it would have been had we got married to each other?' Krish asked .

'I used to think about it a lot. I tried to forget you, but there are reminders of you everywhere. I mean—this is your house too. Anytime you called, your mother would narrate to me in great detail about what was going on in your life. So even though we weren't in touch, you were always on my mind,' she said.

'You know, it the same for me. Anytime I called, I was acutely aware that you might be around. I imagined you listening to the call. Oh Alka, you have no idea how that felt. Like being behind an invisible wall.'

'I am so sorry for what I did, Krish, I had no choice. How could you even forgive me?' Alka said, her eyes looking away from his.

'I have thought about what happened for a long time now. The passage of time changes many things—but mostly it changes our perspectives. We think about the unforgivable things that people we loved did to us, and with time, we forgive them. We think that we will never talk to those who wronged us—and there was a time when I thought I'd never again speak to you—but then, we discover that the love we felt for them is still there. We think we never want to cross paths with someone, but when we do, we're glad it happened. That's how I feel towards you, Alka. I am glad I decided to come.'

Alka was silent, absorbing all that Krish had said. He had practically just declared that he still loved her. Her heart went into a turmoil then. Her cheeks burned. She wanted to throw herself into his arms and kiss him right then, and tell him that she felt the same. But how could she? She was a married woman now, a mother.

She sat still for a while. Krish didn't say anything either. Both stared at the ground, unable to speak, unable to look at each other. Alka swallowed the lump in her throat as she stood up. 'I need to think about what you just said, Krish. Could you find your way back on your own please? Sorry—I just need to be by myself for a bit. I'll walk on my own,' she said.

'Of course. I'm sorry if I upset you. I felt this talk was much needed. See you back at the house,' Krish said as he stood up too.

They walked in the opposite directions—Alka walked towards her plateau, where she usually went, and Krish found his way back to the bungalow.

Alka and Krish both knew something had changed between them. After having openly discussed and acknowledged what both had carried in their hearts for so many years, a stronger understanding had formed between them. This was not a passionate declaration of love fuelled by the impulsiveness of youth. This was more a tacit acknowledgement of what they meant to one another.

As Alka walked briskly up the winding, curved mountain trail of the coffee estate in Sakleshpur, she thought about everything that had happened ever since she set foot in this estate all those years back. She'd never thought that being around Krish would be *this* hard. She had thought of what she would say to him when they met, several times. She knew their paths would cross for sure. But she didn't think that he would ever forgive her. Not after what she had done to him. But today, he had proven her completely wrong.

Sitting on the rock for a while, sipping the cool water, gazing at the chitals had helped to calm her mind.

When she walked back and reached the bungalow, she was glad Krish was nowhere to be seen. She would do her best to avoid being alone with him from now on, till he left. But she was surprised to spot Subbu standing on top of the steps. He was never home at this time usually. She smiled and waved at him. But he did not smile back.

She saw Krish then, emerging from the house, freshly showered, wiping his head with a towel. He came up to the door and stood next to his brother.

'Good walk?' Subbu asked Alka, his eyes never leaving her face.

Alka nodded.

She looked properly at Subbu then. His face was dark with rage. His lips were a thin line.

Alka felt her pulse racing. She felt a surge of guilt submerging her. Panic followed. Did Subbu know about her and Krish? No, it wasn't possible. She knew Krish would never tell him. Krish would never do anything to harm her. Or his brother.

Subbu's eyes were blazing and he was staring at her with a look she had never seen before. It was a look of disgust, hatred and anger.

It was a look that could only mean one thing. Subbu knew her *other* secret. The one she had hidden from everyone, including Krish. She didn't know how he knew, but suddenly, she was certain he did. Her worst nightmare was unfolding in a way she had never expected it to. She looked down, unable to meet his eyes.

'Krish—please excuse us. Alka, we need to talk,' Subbu said, still staring at her. 'Come upstairs,' said Subbu as he marched up the stairs and into their bedroom.

Alka quietly followed.

23

2005

Tired of Being Sorry

THE COLOUR HAD DRAINED FROM ALKA'S FACE AS SHE SAT on the bed, facing Subbu. For a few minutes, Subbu did not speak. He paced back and forth in their bedroom, opening his mouth to speak and then taking a deep breath, as though he was unable to find the words. Alka was getting increasingly nervous by the minute. It was clear that he knew. But how much did he know? What did he know? The longer he paced, the more Alka willed her heart to slow down.

'What is it, Subbu?' she asked, unable to bear this any longer, sweat trickling down in her armpits, under the T-shirt she wore.

'You lied. You lied to me. You lied blatantly,' Subbu came to a sudden halt and locked his eyes with hers. He glared at her, like he wanted to strike her.

Alka squared her shoulders, determined to not let him see how terrified she was actually feeling.

'What do you mean I lied?' she asked, feigning innocence.

'Don't pretend you don't know, Alka. Bad enough you deceived me—you deceived my mother and that is *horrible. Unforgivable.*' His voice rose as he spoke, and he shook with anger.

'What are you talking about?' Alka asked knowing fully well that he was on to her secret.

'You know very well what I am talking about Alka. Your family background. I can't believe you hid it for ten whole years and I did not even suspect once. Your father—he is no industrialist. He is a petty criminal. Who was ... in *jail*!' Subbu spat out the words and then stopped, unable to go on.

'I—I haven't seen my father since my birth—My mother never—'

'Shut up, Alka—just shut up,' Subbu bellowed. 'How could you cheat us like that? What was it that you wanted? Money?'

Subbu's words hit Alka right in the gut.

'What else have you been lying about? Is your mother even dead? Or is it all a ploy? How dare you make your way into this family, you lying bitch?'

Subbu was shaking his head repeatedly.

Alka's head began to hurt. How had Subbu found out? What was he even saying about her father?

'Subbu, I swear I have never met my father. Who told you all this?' Alka had a difficult time getting her words out.

'It does not matter how I got to know. What matters is that I will be the laughing stock in our circles—and your mother—she is a bloody maid in someone's house.'

'Please don't bring my mother into this. She is gone,' Alka shut her eyes in pain.

'How do I even know that's true? Who the hell have I been living with these last ten years? What kind of a con-woman are you? How dare you make a fool of us like this?' Subbu's breath came in short gasps. The veins on the side of his forehead throbbed. With his eyes glowering, eyebrows knitted close together, and his jaw clenched, he looked monstrous. He seemed to have transformed into someone Alka couldn't recognize. He picked up a book that she was reading and flung it at her. Alka instinctively ducked. The book went flying, crashed against the reading lamp on the desk, which tumbled on to the floor.

'Listen Subbu … please let me explain,' Alka's voice was a frantic plea. Her heart slammed against her ribs.

But Subbu hadn't heard Alka at all. His eyes were ablaze with fury, and Alka's words seemed to trigger an explosion of rage within him. Before she could realize what was happening, he had struck her hard across the face. Alka reeled backwards with the blow. She heard the sound of the slap before she felt the sharp pain shoot up her face, and for a few seconds, she saw nothing. As soon as the shock of what had happened registered, something in Alka snapped. She was like a wild animal unleashed.

'How dare you touch me!' she screamed, grabbing the lamp on the bedside stand, which was the nearest thing she could lay her hands on.

Krish, hearing the commotion, raced upstairs and what he witnessed was Alka rushing towards Subbu, smashing the lamp on his head. Subbu ducked just in time but the shade of the lamp crumpled like a paper bag as it struck him on the side of his forehead.

Alka charged at Subbu again and Krish rushed in, between them, holding out both his hands.

'Alka, stop—stop! What are you doing?!' he cried.

Alka was breathing hard, 'Ask your fucking brother. He *hit* me. How dare he?' she said as she lowered the lamp.

'Anna, Alka—what is all this? Stop it, you two!' Krish said. He stood between Alka and Subbu like a referee between two boxers in a fighting ring.

Subbu's eyes still blazed even as he rubbed his forehead where he had received the blow.

'She is a cheat and a liar … that's what she is. Ask her to leave. I don't want to see her face again.'

'Calm down, both of you, calm down. Whatever it is, we can sort it out,' Krish said.

Alka was breathing hard and Subbu's face was so red, it looked like he would explode.

'Here, have some water,' Krish said, picking up the bottle of water on the night stand and offering it to Subbu. Subbu strode out without a word, and Krish offered the bottle to Alka, who took it from his hand and took long gulps.

'You okay? Does he know?' Krish whispered. He was horrified to see Alka's face, where a deep red imprint of Subbu's palm had begun to show up. Her face was swelling up slowly.

Alka shook her head and Krish exhaled.

'Come, let's get you some ice,' he said.

Alka went into the bathroom and looked into the mirror 'Bastard,' she muttered and followed Krish downstairs to the kitchen. Krish took out the ice cubes from the refrigerator, wrapped them in a kitchen towel and handed it to Alka, who kept the pack on her face.

'What happened? Want to tell me?' he asked Alka.

She shook her head. She was too angry and shocked to talk.

Krish looked for Subbu and found him on the verandah. He had poured himself a whiskey and was having it neat. Krish could see that he was still fuming.

'Whatever it was, Anna, how could you hit her?' Krish asked Subbu.

'She isn't who she is pretending to be. She fooled all of us,' Subbu said.

'What do you mean?'

'Her father—he is some petty criminal who was in jail. Her mother worked as a housemaid in Delhi.'

'*What*? What are you saying, Anna?'

'Incredible, isn't it? She didn't speak a word about any of this. She said her mother was a socialite.'

'This sounds preposterous. There's some mistake. I am sure this is a misunderstanding.'

'There is no mistake at all. She is a bloody con artist. I can't imagine how sweet Amma was to her. If only she had known the truth.'

'How are you even sure that all this is true? How did you find out all of this?' Krish still couldn't believe what his brother was telling him.

'Her college professor Mrs Senapathy was at the memorial. She is the mother-in-law of the one of my business associates, who apparently knows Mrs Shetty very well. Mrs Shetty called me. Can you believe the humiliation?'

After a few seconds, Krish said, 'Who is this Mrs Shetty? And humiliation? How?'

'Apparently it was this lady, Mrs Shetty, who took Alka's mother in as a maid, paid for all of Alka's education, after which Alka simply disappeared from her life.'

'What? I don't believe any of this. This just sounds like some wild tale concocted by a madwoman. Why don't you ask Alka if it's true? '

'I don't want to even look at her face. It is true. I am sure of it. Mrs Shetty gave too many details for it *not* to be true. She wasn't making anything up. She was very upset about Alka just vanishing and not even telling her about the wedding.'

Krish sat quietly, thinking about what his brother had just told him. His head reeled at what Subbu had just said. It seemed so surreal. He knew right from college days that Alka was always evasive about her family. It all made sense now. What he didn't understand was the extent of his brother's anger. To Krish, none of this changed who Alka was, and all that mattered was his love for the person she was.

'Listen Anna—all of that is history. You've been married for over a decade now. Let it go,' Krish said.

But Subbu was furious. 'Let it go? Let it *go*? Are you *insane*? This isn't some small thing for me that I let it go. She's been lying for ten years!'

'Anna, how does her past even matter now?'

'Don't you see—she is not *one of us*? She is an imposter. She wormed her way into this place.'

'Are you even listening to yourself? What do you mean by "one of us"? Do you mean caste or financial status or what?' Krish was getting angry with his brother now.

'Everything. The genes she has passed on to our children—I can't even imagine …' Subbu's voice trailed off.

'If it mattered so much, you should have done a family background check at the time of the wedding. I distinctly remember Amma raving about what a nice girl Alka was,' Krish's tone was terse.

'Things are not always what they seem, Krish. I regret agreeing to this marriage—I regret the last ten years. Her father was in jail—can you imagine? When he was released, he went to Mrs Shetty's house, asking for his wife and Alka's whereabouts. He refused to believe that she'd lost touch with Alka.'

'Where is he now?' Krish asked.

'I don't know—this was apparently a year back. He wanted to get in touch with Alka's mother. I don't even know if her mother is actually dead or is hiding somewhere and Alka is secretly in touch with her. I don't know *what* to believe anymore.'

'Didn't you ask Mrs Shetty if her mother was alive?'

'She said her mother was not with them anymore. I didn't ask what she meant. I was too shocked to ask questions.'

'This Mrs Shetty seems like a troublemaker to me. Even if she had found Alka, what is the need to call you up and tell you all this?' Krish rubbed his jaw as he spoke.

'Mrs Shetty felt I had to know the truth. She felt she owed it to me as I am a good friend to Mrs Senapathy's son, whom I've been doing business with for years now. And look at that bitch I've been calling my wife.'

'Please Anna! Don't speak about her like that. Please don't say anything in anger. Hold back you words.' Krish couldn't bear to hear the way his brother was speaking about Alka, but Subbu was too angry to stop.

'She has shown her true class. No woman from a decent family will attack her husband like the way she did. Her father's daughter,' Subbu muttered.

'Come on, Anna. *You* slapped her. That is so wrong. So so wrong,' Krish said.

'And what she did—for ten whole years, fooling us like that? Is that right?' Subbu asked him.

'Why does my background matter so much to you? You didn't think of any of this when you were fucking me, did you?' Alka had walked up behind them and she stood there coolly, her measured words and her icy cold tone hitting Subbu like bullets. Both Subbu and Krish were taken aback by her sudden viciousness. Krish had never seen this side of her. It was as though she had transformed into a completely different person. Her right cheek where Subbu had slapped her had ballooned and her right eye was a slit. Subbu did not even seem to notice how bad it was, or if he did, he was too angry to care.

'What the hell! Listen to her! Instead of feeling ashamed, look at her justifying her behaviour,' Subbu was shouting again, the veins prominent at his temples.

'Alka—please, please leave this for now. We will talk about it,' Krish said trying to pacify them yet again, afraid that another physical fight would break out between them.

'I—I just can't bear to even look at you anymore, Alka. Leave! Leave this estate this very instant. You are not welcome here anymore,' Subbu raised his hand, pointing to the steps.

Alka just stood there, staring at him.

When she found her voice, she said, 'Do you actually want me to leave?'

'Yes! I can't bear to look at you.'

'And what about our girls?'

'Just leave, you bitch! You have no right to them. They are my daughters and I will raise them. I want you gone by the time I am back,' Subbu said as he rushed out, heading towards his jeep.

Krish tried to stop him. 'Anna! Please! You've had a few drinks and you are angry. Please don't go,' he said.

But Subbu was too furious to listen.

Alka walked to the fridge and took out some more ice cubes. She opened the towel and replaced the melted ones. She nursed her face with the cool compress and told Krish, 'Let him go. He will come back when he has cooled down. This isn't the first time I've faced this.'

'*What?* Has he hit you before?'

'Yes, once. Many years back.'

'Oh my god! That's terrible. Why didn't you do something?'

'Like what? Nisha was one and a half and Tulika was just a few months old.'

Alka … that is unforgivable. You should have …'

'Left? Complained to the police? Where would I have gone with two small babies dependent on me?'

'This is domestic abuse, you know. You can't just take it.'

'I was not scared of him then, and I am not scared of him now. I can take care of myself. He says he wants me gone. So I will go.'

'That's not the point. He can't ask you to leave. What will you do? What about the girls? This is plain wrong.'

'Many things are not right in this world, Krish. You can't correct it all. You do what is to be done, and you survive.'

'Alka ... I don't even know what to say. I ... I wish I had known what you were going through ...'

'What would you have done anyway even if you had known? Left Manasi and Sanal, and rescued me? It wasn't like it happened constantly. Most of the time it was just a mundane marriage, like so many marriages. And it was only one time before this that he had lost his temper and hit me. I don't even remember what it was for. And ... your mother knew about it.'

'What? And she did nothing?'

'She apologized for him. She made him apologize to me. She swore it wouldn't happen again. And it didn't ... until today.'

'Oh Alka! I can't even imagine what you went through. Hitting a woman! My own brother ...'

'We think about the unforgivable things that people do and with time ... we forgive them,' Alka repeated Krish's words to him.

He couldn't believe how calmly she was stating it. He took in a sharp breath, trying to imagine what it had been like for her all these years. He couldn't. He had never seen this side of Subbu, who thought it was okay to hit his wife when he got too angry. And while he could see how hard it would have been for Alka to walk out with the two girls, he also couldn't understand how she could be this accepting of it.

'I don't even know what to say. All I know is that this ought to have never happened.'

'I hit him back. Now he won't dare touch me again.'

'Come on, Alka. That doesn't make it any better.'

'Listen, I suggest you don't speak anything about this to Nisha and Tulika. I'll tell them I slipped in the bathroom. Has the hand mark faded?'

Krish couldn't get over how practical Alka was.

He looked at her cheek and said 'Yes, the handprint is no longer there.'

'Oh good. I don't think Subbu will say anything to the girls either.'

'Why didn't you just tell us the truth about your background right at the start?'

'What should I have said? That my mother slaved all her life cleaning that bloody Mrs Shetty's toilets? Do you know after working for them all her life, they didn't even give her a proper funeral? I was the only person there. The *only* one. She deserved much more than what they gave her.'

Everything that was pent up inside Alka came out like a dam, drowning her in emotions she had refused to acknowledge. She had been angry and strong while confronting Subbu but now tears streamed down her face and her voice was hoarse.

Krish had never anticipated it. He didn't know how to comfort her.

'You have no idea what it was like growing up in that house. All my life, I had to clean their vessels, make their beds and she also expected me to be grateful because she sent me to the same school as her daughter. I think I have paid my debts to her. I didn't want her in my life anymore. After my mother's death, I'd cut off from her. I wanted to forget her. I didn't want to remember anything she did. I wanted to be my own person. Was that so wrong? Haven't I fulfilled all my obligations and duties towards Subbu? Towards the kids? Haven't I done every single thing expected from a wife and a daughter-in-law? And I am not complaining. I did it joyfully too. I really had a connection with your mother, Krish.'

'I know,' Krish said quietly. 'She felt the same connection with you too.'

'Then why should my past matter so much? I'm so tired of being sorry about it.'

Krish rubbed his jaw as he thought. Then he said 'I guess it is a big shock. Even I am shaken hearing all of this. Not that it matters to me, mind you. But Anna—he is old fashioned. If there's one thing he detests, it is dishonesty. And let's face it Alka—you were dishonest. No matter what had happened in your past, perhaps you should have laid it bare. And given a chance to Subbu and my mother to decide if they wanted to proceed with the marriage, after knowing about your past. I am not just defending him because he is my brother. I am telling you why it matters, because you asked.'

Alka couldn't believe what she was hearing. Krish's words stung. She had expected him to understand. Instead here he was, pointing fingers at her.

'You know what—I don't think there's much difference between you and your brother, after all. Deep down you are just the same. Class-conscious rich people who think they are better than the rest of us. You—you pretend to care but I don't think you will even begin to understand what it is like. So please take your advice and your judgement and shove it up your—'

'Alka, come on! You know I didn't mean it that way. You know me. I would never judge you. This is just below the belt.'

Alka didn't bother to reply. She marched upstairs, still nursing her face with the ice pack and bolted her door.

24

2005

The Elephant in the Room

ALKA SAT ON THE BED WITH HER HEAD IN HER HANDS. She pressed her forehead with her palms and shut her eyes. She didn't know whether she was feeling humiliated, betrayed or indignant. All she knew was that every single insult she had heard in her life about her social status came flooding into her present, drowning her, pulling her down, making her feel like she was nothing. Her voice, her thoughts, who she was—none of it mattered. All that mattered was where she was born. She would always be the maid's daughter, the maverick trying desperately to fit in. She would never belong. No matter what she did, she would never be one of 'them'. She found it hard to breathe. She forced herself to inhale deeply and took a few slow breaths to calm herself down. She tried to get her emotions in check, so she could think clearly.

What had happened really? All Krish had said was that she should have told them the truth, and given them a choice. When he put it like that, she loathed herself, because she knew he was absolutely right. She couldn't bear the thought that she was a liar in his eyes. She felt she had fallen in his eyes.

But then again, she had been so very young. She'd made those choices at that point in time, with all the maturity she possessed back then. She had done it after taking everything into consideration. The situation was different back then.

But now it begged the question—was it such a big crime to hide her past? Where she was born, to whom she was born— she couldn't control any of that. Subbu's words cut her deep. Had she been Mrs Shetty's daughter, none of this would have mattered. Any which way she looked at it, it was only the question of 'class'. She belonged on the outside, while Krish, Subbu, Manasi and everyone else, were on the inside.

Alka thought about how all she wanted, all her life, was a place to call home. She thought she had created it when she married Subbu and moved into the estate. She still wasn't good enough—even though she had been a devoted mother, a loving wife, and a great daughter-in-law for over a decade. Nothing mattered. Subbu had discarded it all, flinging the words at her—classless, con woman, liar. How easy it was to label someone. The truth was more complicated than that. On top of that, he said he wanted her to leave the house. He said he never wanted to see her again. She sat thinking about where she could go.

Manasi had been the only true friend she had. Now she had nobody to turn to, nowhere to go. What would she do?

A loud knock on the door interrupted her thoughts.

'Alka, open up, please. You know that I, of all people, would have never meant it like that,' Krish's voice was remorseful.

'Krish, please …' Alka's voice was a croak. She was in too much pain.

'Come on, Alka, you know I'm on your side on this.'

When Alka didn't reply, Krish said, 'Please open the door. It's time for Nisha and Tulika to come back from school, and they will be here soon.'

Alka glanced at the clock then. He was right. She didn't want them to see her like this.

'Okay, give me a few minutes, please,' she said softly.

Walking to the bathroom she stared at her face. The imprint on her cheek had faded slightly but the redness was still there. She washed her face, combed her hair, applied some make-up to hide the redness, washed it off again as it made her look even worse. Then she walked out.

Krish was waiting for her downstairs, and he silently handed her a steaming cup of coffee. She took it and walked to the verandah. He followed.

They sat in silence, sipping their coffees.

'You've no idea how ashamed I am that he raised his hand on you. That was simply inexcusable and I apologize on his behalf,' Krish said.

Alka shrugged. 'He wants me to leave the house.'

'He didn't mean it. People say things in anger. You wait and see—he would have cooled down when he comes back.'

'Whether he cools down or not, whatever he said can never be taken back. He should watch his words.'

'I agree, Alka. Look, I am not saying it is your fault, but if tables were reversed, if you found out that Subbu isn't who he led you to believe he was, what would you have done?' Krish asked.

'Ha. What do you think I did? He isn't at all the person I thought he was. He is a male chauvinist and he thinks all that women have to do is be in the kitchen. I put up with it, and stayed with him, didn't I?'

Krish didn't know what to say to that.

Nisha and Tulika arrived then, and they didn't even notice that anything was amiss. Nisha, bubbling with excitement and waving a notebook in her hand, wanted to show Alka that she had got full marks in the maths test. She looked at Nisha's book and asked her how it made her feel. Nisha said she felt very happy. Alka told her that she was proud of her, not because she had got full marks, but because she had worked hard. Even if she hadn't got great marks, she would be proud as she gave it her all, she said. She then noticed that Tulika was upset.

'What happened, baby? What's with the long face? Come here and tell me,' she said.

'I did not get the princess role in the play, Mama. I had tried so hard. I learnt all the lines. The teacher chose someone else. She said I have to play the part of the head-guard,' Tulika was on the verge of tears as she spoke.

'It's okay, my child. We don't always get what we want. That does not mean we are not good enough.'

'Then what does it mean? That girl was chosen. I wasn't.'

'It just means that for now, this is what you are meant to be doing. You know what—you can be the best head-guard the school has ever seen. I will help you practise, and you can shine in the play. It's what we do with all that we have been given which matters, okay?'

That comforted Tulika.

'Really, Mama?' she asked.

'Really,' Alka said.

Watching her with her daughters, Krish wondered how his brother could be so close-minded. How did Alka's past even matter? How could Subbu call her names and say that he didn't want to see her again? How could his brother still cling on to some archaic notions like caste and class?

~

Subbu didn't come back that night. By the time it was 10 p.m., Krish was worried. Alka had put both the girls to bed. Krish and Alka were eating their dinner. Krish tried to call him multiple times, but Subbu had switched off his phone.

Alka said that there was no point in waiting for him. He would be back the next day.

'How do you know? Has he done this before?' Krish asked Alka.

'Done what?'

'Stayed out the whole night like this?'

'Several times. When we've had a fight in the past.'

'Where does he stay?'

'I don't know.'

'Have you ever asked him?'

'I have.'

'And?'

'Just leave, it Krish. I don't want to talk about it.'

She'd long suspected that Subbu was having an affair. On the nights that he stayed out after a fight, she imagined the worst—Subbu staying over with some woman she knew nothing of. But it was simply a suspicion and so she had kept it to herself. She didn't have a shred of proof of anything being amiss. Subbu, in all the years she had been with him, had never mentioned any other woman's name, even in passing. As far as she knew, he didn't have any friends apart from the other planters.

Once during a party at the club, all the men were smoking on the lawns, and the women were by themselves. One of the planter's wives had got drunk and told Alka that she had to watch out, her husband was not as innocent and sweet as he pretended to be. Alka had asked her what she meant and the other women at the group had quickly changed the topic, telling Alka that she was drunk and to ignore her. The next day, when Alka had asked Anandi, she'd said, 'Oh, people always talk. Just ignore it. It's nothing.'

The seeds of suspicion had been sown then. After one of the fights they had, Subbu had marched out and stayed out the whole night. When he returned the next morning, Alka confronted him and asked him whether he was having an affair.

'What a ridiculous thing to ask! Do I ever ask you the same?' he'd said. Alka had replied that that was not an answer. Subbu retorted that the question itself was irrelevant. When she wanted to know where he had spent the night, he said he'd driven around, parked on the side of the road and slept in the jeep itself. He'd driven back in the morning.

Every time they had a fight, he did the same. Eventually Alka stopped asking. She knew they would go around in circles, never discussing the real issues they faced—a lack of emotional intimacy, a lack of proper communication and the fact that their worldviews were very different from each other's. Alka would have preferred if Subbu talked to her so that they could sort it out. But for Subbu, storming off till he cooled down was the solution to all their marital problems. Alka couldn't do anything much about that. So she threw herself into motherhood, focussing on raising Nisha and Tulika, ignoring everything that was wrong with their marriage. She had lived with this suspicion of Subbu's affair for very long, but it was completely baseless and irrational on her part. It would be so foolish to explain all of this to Krish and she felt awkward to go into the details of their marriage. So she skirted his question.

~

The early next morning when Subbu came back, he greeted Krish as though nothing was wrong. Krish, unable to sleep, was walking on the main path of the estate that led to the gate. Subbu stopped his jeep and Krish hopped in, relieved to see his brother coming home safe. His mother's accident had made him jittery, and acutely aware that anything could happen at any time, and he did not like it that Subbu had left the home in anger.

'Where were you the whole night? I was so worried,' Krish said.

'You don't have to worry about me. I can take care of myself.'

'That doesn't answer my question, Anna.'

'I am angry, I don't want to even look at her face,' Subbu avoided meeting Krish's eyes, looking straight ahead as he drove on.

'What are you going to do?'

'I don't know. I haven't decided yet.'

'I think you should just forget it. All of the stupid nonsense stuff like class doesn't matter. It's just social conditioning. Alka might not have revealed her past, but how much does it truly matter? She is such a great mother and has been a devoted wife for a decade now.'

'Leave it to me. I will decide. It's my marriage, so please stay out of it,' Subbu said as he parked the jeep, in the driveway of their home.

'All right, Anna. As you wish,' Krish's face hardened as he turned away.

Subbu knew he was lashing out unfairly. 'Listen Krish, I didn't mean it that way.'

'It's okay Anna. You're right. It's your marriage, your life. You figure it out. I'm going to continue my walk,' Krish said.

~

Krish walked deeper into the coffee estate, this time walking along the path that he and Alka had taken. He thought about how close-minded his brother was and he felt anger coursing through his blood. He thought about how Alka must have felt, hiding her past all her life and feeling so exposed now. He wondered whether his mother would have minded that she had lied about her family history. He was fairly certain that while she would have been shaken for sure, but she wouldn't have cared as much as Subbu did. His mother was a lot more open-minded than Subbu. He knew about the close bond she had with Alka, which she'd never managed to have with Manasi.

He thought about how the last decade must have been for Alka. He knew she did not have a real connection with his brother, and yet she had stayed in the marriage, raising the kids, bonding with his mother, keeping the home running so beautifully. Subbu really did not appreciate her enough.

Then his thoughts meandered to his own marriage. He did not remember the last time when he and Manasi had had any conversation apart from Sanal's issues. Manasi had changed so much. Walking through the estate, he began seeing things with a clarity that he had never possessed before. In Mumbai, in the thick of things, it was hard to even think. He'd been taking an ostrich's approach, burying his head in the sand, hoping that the problem would resolve itself. But it had only got worse. Manasi was right. They hadn't acknowledged the elephant in the room. Their marriage *was* long dead. Both of them had been pulling dead weight all along. The sparring between them had become unbearable, of late.

He could see it so clearly now. If he stayed in his marriage, he would only be unhappy and so would Manasi. If he took a decision to part ways, at least the fights would end. Neither Manasi nor Sanal needed him anyway. Manasi had kept him out and Sanal was incapable of letting him in. With Manasi, it was always about Sanal. She was always 'dealing with him'. When he was at work, he didn't think much about it as there was was always something to bury himself in. But now he had the luxury of time and he began thinking about whether Manasi had any love in her heart for him. She did not speak properly to him and for many years, it had been this way. It was just that he had been too busy hiding under his work, too blind to see it or acknowledge it.

While he had thought about separation many times, he had held on foolishly, thinking there might be a chance to change things. Now he knew he had been deluding himself. All this while, he had been so steeped in the situation that he did not have the perspective which distance afforded him.

The more he thought about it, the more he became certain that a divorce would be the only way forward. At the very least it would mean an end to the insane fights they had every night. He thought about his mother and how fragile life was. It was too short, too unpredictable. Anything could happen anytime. Why was he wasting his life on a dead marriage? He was certain now. He wanted out .

With each step he took, his heart seemed both lighter and heavier at the same time. He didn't know that was possible. He sat for a long time at the stream where he and Alka had sat the previous evening. Marriages ended all the time. He knew it was better for all of them. Yet he didn't know why he felt a sense of emptiness. The sharp pain of rejection engulfed him. Even though he knew he wanted out, it still hurt badly.

~

When he got back from his walk, he said that he would be leaving for Mumbai the next morning. Subbu thought that he had cut his visit short because he had lashed out at him.

'I am sorry, Krish. Please forgive me. I shouldn't have snapped at you like that,' he said.

'No, Anna. I am not leaving because of you. There are just some things I have to take care of.'

After Subbu left for the estate rounds, Krish told Alka that he would be leaving the next day.

Alka said, 'You're going because you're mad at me, isn't it?'

'Why does everyone think I am mad at them? Subbu said the same thing.'

'It seems that way. Your abrupt departure. You'd planned to stay for a week, and now you're suddenly leaving.'

'I have to take care of something, Alka ...'

'All right. Keep in touch, okay?'

'Why haven't you got your own mobile? Subbu has his own phone.'

'It is only this year that BSNL connections started working in the estates. That too is erratic. You don't get any other network. Very few plantation owners have them. There's really no need for my own phone.'

'Everyone has one these days, Alka.'

'Yes I know, but life in the estate is different. We don't even have Internet or computers here.'

'That's true,' Krish said. 'So did you and Subbu sort it out then? Did you talk?'

'No—he isn't even looking at my face. He said he can't bear to look at me and he wants me to leave. He said he would give me three weeks to find something outside the estate.'

'What? How can he say that? What are you going to do?'

'I don't know, Krish. I need to think about it.'

'I am going to talk to him. He can't do this to you.'

'No, Krish. He is angry. Let him cool down. I'll wait till he cools down. Don't worry,' Alka said.

~

Subbu came home only in the evening, and he wouldn't look at Alka or acknowledge her. Whatever he wanted, he told

Gowramma or Selvi. He ignored Alka completely, pretending she didn't exist.

'Listen, Anna, I know you are angry. But ignoring someone doesn't solve any problems,' Krish said as the two brothers sat talking on the verandah. Alka had busied herself with supervising the girls, their homework, giving them dinner and putting them to bed. Then she said that she was having an early dinner and she vanished upstairs as soon as Subbu came.

Krish and Subbu had dinner, which Gowramma served. She knew there was something amiss but she was too polite to ask what had happened.

'I need time to think about it. This is a deliberate deception she carried on for so many years.'

Subbu didn't tell Krish that he had asked Alka to leave the estate. Since Alka had told Krish not to bring it up with Subbu, he pretended he didn't know about it.

The next morning Subbu hugged Krish and bade him farewell, just before he left for the estate rounds.

When the girls were leaving for school, Alka told them that Krish was leaving for Mumbai and he wouldn't be home when they returned.

'Chickappa, you must come again soon okay?' Nisha told him.

'Yes and we will play Pictionary,' Tulika added.

'Yes, we will,' Krish said.

'Promise?' Asked Tulika.

'God-promise,' Krish said pinching his throat and both girls giggled.

~

When it was time to leave for the airport, Krish badly wanted to hug Alka. He wanted to take her in his arms and tell her she deserved better. He wanted to tell that he was there for her, always.

But he didn't. It took all his self-control to resist. He knew if he hugged her, he wouldn't be able to leave.

Instead, he said, 'Get that phone, will you?'

Alka just smiled and said, 'You better keep your promise to Tulika.'

'I will,' he said.

Alka hung on to those words. With Subbu treating her like she did not even exist and telling her she had to leave the estate, she didn't know what the future held. Krish's promise that he would come back gave her some happiness. But she wasn't sure if that was for the best for both of them. It would only make things messier. Yet, a small part of her couldn't help hoping that he would return.

Part Four

A Place Called Home

'How beautiful to find a heart that loves you, without asking you for anything, but to be okay.'
—Khalil Gibran

25

2005

Leaving

IN THE DAYS THAT FOLLOWED KRISH'S DEPARTURE, ALKA kept expecting to have a conversation with Subbu about everything that had happened. She felt guilty at having hidden her past from him. But she also wanted him to realize that it was simply not okay to hit her, no matter how angry he got. She wanted him to apologize for striking her. But that wouldn't be possible unless they had a conversation about it. She thought that once he had calmed down a little, she would be able to explain to him her side of things, but Subbu continued to pretend that she didn't exist. He would return from his estate rounds long after the girls had gone to bed, remove his boots, pour himself a drink and then he would blast his music, all the while not saying a single word to Alka.

He had also taken to drinking heavily, and this worried Alka. Earlier, he drank only occasionally and never more than two or three pegs of whiskey. These days, Alka was alarmed to see that he was finishing almost three-fourths of a bottle in a single night.

After a couple of hours of drinking and music, he would walk to the table, eat his food, trudge into his room on the ground floor and sleep.

Alka also missed Krish a lot. It was strange, she thought, that after being out of touch for over ten years, she so badly wanted to hear his voice and speak to him; tell him about what was going on with her and Subbu and how worried she was. He would know how to handle Subbu, and she was so tired of this stalemate situation that she was more than was ready to take his advice.

The only thing stopping her from contacting Krish was that she didn't want to complicate things further. After all, it was keeping secrets that had landed her in this mess in the first place. If she went behind Subbu's back and spoke to Krish, it would be yet another secret that she would need to keep. She knew she still had intense feelings for Krish, and she was certain he felt the same way about her. The last thing she wanted was to add fuel to the already burning fire. So she resisted involving him in this matter. This was between her and Subbu and she had to sort it out.

~

Both Nisha and Tulika noticed this change in their father.

'Are you and Papa getting a divorce?' Nisha asked.

'What is a divorce?' Tulika piped in before Alka could answer.

'It means they will live in different houses. Appa will be in one house and Mama will be in the other,' Nisha answered.

'So will we have two houses? That's good! Where will our new house be?' Tulika said.

'Shhh … no one is getting a divorce. And it's not as simple as getting two houses. It's far more complicated than that. Anyway, how do you know about divorce?' Alka asked Nisha.

'My friend told me. Her parents don't live together. She lives with her mother and grandmother in her grandmother's house. Their father doesn't live with them now. Her mother has to spend a lot of money now because she has to see lawyers and go to court.'

'You girls don't have to worry about that. That won't happen in our case. Your Appa is just angry about something. Once he cools down, I will speak to him and everything will be fine, okay?' Alka promised them.

She desperately hoped that she was right.

~

After three weeks, when Subbu still wasn't relenting or willing to talk, Alka decided that she'd had enough. She would confront him. She would tell him that this couldn't go on. He couldn't treat her like this. They would talk like two mature adults, and whatever it was, they would sort it out. She would insist upon it.

'Listen Subbu, this just won't do. We need to talk,' she said that evening as he trudged in from the estate rounds and removed his boots.

Subbu ignored her and headed straight to the bar cabinet. Alka blocked his way and stood in front of him.

'I said we have to talk,' she asserted, staring at him.

'And I said you need to leave this house, but you didn't listen to me either. You aren't welcome here anymore. So why are you still here? Now move out of the way,' Subbu said as he took a step forward.

Alka stood there, glaring at him, challenging him.

'Move—don't make me angrier than I am,' Subbu's voice rose as he took another step forward.

'Don't you dare touch me. And no, I am not moving,' Alka said. Her face was flushed and she raised her chin as she locked eyes with him.

'Ha! Suit yourself. You're nothing but a leech,' Subbu scoffed, gave a bitter laugh and walked away.

Alka stood there for a few seconds, staring at his back as he walked towards his room. His words had found their mark. They stung. Deep. Her shoulders slumped. Her glowering eyes lost the anger and were now downcast. She walked to the sofa and sat down.

A leech—that's what he said she was. A predatory worm that sucked blood out of people till it was satiated. What Subbu had said just now had hurt her more than the slap. His remark cut her deep. Was that how he saw her?

Why did it hurt so much? Was it because he had robbed her of her dignity, her self-respect and all that she believed in with that single remark? She blinked a few times. She had never expected that from him. She thought he would calm down in time and they could speak again, but the disgust in his voice and the look in his eyes wounded her. Suddenly she knew why it cut deep. It was a look she recognized. It was exactly the same look Tanvi and all those girls at the party during her schooldays had had in their eyes, all those years ago.

Alka got up and fled into her bedroom. She buried her face in the pillow and wept. *Leech ... leech ... leech*—the words kept going around in her head. Alka wished she could just curl up and die. Perhaps his words hurt her so much because there was some truth in it. She had latched on to him, like a leech, the moment Anandi had brought up the proposal. She had been looking for security, for comfort and a place to call home. Now he had made it clear that she was unwelcome.

What was she doing here? Why was she even making an effort to talk to him, to sort things out? Clearly, he couldn't see beyond her social background. If that mattered so much to him, was it even worth holding on to this relationship? Were all these years that she had spent here a lie? She didn't know whether there was even a tiny bit of love left in his heart for her.

She couldn't stay here anymore after this. She had to get away. Subbu had made it clear multiple times. She decided she would leave, at least for a few days. She couldn't think long-term just yet, since she couldn't possibly imagine abandoning her girls. She needed to think carefully about what her future course of action could be, and she needed to be absolutely sure of her actions. Perhaps time away from Subbu would bring her some clarity. Right now, she felt so stifled in this house that she was unable to think clearly.

Alka got out of bed and paced up and down her bedroom floor. As she packed her bags; she thought about her two daughters, who were sleeping in the adjacent room. She would have to explain to them why she was going away for a few days. She would have to assure them that it was just a temporary thing and that she would be back. She had never left them alone for more than an evening before this. But she decided that Selvi could take care of them for a couple of days. They would be at school for most part of the day anyway, and so it might not be too hard.

~

The next morning, Alka explained to Nisha and Tulika that she had to go on a little trip and would be back in two days.

'But why? You don't have a job,' Nisha said.

'It is not only people who have jobs who can travel. Mummy needs a break. A little vacation.'

'Are you tired of us?'

'Never! How can I be tired of you?'

'Then why are you going away without us? What do you need a break from? From Appa?'

'It is like this—you go to school for five days. Then you get two days off. Mama never gets holidays. So think of this as Mama's holiday, okay?'

Nisha paused to think.

'Okay. You are right, Mama. Papa gets holidays when he goes to Bangalore. But you have never taken a holiday. You take a nice big holiday, Mama' she said.

Tulika wasn't too happy about it, but she agreed too. Alka kissed them and hugged them, and sent them to school, reminding them to listen to Selvi. She instructed Gowramma on the menu for the next few days and explained to Selvi that she had to visit a friend. She left detailed instructions with the younger woman on what to pack for their lunch, when to enforce bedtime and how much TV she could let them watch.

'Don't worry, Akka, I will take good care of them. You have a good time and come back safely,' Selvi said.

Subbu had already left on the estate rounds as usual, without a word to Alka. She told Selvi to inform him when he came back that Alka had gone away for a few days. Serves him right, she thought. Let him come back and discover that I have left.

Once the girls left, Alka told Shanker to drop her to the main bus stand at Sakleshpur. She'd decided that she would take a bus to Bangalore and she would check into a hotel.

Then she would decide what she had to do.

26

2005

Learning to be Invisible

As ALKA CLUTCHED HER LARGE BAG AND WAITED FOR the bus, her shoulders hurt with the weight. She didn't want to place it on the floor—it was too dirty, strewn with discarded cigarettes, empty coffee cups and paan stains. The ticket office had told her that the bus would arrive in fifteen minutes.

'It is an ordinary bus, not a luxury one. Okay?' The guy at the ticket counter declared, looking at Alka. He wasn't used to a passenger like her. Most of the people who travelled to Bangalore from Sakleshpur on ordinary buses were construction workers and estate labourers.

'Yes, okay. One ticket, please,' Alka said.

Now she stood wondering if this had been a wise decision. She should have asked Shanker to drop her to Bangalore instead of bravely venturing on this journey in a bus, she thought. But then Subbu had called her a leech, and her pride hadn't permitted her to use his vehicle.

She wished the bus would come soon. She didn't want to sit on the benches either. They looked filthy. An old man in a white turban cleared his throat loudly and spat next to her. A family of five, sitting on the bench peeled some oranges and discarded the peels at their feet. A young man who was selling tea shouted loudly as he weaved his way between the crowds. When he came to Alka, he stopped and asked 'Special chai, Madam?'

Alka was dying for a cup of tea. Her head hurt. She looked at the flask he was carrying the tea in and the glasses in his bag. They didn't look like they had been properly washed, and so she declined reluctantly.

When the bus pulled up at the stop, she got into it and found her seat easily. She shoved her bag in the stand over the seats. The seats were hard and uncomfortable. Soon the bus filled up and it was packed to the capacity. There wasn't a single seat left.

Alka was happy that she had gotten a window seat. An old lady squeezed in right next to her. With her were two children, a girl and a boy, who looked to be around the same age as Nisha and Tulika. The old lady made them sit together beside her.

'Please adjust,' she told Alka in Kannada and gave her a toothless grin as she moved closer. Alka was pressed against the side of the bus. Alka hated how the old lady had pushed against her and she hated the general atmosphere in the bus. The smell of so many unwashed bodies packed tightly together made her want to retch. She put her head outside the window and tried to ignore the noisy chatter and the stench inside the bus.

As the bus sped to Bangalore, Alka looked at the scenery she'd passed in the Scorpio a hundred times. She was so familiar with the roads, but the view from the bus was a bit different. Since it was at a higher vantage point, she could see the ravines and the valleys that weren't visible from the Scorpio.

'Visiting your husband?' the old lady asked Alka in Kannada.

Alka was in no mood for conversations with strangers, but the old lady was cheerful and Alka couldn't possibly ignore her without appearing rude.

'No,' she said shortly. Then she added, with a trace of bitterness, 'Running away from him.'

'Hahaha!' The old lady seemed to find this hilarious, and slapped her hands on her thighs as she laughed heartily.

'It's a good thing you have done. Once in a while, they need that,' she said and laughed some more. She was missing a front tooth. Her remaining teeth were crooked and they were stained red with paan. Her laughter was so infectious that, absurdly, Alka found herself laughing with her. It had been such a long time since Alka had laughed with such carefree abandon. The last time she had laughed this helplessly was with Anandi, when Anandi had imitated one of the ladies in her card playing group.

Suddenly the engine of the bus spluttered and the bus bumped roughly before coming to a grinding halt. As the driver got up and announced that they'd had a breakdown, a collective groan went through the bus. He added that while they'd contacted another driver to come pick them up, it would take three hours for that bus to get here.

'Those who want to return to Sakleshpur, there is a bus which is headed that way and it will cross us in half an hour. No extra tickets—you can go back for free,' the conductor announced generously.

'Ayeeee! If we wanted to go back why would we have boarded the bus? Fool!' one of the old men sitting in the front shouted and everybody laughed.

'Ajja—we are midway between Bangalore and Saklehspur. So I just gave you the option. That's all,' the conductor said.

'So, do you mean that we have to pay extra if we choose to go to Bangalore?' one of the women sitting in the front asked.

'You have to pay half-ticket charges. The bus is coming all the way from Bangalore just to pick you all up, but if you go back to Saklehspur and board the bus tomorrow from there, there will be no charges. We will fit you all in the regular bus along with other passengers,' he said.

'If we board the bus tomorrow, they will pack us all in like fish in a fish basket. There won't be space for even a grain of sand. We will pay extra and go to Bangalore,' the old lady told the children.

An argument broke out then. The passengers said that it wasn't their fault that the bus broke down. The driver and the conductor said that it wasn't their fault either. After debating for a while, many of the passengers said they would go back to Sakleshpur and catch the bus the next day. In half an hour, the promised bus heading towards Sakleshpur arrived and they boarded it.

The ones who chose to stay back grudgingly paid half price for the ticket and waited for the rescue bus to arrive from Bangalore. Alka chose to wait too. There was no way she was going back. She wondered now if she should have bought that mobile phone after all. She could have then called Shanker and asked him to pick her up. Instead, she was stuck here, in the middle of nowhere, waiting for a bus.

She was tired and hungry. She hadn't packed any food, presuming she would reach Bangalore in a few hours. She reached for her bag to pull out the bottle of water she had put inside. When she took it out, she saw that the bottle was empty and the entire side of the bag was dripping wet.

'Oh, hell,' she muttered.

The old lady saw what had happened.

'Don't worry, I have plenty of food and water. You can join us,' she said as she got up from her seat, and gestured for Alka to follow her.

Alka got out of the bus with the old lady and the two kids. The passengers who were waiting to go to Bangalore had spread themselves out in groups and were scattered across the small clearing by the side of the road.

'Come! We can't do anything; we might as well have a good time here,' the old lady said as she fished out a blanket from her bag, spread it on the grass, and made the children sit on it.

'Come, akka, sit, sit,' the girl, the older of the two children, called out to Alka.

Alka looked around. She didn't have much of a choice, and so she joined them.

The old lady took out plates made of leaves woven together, and two plastic boxes filled with a red curry of some sort and a few Jwala rotis. She served Alka and the children.

Alka ate the food gratefully. It was a simple meal, very different from what Gowramma made every day, yet it was so delicious and filling.

'Thank you for sharing your food with me,' Alka told the lady.

The lady just smiled in reply.

'Akka, you are so beautiful. I want to be like you when I grow up,' the girl told Alka.

'Beauty is only external. It will fade with time. What matters is how much you study. Then you can be anything you want to be. So study hard, okay?' Alka replied.

'But I only want to be beautiful. I don't want to study,' the girl said.

'She wants to act in the movies. All the time she is making faces in front of the mirror,' the little boy said, and the girl gave him a smack on the head.

Then the two children ran off to play.

Alka learnt that the old lady's name was Yellama. She was originally from Maharashtra but had migrated to Karnataka many years ago, when her parents had moved here in search of jobs. Her husband had left her for a younger woman and she had raised her son alone. And then fate intervened, Yellamma told her. She'd lost her son and her daughter-in-law in the stampede that had happened in Mandhar Devi temple in Satara district a few months ago. Her son and her daughter-in-law had left the kids in her care, and were on their way to a new job at a hotel in Mumbai where they were to join as cleaning staff. They had decided to go to the temple before taking up the new job to seek the deity's blessings. Her son had been excited about the job, as the pay was far higher than what he made as a temporary labourer at the estate. He and his wife would settle down there, he'd said, and they would send for the kids and Yellama soon after. Instead, they'd become victims of the tragedy.

Alka was shocked.

'My God. I would have never guessed. You seem so—' Alka shook her head in disbelief and sadness.

'Jovial?' Yellama completed the sentence for Alka.

'It really destroyed me. I was in shock. But you can't fight fate. I do feel extremely sad. But whether I laugh or cry, I have to work and raise these two. I don't want to be morose and brooding. These two children are dependent on me now. Being sad won't bring dead people back, will it? ' Yellama said.

'So have you found a job in Bangalore ?' Alka asked.

'Yes. A rich couple has just had a baby. They need someone to look after the baby full-time—day and night. They have servant quarters at the back in their compound. It is a small room with a bathroom, which I have to share with a boy from my village, who is a cook there. The main thing is they are okay with both these children living there with me. Their only condition is that we will have a separate entrance from the back, and they don't want to see the kids anywhere in their compound. I will have to tell these two to be very careful. You've seen how naughty they are. I don't want to get thrown out because of their behaviour,' Yellama said.

Yellama's words took Alka right back to her time in Mrs Shetty's house. She remembered how she had hid in her room, and become invisible whenever Tanvi's friends came. She recalled how Mrs Shetty said she wasn't to play in the house, and if she entered the house, it had to be only for work. Alka had gotten so used to Mrs Shetty's rules that she'd always stayed in the room, never venturing out unless it was for her daily chores. She remembered that one time when she couldn't resist her temptation and had helped herself to the chocolates that Mrs Shetty kept for Tanvi in her kitchen. She never offered them to Alka. Her mother had given her a scolding and then rushed out to replace the chocolates. She told Alka not to do it again, as the chocolates were expensive and her mother said it ate into their savings. Recalling that incident still hurt Alka deeply. How could Mrs Shetty have been so insensitive? Alka had only been a child. How could she treat a child that way? In contrast, here was Yellama, who was ready to share her food with Alka, a complete stranger.

Alka went very quiet and Yellama noticed her expression. She presumed Alka was feeling sorry for her.

She said, 'What happened? Don't feel sad for me. The children are getting a good life.'

That made Alka feel worse. What right did these rich people have to treat their help this way? Just because someone was working for you, why should they be invisible till they were summoned? Mrs Shetty had treated her and her mother very shabbily.

And now, even after all these years, she hadn't left Alka alone. She had called up Subbu under the pretext of 'revealing the truth about Mrs Senapathy's son's business associate's wife.' How dare she? What business did she have to do that?

If she hadn't called Subbu, life would have continued as usual for Alka. Alka was filled with a bitter, blinding rage towards Mrs Shetty. Hatred for her, and frustration over her unfair behaviour, came flooding back to Alka.

~

When the bus to Bangalore finally arrived, Alka got in, along with Yellama, the two children and all the other passengers.

This bus was a slightly nicer one. The two children were excited about it and ran their hands on the seats, which were single seats with soft cushioned upholstery. How easily they were pleased, Alka thought.

She felt sad as she looked over at the kids. They didn't know what awaited them in this new house their grandmother was taking them to. They would have to go through their childhood learning to be invisible, just because their grandmother's employers didn't want to see them around. She saw herself in the young girl with big dreams. She saw her mother in Yellama, who was ready to work day and night, in exchange for a place she could call home and a few thousand rupees.

Alka's heart felt heavy. She wiped away a tear discreetly. She was filled with a mixture of sadness and rage and helplessness that came in waves, as she sat thinking, with her head resting on the side of the bus, looking out of the window with the cool breeze blowing on her face. The sun was setting and the sky was a dark orange, with streaks of deep red.

Suddenly, she knew what to do. She changed her mind about checking into a hotel in Bangalore. She would travel to Delhi, instead. She would confront Mrs Shetty and tell her exactly how she felt about the way she and her mother had been treated. She would tell Mrs Shetty exactly what she thought of her.

Alka knew, without a doubt, that this was something she simply *had* to do.

She had to make peace with her past.

27

2005

A New Charity Project

As Alka walked out of the Delhi airport, she called a taxi with her newly bought mobile phone. After getting out of the bus in Bangalore, Yellama had asked Alka for her mobile number. Alka had replied that she didn't have one, but had written her home phone number on a piece of paper and given it to her. Yellama had declared proudly that she would be getting a mobile phone soon. Her employers had promised her one and she said she would call Alka on the number she had given her.

It was only then that Alka saw the need for a mobile phone. While she was at the estate, she hadn't needed one, since only the BSNL connection worked there. But here in the city, she saw that most people, including auto drivers, seemed to have a phone. So she stopped at a store and got herself a Nokia handset as well as a sim card. The store had a tie-up with a mobile operator and they did everything that was necessary for a new mobile connection.

Before she took off from Bangalore, her number had been activated. Alka looked around at the Bangalore airport and saw how much it had changed since she had last flown. There were a lot more shops now. She bought a ticket at the airport counter, and learnt to use her new phone while waiting to board. She had the whole night to kill as the next flight was only in the morning at 5.30 a.m.

She thought of messaging Krish, but decided against it. It was past 10 p.m. and too late to disturb him now. Also, if she messaged him, she would be rekindling their unfinished business. She didn't want that. That was in the past, and her present was messy enough already.

Alka wanted to call home and check on the girls, but she knew that Selvi would have gone to bed, and she didn't want to speak with Subbu, who would probably be drinking by now. She dozed off briefly for a few hours, resting her foot on her bag.

Though she'd left home only that morning, it seemed to Alka like many days had passed since she'd last seen the estate.

~

Upon landing in Delhi, Alka freshened up in the bathroom, still fighting the decades old resentment which had been rising within her through the journey. She combed her hair, applied eyeliner and deep red lipstick, changed out of her travel clothes in the bathroom, and put on a pale cream silken blouse and trousers. With a final generous spritz of her favourite perfume, she was ready. Her clothes and make up felt like an armour—her shield against the world. She had realized long ago that people respected you when you looked a certain way. Today, Alka was dressed to kill.

~

In the taxi, she sat back as they sped towards Mrs Shetty's house. Peering out of the windows, she discovered that she couldn't recognize the area at all.

'Are you sure this is the right place?' she asked the cab driver.

'Madam, are you new to Delhi?' he asked in return.

'I used to live here a long time ago, and this looks different.'

'Trust me, madam, I have lived here all my life. This is the address you gave me,' he said as he stopped the car in front of the complex. It was just the way Alka remembered it, except that it looked old and faded now. A massive glittering mall had come up right next to it. The old double-storied buildings that stood next to the complex had all vanished and were replaced by swanky new skyrises.

Alka paid the cab driver and as she entered the complex, a familiar feeling of dread rose within her when the guard stopped her at the gate.

'Which flat madam, and what's your name? I have to inform them,' he said.

Alka stood a little straighter then. He had called her 'madam'. She told him the flat number and asked him to inform her that Mrs Shekhar needed to see her, and it was about the Inner Circle Club.

'Please enter it in the register madam. The lift is to the right as you enter the building,' the guard said, as he pushed the register towards her and went inside the cabin to make the call.

By the time Alka wrote her name in the register, he had come out and asked her to proceed.

'May I leave my bag here with you? I won't be long,' she said.

'Of course, madam, I shall take care of it for you,' he said as he bowed and carried her bag into his cabin.

~

Alka's fingers quivered as she rang the doorbell. She clenched her fists and took a deep breath to calm herself down as she waited for the door to open.

She heard footsteps on the other side and her breath quickened. The door was opened by a young girl, who looked about thirteen.

'Please come in and sit down. Madam will come out soon,' the girl said.

Alka entered and sat down on the sofa—the sofa that she had cleaned all through her childhood, the one she had never been allowed to sit on. She looked around triumphantly. Nothing had changed. Mrs Shetty had not even replaced the curtains. The centre table, the furniture, the paintings—all of it were the same. The only thing that was different was the large television mounted on the wall.

The girl got her a glass of water on a tray—exactly like Mrs Shetty had trained Alka to do, all those years ago.

First offer water to any guest. Always use the good glasses. Serve them on the tray.

Alka thanked the girl and asked her in Hindi what her name was, and how old she was. The girl replied in perfect English that she was twelve.

Alka asked her which school she went to and discovered that she went to Alka's school.

No surprises, Alka thought. Mrs Shetty had not changed at all. This girl was her new charity project.

Alka forced herself to sit coolly on the sofa when Mrs Shetty entered the room. She looked slightly older and she walked more slowly than she had once. Apart from that, she looked just the same. Even her hairstyle was the same.

'Hello, hello, welcome. You must be the new member Mrs Hoon told me about, right? I thought you were supposed to come here on Friday morning?' Mrs Shetty said as she entered the room and sat across from Alka.

Alka was simmering with anger and she felt it bubbling up inside her. She forced herself to drain the glass of water that the girl had offered.

Then she looked Mrs Shetty in the eye and said, 'I am not the new member. You don't recognize me, do you?' Her voice had turned to ice.

Mrs Shetty stared at Alka for a few seconds. She looked confused.

'Really sorry. You do seem familiar. Have we met through the club?'

'I should say so. Except I was the one serving all your guests,' Alka said.

Mrs Shetty gaped at her and then stood up like she had seen a ghost.

'Alka?' she nearly shrieked.

Alka stared back, her gaze burning with so much rage that she was surprised Mrs Shetty hadn't turned to ashes.

'How dare you—how dare you come in here and—'

'And what? Sit on your sofa? Have water from your glass and not from the maid's glass that you kept aside for me and my mother?'

'Leave! Leave this instant, you—you ungrateful, wretched woman,' Mrs Shetty's voice rose.

Hearing the commotion, a younger woman came hurrying out from within the house. Alka stared at her. Tanvi. Here was her childhood nemesis. Alka saw dark circles under Tanvi's eyes. She had gained a few kilos over the years. She was still dressed in her night clothes and her hair was uncombed, piled on top of her head. Alka saw that she had greyed too.

'Maaa, what happened? Is everything okay?' Tanvi asked, and then she spotted Alka. Like her mother, she didn't recognize her.

'Ask her to leave! Call the security guards,' Mrs Shetty was screaming once again.

Alka sat there coolly, watching them both with a perverse satisfaction. Nothing had changed. Mrs Shetty was still the same.

'Why Ma? What happened?' Tanvi looked confused.

'That … that is Alka. *Alka!*' Tanvi gasped, finally recognizing the woman before her.

'I came here to tell you something. I want to tell you that neither my mother nor me deserved the treatment you gave us. You thought you had done my mother the biggest favour in the world, sending me to the same school as your daughter. But she gave you far more in return, didn't she?

She did everything for you, including cleaning up your vomit when you were ill. Ask yourself whether how you treated her, how you treated *us*, was fair. Did you think we didn't deserve kindness just because we didn't have money? What exactly was your thought process? Did you believe that we were somehow lesser than you?'

'What didn't I do for you eh? How can you barge in here and talk nonsense! Tanvi, call the guards this instant!' Mrs Shetty told Tanvi.

But Alka wasn't done.

'And you Tanvi—you thought you were better than me because my mother worked for yours? Do you even remember the party where you and your friends laughed at me, just for being invited to it, and the fact that I had "dared" to come for it? You know what—I thank you for it. I saw your true colours because of that, and it taught me who to stay away from. A big lesson in my life. Thank you,' Alka said.

The intensity in Alka's voice made both Tanvi and Mrs Shetty gape at her in utter shock.

'Just a few minutes ago, you said "welcome, welcome" to me, when you thought I was a member of your precious club. And now, when you know who I am, you want me to leave? And what did you hope to achieve by calling up my husband and telling him about my past? I came here to warn you to never again interfere with my life. My mother and I have more than paid our debt to you. Now stay the hell out of my life,' Alka said, her eyes flashing.

Then she stood up and marched out, thinking of her mother, thinking of everything that had happened in that house, thinking of how far she had come.

She didn't look back.

28

2005

The Best Matar-Paneer in Delhi

OUTSIDE THE COMPLEX, ALKA HAILED A TAXI AND GOT in. She directed the driver on the route to take. There was one more person she had to see; one more place she wanted to visit.

Though the area looked different, she remembered her way perfectly. It was the same path she had once walked with her mother, all those years ago, to Renuka's house.

The cab came to a stop in front of the narrow lane between the buildings. As she got out, she remembered the spring in her mother's step and the joy on her face that day. The lane was too narrow for the cab to enter, so she paid the driver and thanked him.

As she walked on, carrying her bag, she noticed that the lane was a paved path now. There were no open drains anymore. The area had transformed into a clean, middle class neighbourhood. On both sides stood three-storied buildings painted in various bright colours, constructed very close to each other. Gone was the slum that Alka had walked through.

Alka was confused. She didn't know where Renuka could be. Was she even in the same area? Would she have moved out? As she walked on hesitant and unsure, she spotted the peepul tree. It had grown bigger and someone had tied read and yellow sacred threads all around its trunk. There was also a circular platform constructed around it, which hadn't been there before. Next to the tree, where Renuka's home had stood all those years ago, there now was a small eatery with a bright red board that said 'Manish Tea House'. It seemed to be a cheerful place, with canary yellow plastic chairs and deep green wooden tables. A blackboard stood just outside it, announcing the dish of the day. Alka's mouth watered when she saw that the special dish was paneer matar masala and rotis. The interaction with Mrs Shetty and Tanvi had left her drained and hungry. So she walked into the restaurant, and sat down on the chair, hoping to have some delicious food. She also thought she could speak to the restaurant owner about Renuka.

The bright sun beat down on Alka's face as she sat right near the entrance. Even though the restaurant was tiny, it was pristine. The counters were wiped down. In the corner, above the cash counter, was a metal stand mounted on the wall. The stand held a lamp and some incense, which was lit. The smell of sandalwood flooded the place. On the wall behind the lamp hung a gold-framed picture of Lord Vishnu. Alka loved this small, quaint place.

The waiter appeared and took Alka's order with a cheerful smile. She asked him who the owner of this place was.

He shrugged and said that he was the waiter as well as the owner. He said his mother was the cook.

'Madam, this will be the best matar-paneer you eat in Delhi. It's my guarantee,' he said.

It was then that Alka carefully looked at his face.

'Manish?' she asked.

'Yes, madam, I am Manish,' he replied.

'It's me, Alka,' she said.

But he looked at her blankly. He didn't remember her at all. Alka was beside herself with excitement.

'I had come to your place as a child. You had got me Fanta and samosa, do you remember? My mother Seema—she was good friends with your mother, Renuka. Is Renuka mavshi here?' Alka asked, her eyes dancing with excitement and anticipation.

'Oh ho ho! Alka! Seema Mavshi's daughter. By God! I would have never guessed. You look completely different now. I didn't recognize you. Sorry!' Manish said tapping his forehead and giving Alka an embarrassed smile.

'It's okay. It's okay. Where is your mother?' she asked.

'Come inside. You can enter our home through this door at the back,' Manish said as he led Alka to the back of the restaurant, which then opened out to a house with a courtyard.

'Ma, look who is here!' Manish called out to his mother, who sat by the side of the Tulsi plant in the courtyard, cleaning rice on a tray.

'Who is this?' asked Renuka as she adjusted her glasses and squinted at Alka.

'Renuka Mavshi, it is me, Alka.'

Renuka stood up and stared at Alka. 'Oh my god! It's really you,' she said and the next moment she had enveloped Alka in a warm hug. 'So many years now it has been! So many years. Come, sit,' she said as she led Alka to a charpai, which stood in the courtyard on one side. The courtyard had many plants in beautiful painted pots. Alka sat and Renuka sat beside her. Alka gazed at the bright blue skies just as a flock of white cranes flew overhead.

'What took you so long to find us?' she asked. 'I waited for so many years. What have you been up to? There's so much to catch up on. But wait, first you must eat,' Renuka said.

'Oh my god! I forgot about the matar-paneer. Alka had come to the restaurant and placed an order,' Manish said before Alka could answer.

'Ha! That's okay. I was trying to find your house and I couldn't recognize it. It's so wonderful that you started this restaurant,' Alka replied.

'I didn't start it. My mother did. She named it after me.'

'And now you are going to taste the best matar-paneer, in all of Delhi!' Renuka said, echoing what Manish had said earlier.

Alka smiled.

'I'll make it. You can catch up with Ma,' Manish said.

A young woman, dressed in a pink and yellow saree, emerged then from inside the house. She had a chubby baby on her hip and another toddler trailing behind her.

'This is my wife Kavita and these are my children—the older one is Ritvik and the baby is Meera,' he said. 'Kavita, this is my mother's friend Seema Mavshi's daughter. We knew each other when we were children, ' he said proudly.

'Namaste', Kavita greeted Alka. Then she said 'She resembles her a lot!'

'You know my mother? Have you met her?' Alka was surprised. Kavita looked very young and it had been more than ten years since her mother had passed away.

'I've seen the photo and heard a lot about her,' Kavita said as she pointed to the wall on the verandah of the courtyard.

Alka looked at the wall, and on it hung various framed photographs, including one of her mother and Renuka. It was a black and white one that was clicked in a photo studio. Her mother was laughing in the picture and so was Renuka, as they leaned over a fake bridge which was in the foreground as a prop. The backdrop was a hand-painted picture of a forest and a river flowing through it.

'I've never seen this picture of my mother. In fact I don't have a single photograph of her; how happy you both look. When was this clicked?' Alka asked.

'She was so happy that day. It was the day you got admission in Bangalore. She came here and told us we had to celebrate with her. I insisted on clicking that picture. Little did I know it would be her last,' Renuka said. 'And I have waited all these years for you. I hoped to see you when she passed.'

Manish appeared with the food then.

Kavita lay the baby in a floor cradle on the verandah. She fetched a small wooden table and placed it in front of the charpai. Manish served Alka the food.

'Special service for you. Breakfast under the bright blue skies,' he announced.

'Aren't you all going to join me?' Alka asked.

'All of us have finished eating. By 9.30 a.m., the rush hour starts. So we all eat before that,' Kavita said.

Alka's stomach growled with hunger. She a took a bite of the mouth-watering food and declared that it was indeed the best matar-paneer in the whole of Delhi. Both Renuka and Manish looked pleased.

Kavita brewed tea and served Alka and Renuka in porcelain tea cups. Alka missed her mother intensely. She remembered the last time she'd been here.

'Yes, I miss her so much too,' Renuka had noticed the faraway look in Alka's eyes. 'How is it that I didn't see you when she passed away?'

'I did come! I felt terrible that Mrs Shetty had kept her body in the servant's room. There was no one near her. I couldn't go to the crematorium either,' Alka's voice shook and she sipped her tea to hide that she was blinking back her tears.

'She was not alone there, Alka. Manish performed the last rites for her. He was waiting at the cremation ground. I was there too, but outside, as women weren't permitted inside back then. Nowadays, it is different. But she wasn't alone. Do you remember my sister Manjula? She was there too, and so were all the men from our community. We'd made all the arrangements too. Don't you worry. She was given a proper send-off,' Renuka wiped her eyes with the corner of her saree.

' I … I never knew … How did we miss seeing each other?' Alka said.

'Mrs Shetty told us she wasn't sure if you would reach in time. She asked us to move the body to the crematorium. I think she wanted us all out of the house, I am not sure. Manish was coming from the hospital in the ambulance. When Mrs Shetty shooed us out, everyone left for the crematorium.

But since Manish wasn't sure of the way, I stood at the end of the road for a while, to guide the ambulance folks so that they would find the building. After that, the guard said only the people who were removing the body could go upstairs. You must have entered the building when I was standing at the end of the road. Mrs Shetty didn't give any of us permission to enter the building. I think she thought we wanted to demand money or something,' Renuka scoffed. 'I was waiting to see you, but when they didn't let any of us enter, we left for the crematorium. I thought you would come to my place afterwards, but you didn't.'

'I was in shock. It was very unexpected. I felt so alone. And I wasn't thinking.'

'She'd been ill and I suspect she'd been unwell for a few months. I was concerned about it when I saw her. It was me who had dragged her to the doctor. She was steadily losing weight. The doctor said that she had to rest for at least fifteen days. She had some sort of a respiratory infection—probably pneumonia, we do not know. But she insisted on steroid injections from the local doctor, because she said she had to work and she couldn't take leave. I'd told her many times to tell you. But she insisted she would be fine. She said she didn't want to worry you, as it would interfere with your studies. The next thing I knew, she was gone.'

'I think it was overwork that took her life, mavshi. That horrible Mrs Shetty worked her too hard.'

'Your mother was such a timid soul; I told her so many times to speak up, but she was terrified Mrs Shetty would throw her out. Her only concern was to protect you.'

'I know, mavshi, I know …'

'Anyway, Manish tried to find you after that. We even tried to find out the name of the college you were studying in. But after your mother passed, I think you never kept in touch with Mrs Shetty. I tried to approach her to ask her for your number, but the guards wouldn't let any of us in. There was something important I had to give you,' Renuka said as she got up and went inside. She returned with a small wooden box. It had a carved peacock motif on the lid and it was polished a deep rich brown.

'You mother left this with me for you. I think she knew she would soon be gone. I've kept it safely all these years, hoping I would see you again,' Renuka said as she handed the box over to Alka.

Alka took the box from Renuka and ran her fingers over the peacock motif and the smooth metal clasp. She didn't know what the box contained and she closed her eyes briefly steeling herself for the flood of emotions that she knew would overtake her upon opening it.

'Would you like to open it alone?' Renuka asked gently.

Alka nodded and Renuka led her into a small bedroom inside. Then she closed the door, leaving Alka alone. The cool dark bedroom, felt comforting as Alka sat on the bed and opened the box.

28

2005

Fight for What Is Yours. Never Give Up.

A FRESH WAVE OF GRIEF WASHED OVER ALKA AS SHE opened the box. The box was lined with deep red velvet. Inside it, was a spectacular, thick silver necklace made entirely of tiny balls placed close together, and two matching silver earrings made in the same pattern. There was also a photograph of her mother and Renuka, the same one which Alka had seen on the wall outside. The box also contained a white envelope, sealed carefully. The tape had yellowed and so had the outer paper. Alka held it up against the window where a trickle of light was streaming in, so that she could see where to tear open the envelope from. The ache of her mother's absence pierced her heart like an arrow and she took out the paper from inside the envelope, with trembling hands.

It was a letter, written in Hindi. The handwriting was neat and careful. Alka had to blink away the tears as she began reading.

My dearest Alka,

I know you must be in pain as you read this. You are perhaps angry with your Aayi for abandoning you. I tried to hold on my child. I could not. Please forgive me.

Renuka took me to the doctor. She insisted I see him. But what I did not tell her was that doctor said he wanted me to do some advanced tests. It would cost a lot of money and from the doctor's tone I get a feeling that it would be a lost cause. Hence I decided to write this letter. Please forgive me for not informing you; I really want you to focus on your life.

This box contains the traditional Silver Thushi and the earrings that I had worn for my wedding. I had packed it away carefully, because I wanted to get it plated with gold, so you could wear it on your wedding. I have saved money for this, and it is in a fixed deposit, the details of which are at the bottom of the box (Lift the lining at the bottom and it is hidden there). Please use it and get the necklace and earrings covered in gold. My parents couldn't afford any gold and I am proud that I am able to buy gold for you.

Please don't ever think that you are alone, just because I have gone. I am leaving you another treasure. Renuka. She has a heart of gold. She is the sister I never had.

Manjula too is a gem of a person. You can approach them for anything, any time, and they will welcome you warmly. If we find such people in our life, we have found true wealth and we must hold on to them. Do everything you can to keep in touch with them.

The world is a cruel place, Alka. But if we have strength of character and strength of mind, we should fight for what is rightfully ours. But we must also know when to let go. It is not worth our time or effort to fight for every single thing. So choose what you want wisely, and work towards it.

I was too timid to stand up for myself. But then, I had to protect you. When you face the world, I want you to be fearless.

Never give up. Be a fighter.

Please remember I am always with you even though I may not be present in physical form. I am watching over you and I know you will fulfil all your dreams.

With love and hugs,
Aayi

PS: I am asking Renuka to write this letter for me, because she writes better, and is more educated than me. I told her what I wanted to say, and I made her tear up the paper thrice before I was satisfied. Her writing is beautiful, isn't it?

Alka was still crying as she folded the letter and put it away in the envelope. Then she lifted the lining and as promised by her mother, she found a passbook that had details of the fixed deposit. Alka was the nominee and she would get a sum of five lakhs.

Alka sat for a while in the comfort of the dark bedroom, running her hands over the box, and sniffling away her tears. At last, when the tears stopped flowing, Alka got up and walked outside.

The mid-morning rush at the restaurant had already started. Kavita and Manish were busy cooking. Renuka was helping them to look after the kids. She was rocking the baby in the cradle, and she watched over the toddler as he wandered about in the courtyard,

Alka walked up to Renuka and hugged her tightly, and she apologized for not being in touch for so many years.

'Don't say sorry and all that. I am just glad I could carry out her final instructions to me, which was to entrust the box to you.'

Renuka then asked her what brought her to her home that day. She wanted to know why Alka had decided to visit after so many years. She wanted to know all about Alka's life.

'What have you been up to? Did you get married? Do you have children? Are you working? I don't know what happened after you left Delhi,' she said.

Alka replied that it was a long story.

'I would love to know what happened, only if you want to share, that is,' Renuka added.

The baby had gone to sleep. Renuka covered her with a thin cotton quilt and she got up and sat on the charpai. Alka joined her.

'I got married within a year after my mother's death,' she began. She didn't tell Renuka about what had happened between her and Krish—that was something she decided she was not ready to share.

But apart from that, she told Renuka everything. She told her about her daughters, about her life at the estate, about how close she was to Anandi, about the memorial and finally about Mrs Shetty exposing her to Subbu, and the fight that Alka had with him.

Renuka listened in silence.

'That's quite something you have been through. We've also been through a lot,' she said.

'What happened after I left? How did you start all this? And where is Manjula Mavshi now?' Alka asked.

'Manjula is doing really well for herself. A couple of months before your mother passed away, she left her husband and she joined me here. It was a good thing she had wisely refrained from having kids with him. He was a useless lump of a man. Manjula and I both started a small business, selling vadas, samosas and bhajjas in the evening. We only had a single table here, and we used the stove from our kitchen to cook. We would start making everything by 3.30 p.m. and by 7 p.m., our entire stock would be sold out. We had a regular customer, Hamad Bhasin. He was a handsome young man. I suspected he came every day for Manjula rather than for the stuff we sold! Theirs was a crazy love story. Everyone in the community disapproved. But they both didn't care. He found a good job in Dubai and when he moved, everyone said he had left her, and he would marry a nice Muslim girl and settle down there. But he proved them all wrong. He sent for her within a year. She joined him, and they are doing very well now. They have a son too. She lent me the money to expand our business. By then Manish had dropped out of class 12. He helped me to set it up. The neighbourhood too has really prospered. It was taken over by an urban development organization, and they tied up with some corporates. They did a lot for the community. Most of us are doing well now. All by the grace of God,' Renuka said.

'You all have been through a lot too. I am really happy to see all of this,' Alka said,

Renuka told Alka that since she had anyway told her husband that she is taking a break to think things over, she might as well stay with them for a couple of days.

'Renuka Mavshi—I can stay in a hotel. That was the original plan.'

'Chup! With me being here, you aren't staying in any hotel. But I know you now have a lot of money, so if our house is too small and uncomfortable for you—'

'No! Not at all. I can't tell you how much this means to me. Truly. When Subbu told me to leave, I felt like I was alone. Now I feel like I have found a family,' Alka said.

'Let him see what it is like without you. Then he will realize your value. Trust me—all these men are like that. They are all big babies. They think they can manage everything but you wait and see how he struggles and then he will wag his tail and come running after you,' Renuka said.

Alka was touched by Renuka's hospitality and concern, but she didn't know how to explain to Renuka the disdain and hatred she had seen on Subbu's face.

'I don't know. I don't think Subbu will do that,' she said.

'Then you must remember what your mother wanted you to do. Fight for what is yours. Haven't you invested ten years of your life in that estate? Haven't you cared for his mother like she was your own?'

'Yes, I have,' Alka said.

'Then there's no question of him turning you out. Take a small break and then go back and claim what is yours,' Renuka said.

Renuka then asked Alka to show her pictures of her daughters and the estate on her phone.

'I bought this phone only yesterday when I was on my way here. I have no photos. We don't get good network in the estate; so I had never felt the need for a mobile phone till now,' Alka explained.

The rush hour in the restaurant had eased and Manish joined them and he heard the last bit of the conversation.

'How did you manage without a phone?' Nowadays everyone has one,' he was puzzled.

'Ah—there's a world out there where we still don't have Internet and mobile phones. It's a beautiful world,' Alka smiled.

She then excused herself and said that she wanted to speak to her daughters.

'Yes, yes—please go call them. Tell them you will come after a few more days. Stay with us!' Renuka said.

'Oh no, definitely not a few days! I'll stay for the night and leave tomorrow. This is the first time I am leaving my girls alone. Two nights on their own is good enough for the first time,' Alka said.

'Yes, that's also true. But remember Alka, you are never alone. You always have us and you are welcome here anytime, okay?' Renuka said.

Alka nodded gratefully, thinking how fortunate she was to have decided to meet Renuka.

'So how are the girls doing? Are they okay without you?' Renuka asked when Alka returned from the phone call.

'Yes, they seem perfectly okay. Selvi—that's the girl who helps me look after them—told me they ate all their meals and they are doing their homework too,' she replied.

~

Alka slept in the same room as Renuka that night. Manish and his family slept in the other room. Alka couldn't help thinking how large-hearted Renuka and her family were. Mrs Shetty had a large house but she wasn't willing to give Alka and her mother even a room heater in the winters. Renuka had just a tiny two bedroom house, yet she was happy to share everything they had, and she did it without even thinking twice.

As she drifted off to sleep that night, Alka felt peace and contentment that she had never experienced before. The genuine love and acceptance that she had experienced here, for exactly who she was, filled her heart with joy.

Her mother's words and what Renuka had told her rang out loud in her head. *Claim your space. Fight for what is yours. Choose what you want.*

Alka decided that that was exactly what she would do.

30

2005

Every Ending Is a New Beginning

THE NEXT MORNING, RENUKA TOLD MANISH TO accompany Alka to the airport.

'No, no, Please. I can manage on my own. He has this restaurant to run,' Alka said.

'We don't see off family members like that; if you don't want him to come along, then I will,' Renuka said.

'Please don't! Why should we pay double fare for the taxi? It will have to drop me to the airport and then bring you back. It's a big thing for me that you have said I am family,' Alka insisted.

It was with some reluctance that Renuka agreed for Alka to travel on her own to the airport.

'The next time you come, bring your daughters and your husband too, okay? They are all welcome here,' Renuka said.

Alka smiled in reply. She couldn't imagine Subbu staying in Renuka's house.

She kept thinking about it while waiting to board her flight to Bangalore. Krish had accepted her completely. He never bothered about her family background or who she was. Then why hadn't Subbu done the same? Why was he so steeped in societal conditioning and his own prejudice?

Then Alka realized that she too had been influenced to some extent. In the bus, on the way here, she had looked down upon the villagers who had travelled with her. Yet Yellama turned out to be such a kind soul.

Alka had also seen Mrs Shetty hadn't changed at all. She had so much of money, and yet her heart was so small. She was continuing to lead her life exactly like she always had. Why couldn't Subbu see that it was only when your mind and heart were open that there would be room for growth?

Then she thought about Krish.

Message him. Call him. Message him. Call him.

The voice inside her head had piped up again. Did she owe him a phone call? She thought long and hard. The connection she shared with him was genuine. He had declared her love for her. He had promised to come back. But what future did it have? She thought of her little girls. They came above all else. She would never be able to face them if in the future she had to explain to them, that she left their father to be with their uncle. The thought horrified her. She had to kill this relationship. She couldn't allow it to sprout. She put away her phone inside her bag.

Though she'd made her choice, her heart felt heavy. Yet she was certain about her decision. She was walking away from him a second time. She knew he had promised to come back. She would deal with that when it happened, she thought. For now, she had to put away his thoughts firmly in a box, and lock it up. She had to focus on mending things with Subbu.

She would speak to Subbu and convince him. He could call her all the names he wanted. She wouldn't take offence. She didn't care anymore. She wasn't a leech. She was a lioness, a fierce one, she decided. Subbu had to see that. She had invested ten years in this marriage and she wouldn't back down. Like her mother said, she would fight for what was hers. She would let Krish go.

She called up Selvi and told her the approximate time of her arrival.

When she got back to the estate, feeling rejuvenated like never before, Selvi was there to welcome her.

'Akka! My mother has made all your favourite dishes for lunch,' she said, delighted.

'Thank you, Selvi. And thank Gowramma too. How were Nisha and Tulika? Were you able to handle them?' Alka asked as Selvi took the bag from her hands.

'They were fine. I did everything as you instructed.'

'Did they miss me?'

Selvi didn't know how to answer that. The girls had not even asked about Alka. They'd felt all grown up as they managed everything on their own for the first time, without their mother hovering about them.

'Errr … Akka, actually they—,' Selvi hesitated.

Alka burst out laughing. 'They didn't miss me at all, did they?'

'No Akka, they didn't,' said Selvi, scratching behind her ear, looking at the floor, as though it was her fault.

'That's a relief! It means I've raised them to be fully independent.'

'I think Subbu Anna missed you, though,' Selvi said softly

'Did he say so?'

'No, Akka, but I could make out he did.'

'Alright, lay the table for lunch please. I need to freshen up,' Alka said, feeling strangely happy at the thought of Subbu missing her, although she wasn't sure if Selvi was right in her assessment.

She skipped up the steps, two at a time, humming a song that she had heard being played at Manish and Renuka's restaurant.

~

When Subbu came back for lunch, Alka was there to greet him. Her hair was damp from the shower, and she had changed into a white salwar kameez which she knew was his favourite. She had also used an eyeliner, applied some lipstick and worn his favourite perfume. She didn't remember the last time she had dressed up this way at home.

'Hello, Subbu.' She greeted him with a warm smile.

Subbu noticed immediately that she looked beautiful, but he didn't want to pay her a compliment.

He hadn't expected Alka to leave home. He had been shocked when Selvi had told him that Alka had asked her to tell him that she would be gone for a couple of days. Subbu was too proud to ask her where she had gone. So he had grunted in response.

The two evenings that Alka was away, Subbu came back early from the estate rounds. He didn't want to leave the girls unsupervised. And since he was the parent in charge, he didn't drink either.

Both girls were delighted at his unexpected presence. They showed him all their school work. Nisha recited poetry she had learnt that day. Tulika made him listen to the multiplication table of 16 which she had memorized. They both showed him the drawings that they had made. Subbu felt a swell of pride in his chest as the girls were smart, articulate and expressive. They asked him if he was angry with Mummy and whether that was why she had gone away.

Subbu—looking at these two innocent girls, answering all their relentlessly honest questions and thinking about what Krish had told him, asking him to be a bit more open minded—had been forced to confront his own belief about Alka. It was true that she had lied about her background. But it was also true that whatever she had done for the family, for his mother and for him, was unquestionable.

There was also another thing that Subbu realized—when she was gone, he missed her. The house already felt empty when his mother died. And when Alka had gone just for a few days, it had felt even more hollow. He couldn't really imagine a future without her in the house. But he wasn't ever going to admit it to her.

'Hmmm ... so you are back?' he replied to her greeting.

'That was always the plan,' Alka smiled.

She marvelled at how light she felt, how confident she was. It was funny how a little break could do so much. A little break that had changed so many things within her. Her mother's letter had given her confidence. Her confrontation with Mrs Shetty had given her courage. Her stay at Renuka's place had given her the much needed care and acceptance. Alka was a new person now and she glowed with her new found wisdom.

Subbu and Alka sat at the table, and helped themselves to the steaming hot rice, Koli Saru and Thambuli, which Gowramma had prepared.

'How am I looking?' Alka asked, emboldened by the new feeling of optimism that she was swimming in. When she confronted him with a direct question, Subbu was forced to answer. 'Lovely as ever,' he caught himself saying.

With that, the ice between them melted a little.

'Oh Subbu, I never, ever meant to hide things from you,' Alka said.

'I am still angry. I haven't got over it.'

He avoided looking at her as he dug into the food.

'Come on, Subbu, I get it that you are mad at me. But can we at least talk about it? We can't change the past. But I wish you would give me a chance to tell you my side of the story.'

'What is your side? Every way you see it, you lied,' Subbu said. His words came out a little harsher than he intended.

He finished his meal and walked towards the table in the hall. Alka saw that as a victory that she had managed to get him to speak at least so many sentences, which was a progress from earlier, whenever she had tried to converse with him.

'Want some hibiscus wine?' she asked.

He nodded. 'Thanks,' he said.

She poured a glass of wine and gave it to him. He silently took it from her and sank into the sofa.

'I did lie and it was wrong. I admit it. But remember—I was only twenty-three. I had lost my mother. I was full of insecurities. I was a different person then,' Alka said as she sat down in the chair next to the sofa.

'I get all that but—'

'No Subbu, you don't get it. Do you remember how it was for you, when your own father died when you were in school and you had to drop out? You had your mother, you had the coffee estate to run, you had a younger brother to take care of. All these were your safety nets, though you might not have seen them that way, at that point. You were firmly rooted. But what did I have? I'd grown up in Mrs Shetty's house, my mother doing her housework. I did a lot of their housework too and I am not ashamed to say that now. But back then, I would have died rather than admit to it. I was bullied and teased about it by kids I went to school with. I grew up in terror of my secret being discovered—and what about the secret was so terrible? Just that we were poor and my mother was a maid. I couldn't help where I was born. Yet, I was made to feel ashamed about it. Why? Why does society place so much emphasis on class and caste?'

Subbu looked at Alka, Her eyes reflected her anger and helplessness at the unfairness of it all.

Subbu saw the point that she was making and felt a bit ashamed, as he was guilty of the same. She was right. She couldn't help where she was born. Yet to discover that he had been lied to in this way—it was humiliating. It just signalled to the world that he had been made an utter fool of. He found it hard to accept that.

'You still shouldn't have lied about it.'

'Would you have married me if you had known the truth about me?'

'I don't know, but don't you think I should have been given that choice?'

'Yes, Subbu. You should have. For that I apologize. I apologize sincerely. I am sorry, Subbu. I do get what you are saying. You think you know a person for your whole life and then you discover something about them that changes everything you believed about them. But that doesn't negate the person I am. Come on! You have seen how fond I was of your mother. I cared for her, looked after her like she was my own. I missed my mother so much and I can't tell you how grateful I was to have your mother's company, to have you, to have a family of my own. You might never understand how much it all meant to me—to have a family of my own. You grew up with a loving, kind family. All my life I have known only one kind of life—being at someone's mercy for even the home we stayed in, and having only my mother as my family, who was snatched away so early. You have no idea what that was like. When your mother came with that proposal, I felt it was godsend and I grabbed it. Maybe I was selfish—for that I am sorry. I should have told you all the truth. I simply couldn't. I never speak about my past, but it is a part of who I am.'

Subbu sat back leaning on the sofa, Alka's words slowly sinking in. He had never considered what her life must have been like. He had been too blinded by his anger till now. The two days that she had spent away from him had helped him cool down.

'I understand you are upset. For that I am genuinely sorry, Subbu. I cannot undo the decisions I made. But going forward, I know I cannot live like this, ignoring each other, without addressing the problem. How long will we continue this war of silences?'

'I ... I get what you are saying Alka. But ...'

'No buts, Subbu. You need to think. You need to think what your values are. If the values no longer serve you, you need to reconsider them. Only then will you grow. Do you know where I had gone the last two days?'

'Where? I thought you might have gone to Bangalore. I did think about it and that was what struck me as the most likely place.'

'That was the initial plan. But then I went to Delhi. I confronted Mrs Shetty. You know what? She has a big house but she is living that same pathetic life. She has got another girl as her maid and she is educating her. I guess from her perspective, she is doing her a great favour. But I can only see exploitation in this, because I was badly affected by it. I met my mother's friend Renuka. They welcomed me with open arms. They don't have much themselves. Renuka used to work as a maid in someone's house too. Now she has her own restaurant. That doesn't make her any lesser than us. They shared everything they had with me—everything. I felt welcomed there, Subbu, and I stayed with them. And for the first time in my life, I felt I was not alone. You have no idea how that feels. And you are telling me to leave my own house? For what? Because my mother didn't have money? How does that change who I am? '

Subbu sat back and thought about everything Alka had just said. She was right. He had been so infuriated at being made a fool of by her that this other perspective of seeing it, which she had passionately espoused, hadn't even occurred to him. He too had fallen in the trap that society had laid—

of 'us' and 'them', of 'right' and 'wrong', of social classes and divisions. Who made them anyway?

If he followed the norms and asked her to leave, he would be an idiot who was dancing to tunes of an arbitrary social construct that did not care about him at all. It was his girls who would lose a great mother. He would lose this family.

He sat in silence for a few minutes. Then he closed his eyes. He thought of his mother. He thought of the bond that she had with Alka. He wondered if she would care that Alka had lied about her background. He knew the answer instantly then. His mother wouldn't have cared at all. He thought about Krish's words. Krish didn't care too. Then why was he holding on to the fact that she had lied? Was it worth throwing away the last ten years just because of his stubbornness of not forgiving her. He knew the answer then. If they had to move forward, he had no choice but to forgive her. She was right. They couldn't keep continuing living like this, without speaking to each other.

Then he opened his eyes. He took a sip of the wine. He looked away as he quietly said:

'I owe you an apology for striking you and asking you to leave. I am sorry I lost my temper. Let's try again.'

Alka smiled in response. She poured herself a glass of wine too.

'To us,' she said as she raised her glass.

'To hell with Mrs Shetty and all the rest of them. They don't matter,' Subbu said as he clinked his glass with hers.

Alka sat down in the drawing room on her favourite chair, with her feet up on the ottoman. Subbu sat opposite her. They sipped their wines, sitting in silence, surrounded by the chirping birds in the lush green estate.

Alka closed her eyes. She thought of Krish. She wondered when she would hear from him and how she would deal with it. Then she pushed the thought aside.

Subbu was smiling at her now. She smiled back at him and took another sip of the wine.

She was home, at last.

Acknowledgements

To my father K. V. J. Kamath, for the first visits with him in my childhood, to the various coffee estates in Chickmaglur and other parts of Karnataka. He'd have loved this book.

To my brilliant editor Swati Daftuar, for the countless phone calls, for being in love with the book as much as me, for her sharp, precise inputs and the countless revisions we did. I can't describe how wonderful it was to work with an editor like her. I am lucky!

To the super-efficient team at HarperCollins India: Ananth Padmanabhan, Diya Kar, Shabnam Srivatsava, Rahul Dixit, Akriti Tyagi, Aastha Verma. It's such a joy to work with you all.

To the cover designer Saurav Das, for the brilliant cover and layout of the book.

To my technical support team Pranav Shah, who is super responsive.

To Sathish of Sakleshpur and to Sahishnu for inputs about life in the coffee estates. They took out the time and explained things to me in detail. Any mistakes I have made are totally mine.

To Purvi and Atul, for being my first editors and beta readers.

To Satish, for being a rock!

To my mother, for being so proud of whatever I have achieved, and for her pragmatic view of life.

To my closest friends, whom I am in touch with on a regular basis—you know who you are!

To all my fabulous readers, who read everything I write, and tell me that they wait for my next books eagerly. You give me strength.

About the Author

Preeti Shenoy, among the highest selling authors in India, is on the Forbes longlist of the most influential celebrities in India. Her books include *When Love Came Calling, Wake Up Life Is Calling, Life Is What You Make It, The Rule Breakers, A Hundred Little Flames, It's All in the Planets, Why We Love the Way We Do, The Secret Wish List, The One You Cannot Have* and many others. Her work has been translated into many Indian languages. Preeti is also a motivational speaker, and has given talks at many premier educational institutions and corporate organizations like KPMG, ISRO, Infosys and Accenture, among others. An avid fitness enthusiast, she is also an artist specializing in portraiture and illustrated journalling.